Inches from the Abyss

The chuck wagon continued to rattle but the horses in front and behind created stability. They never swerved and turned only when Griswold followed the gentle curve of the stone face. He always let the men in back know when a turn was coming so they were not alarmed.

It was after taking one such curve that the wagon sloped slightly to the front right, off-center; Griswold whoa'd and reined the team to a hard stop even as the earth and stone beneath the front right wheel gave way.

"Lost some lip on the ledge!" Griswold said. "Just fell away!"

Fremont swore and both he and Buchanan pressed themselves harder against the ribs of the wagon.

"Griz, get off and cut the team free!"

RALPH COMPTON

THE EMPIRE TRAIL

A RALPH COMPTON WESTERN BY

JEFF ROVIN

BERKLEY
New York

BERKLEY
An imprint of Penguin Random House LLC
penguinrandomhouse.com

ISBN: 9780593102442

First Edition: February 2021

Printed in the United States of America
1 3 5 7 9 10 8 6 4 2

Cover art by Steve Atkinson
Cover design by Steve Meditz
Book design by George Towne

THE IMMORTAL COWBOY

This is respectfully dedicated to the "American Cowboy." His was the saga sparked by the turmoil that followed the Civil War, and the passing of more than a century has by no means diminished the flame.

True, the old days and the old ways are but treasured memories, and the old trails have grown dim with the ravages of time, but the spirit of the cowboy lives on.

In my travels—to Texas, Oklahoma, Kansas, Nebraska, Colorado, Wyoming, New Mexico, and Arizona—I always find something that reminds me of the Old West. While I am walking these plains and mountains for the first time, there is this feeling that a part of me is eternal, that I have known these old trails before. I believe it is the undying spirit of the frontier calling me, through the mind's eye, to step back into time. What is the appeal of the Old West of the American frontier?

It has been epitomized by some as the dark and bloody period in American history. Its heroes—Crockett, Bowie, Hickok, Earp—have been reviled and criticized. Yet the Old West lives on, larger than life.

It has become a symbol of freedom, when there was always another mountain to climb and another river to cross; when a dispute between two men was settled not with expensive lawyers, but with fists, knives, or guns. Barbaric? Maybe. But some things never change. When the cowboy rode into the pages of American history, he left behind a legacy that lives within the hearts of us all.

—Ralph Compton

CHAPTER ONE

I'M SUPPOSED TO be afraid . . . of *this*?"

Andrew Pierce Buchanan looked at the orange a moment longer, then squeezed it in his big bare hand. The rind gave easily and pulp and juice oozed around his fingers. He opened his palm, turned his hand over, and let the fruit drop to the rusty red dirt. Then his dark brown eyes returned to Chester Jacob, the man who had given him the fruit.

"You proved absolutely nothing except that you're a stubborn man—a *good* man, don't mistake my meaning, but one without a good head for business."

The speaker, Chester Jacob, pulled the drawstrings on the canvas sack. He threw it back over the shoulder of his brown suit.

"And you, my friend, are like my kid brother used to be," Buchanan said. "Always impressed with things that are new."

Buchanan's young, devoted Australian shepherd, King, came romping over, following the strange scent.

The six-foot-three rancher lowered his hand to where the dog could lick it.

"He don't seem so fond," Buchanan said as the dog turned elsewhere.

"They're for people," Jacob replied with frustration. "Oranges are not just new, Andy. They're vital, alive."

"Not so alive," Will Fremont chuckled. The foreman of the AB Ranch was standing beside Buchanan. Each laugh caused his outsized chest to expand and contract like a blacksmith's bellows.

"That was one," said the disgusted Jacob. "Imagine thousands."

"That's what I'll have to, friend," Buchanan said. "Imagine them. They're not coming. Not to my land, anyway."

"Like Indians, they will surround you before you know you're in danger," Jacob said.

"Then you will have the satisfaction of knowing that you warned me and I didn't listen."

"Besides, boss needs something to rope," Fremont said. "He loves throwin' a lariat. Can't do that with an orange."

The agent for Widmark Shipping sighed and hoisted the sack over his shoulder. The man was a fit, bronzed statue in a brown suit that had been battered about the seams by constant travel and too-little darning.

At least he doesn't have to worry about being stopped by the hands-up crowd and robbed of his clothes, Buchanan thought. There were still outlaws, renegade Rebels among them, who dogged the routes he took.

Fremont was watching the dog and chewing on a dead cigar. "Boss, you remember that hailstorm that smacked us about, oh—four, five years ago?"

"Summer of '65, right after the war. What about it?"

"Yes, what does that have to do with anything?" asked Jacob, taking out his impatience on the shorter man.

Fremont puffed on the cigar, with no success. He was glaring at Jacob and did not seem to notice.

"Those hailstones tore heck out of the silo, the barn, and the house Andy had built. Even worse than the quake that came right before. Roof of the sod shed looked like Old Greyback turned a scatter gun on it." He had pointed at the distant mountain, then looked down at the mash even the dog had abandoned. "If this 'dangerous' orange of yours fell from the sky, this is what woulda happened."

Buchanan and Jacob both looked at the speaker with confusion, Jacob with impatience as well.

"I am pretty sure, Fremont, that Chester meant a different kind of fearsome when he showed us the orange."

"I *know* that. I was making a *metaphor* for the purpose of educatin'."

Buchanan grinned. "Next time I see Miss Sally, I will report to her that you can both read *and* philosophize."

"Among my other attributes." Fremont inflated and winked.

"For the love of Pete," Jacob complained.

The three men were standing under a charitable spring sun at the strong oak gate that stood below the sign of the AB Ranch, a five-hundred-acre spread established by Buchanan in 1852. That was the year the U.S. government drew up the San Bernardino meridian, a survey that had helped to divide public and private parcels. Then just twenty, he was working as a cowboy up north, in the San Joaquin Valley. He had paid $1.01 an acre using money he had inherited when his mother, Rachel, died.

The shipping agent looked down at the sweet remains where flies were now beginning to cluster. "I did not mean, Mr. Fremont, that you should fear this as some kind of . . . of celestial thunderbolt. What I meant is that this fruit can either be an instrument of your financial ruin *or* your salvation."

"We're doing okay, ain't we?" Fremont asked his employer.

"We're not starving."

"What about your herd?" Jacob pressed.

"They're eating, too," Buchanan replied.

"But farther out than before. Double-D hands say they saw Reb Mitchell making his rounds wider than before."

"Grasses grow on their own time, not mine."

Fremont said, "Double-D hands and rustlers were also ridin' wider than before. Dawson tries every way he can to hurt every small ranch he can."

"Then, for God's sake, get out before there's bloodshed," Jacob said. He shook his head. "Mark me, one way or the other, the Valencia orange is coming to this region, and soon."

"The appetite for beef ain't goin' anywhere either," Fremont said.

"But there's still a glut—"

"I am just gonna have to ride that out."

"—and you're farther west than Wyoming and Texas, so you still have to walk your herd in. How many pounds do they lose each drive? That's cash they're shedding."

"Train'll be here someday soon."

"Another wait you have to 'ride out.'"

"Maybe not. I got another notion in the meantime, one that may cure the problem entirely."

"Involving cattle?"

Buchanan shrugged. "That's what we raise here."

"That's my point. I have an option for you, too, Andy. The state is going to subsidize orchards and there will be more and more of them. They'll come in and then go out on Mr. Widmark's boats. Even now he's up north commissioning a ship with one of those fancy screw propellers so he can scoot across the Pacific. If not for cleaning and feeding beef, I'd say the Far East was a market for you—but it isn't."

"And you'd need more ice than cow to ship carcasses, I know. I talked to the clipper captains along the *Golden West*'s route. Asked me if I could get them guano. Big demand for that, too."

"There is?" Fremont said.

"Fertilizer," Jacob informed him without turning from Buchanan. "You're always ahead of me, and you're always thinking. Which is why I've come to you, to give you a chance to become part of something else before everyone else."

"Including Dawson?" Fremont asked.

"He's a different case," Jacob said. "Some ranchers do that as a means to empire building."

"Thank you," Buchanan said. "I mean that, Chester. But groves and vineyards are a little tame for me. And for my men, too, I think. We're family."

"I bet it wouldn't take much to convince Joe to switch to whittling," Fremont said. "Give him more time for Bible studies." The foreman made a fist and swung it up and down. "What do you call those sticks on ships?"

"Belaying pins?" Buchanan said.

"If you say so. Or a big longhorn steer scowlin' out at the water."

"Figureheads," Buchanan said.

"That's it," Fremont said.

Jacob's bony fingers tightened around the neck of the canvas. "This is not a joke, gentlemen. By my soul, change is coming."

Fremont snorted. "It always does. Miss Sally says that a lot, but she thinks it's good for us. Keeps us educated, like this next drive. And change'll show your oranges the saloon door when the next paying customer rolls in. Maybe wild turkey meat or snake hide."

Buchanan, however, was silent. He turned his eyes east, toward the stable where over a dozen horses were being fed and groomed in preparation for the next drive—the most dangerous one any man had ever taken. His gaze drifted south to the sky-scraping peaks beyond, their sharp edges and snowy crags bright against the rich, blue heavens.

"Like I said, we've been doing okay here," Buchanan said, more to himself than to the others. "We'll keep on doing okay. I feel it."

The rancher raised the brim of his off-white Stetson and let the noon sun shine on his forehead. He had possessed that sense for weeks now, like something was coming. He squinted now to the west, where small shadows fell from the occasional oak and cactus, to the posts and sign a short walk away at the front of his property. He watched as King, who had been fighting the rind like it was a dead bird, suddenly dropped it and took off after a gopher. Both animals scrambled into a gully that had been created when an earthquake rearranged the landscape on a very hot July morning the summer previous. He thought back. Everyone knew then that something was coming. It wasn't like a puma stalking just beyond a campfire and the horses tugged at their ropes, or a black bear foraging in the compost mound, making all the cattle restless. For days before the tremblor happened, every animal—domestic, flying, crawling, or burrowing—was still. Buzzing was nowhere to be heard. The twilight bats stayed in their caves. Even King stuck to lying beside the well. Then the quake hit and everything was in motion. The house and barn twisted one way, then the other, like when his daughters made up their little dances. Fence posts swayed, trees groaned, dirt danced, and rocks shifted. Only the mighty San Bernardino range anchored by San Gorgonio Mountain, Old Greyback, paid the thing no attention. He saw later upon exploring that they'd shook off a few rocks but nothing more. Then, as soon as the rumbling was over, the animals returned to life. They didn't even pay heed to the little tremors that followed.

Buchanan wondered if his own sense was like that—something animal.

"What about your wife and the girls, A.B.?" Jacob asked.

The rancher was startled out of his thoughts like a sleeper suddenly woken. "I don't get your meaning."

"Maybe you should talk to them. You met your wife while planting crops, did you not?"

"That was very different."

"Yes, but maybe it was a sign. Someone who's been to war and back—I would have thought such a man would want to stay home, count his many blessings, enjoy his family instead of crisscrossing half a country for half a year."

"Two countries."

"Pardon?"

"Nothing. And what is your solution, Chester. To watch orchards grow?" Buchanan shook his head. "I'd be so ornery each and every day, my girls'd throw me out. You can only fix thatching so many times, replace a few warped floorboards once every spring."

"What are you, thirty-eight?"

"Bordering on thirty-nine."

"Aren't there other things you want to do?"

"What man would say there aren't?" Buchanan turned a thumb south. "Never been to the top of Old Greyback to see if Saint Gorgonius actually lives there, like the missionaries say. Never crossed the Inland Empire to the sea down there."

"Y'mean Big Salt Creek," Fremont said. "Miss Sally calls that a misnomer, seeing as how it's much larger than that, according to books she's got."

"What about something bigger than a sea?" Jacob pressed. "You can plant orchards and let your men tend them, come and see a blue ocean, not like the dreary one you grew up on. I tell you, there are sunsets that light a fire in the soul. I can arrange that—"

"You just told me to stay home and count my blessings."

"Mr. Widmark has short runs up and down the coast and is looking for deck officers. In fact, if you want, you can bring some cattle."

"What's 'some'?"

"Maybe twenty head? There's a market in Guaymas on the Gulf of California. We already sail there to swap woven goods for shrimp."

"From steer to those shellfish?" Buchanan shook his head. "Chester, I don't think so."

"Don't think of your job as beef. You command men. Why does it matter where?"

"Because I *know* this," Buchanan said.

"Men are born to learn, to grow."

"I saw balloons that can carry men to the sky, too," Buchanan said. "When you're ready for that, we'll talk."

"I'm sorry?"

"I would like to try that, flying among the clouds. Imagine meeting Old Greyback as an equal. Imagine hitching balloons to cattle to move 'em."

Jacob frowned. "Now you're just wasting my time."

"Oh, no he ain't," Fremont jumped in, his chest inflating again to announce knowledge. "Did you know that a coupla French boys figgered it all out back in the 1780s? Miss Sally told me all about them. I forget their names but they were paper makers who watched ashes rise—"

"Thank you, Fremont," Buchanan said. "I think you do need to get back to work, help Griswold with the table grub. He's been a little held back since he hurt his arm."

"I am on the hoof," Fremont said, nodding at both men in turn and walking off, bowlegged and rolling the dead cigar around his mouth.

Jacob regarded the rancher. "You don't get hurt picking oranges, you know."

Buchanan turned his bronzed forehead toward the mush on the ground. "Except if you're an orange. How're you going to fight them?"

"They don't sail to the West Coast or Asia."

Buchanan grinned. "Come on, I'll see ya off."

"Thanks, but fair warning: I won't stop asking."

"Doggedness is one of the things I admire about you," the rancher slapped the man's bony shoulder.

CHAPTER TWO

BUCHANAN AND JACOB walked through the still, warm air to the agent's buckboard. The dirt of the AB Ranch glowed golden under a cloudless sky. It did not seem arable to the rancher, since nature had not by its mighty self produced anything here. But the well had never gone dry even in the worst of any drought, and the state had men and equipment enough to irrigate a desert. He had seen that up Los Angeles way.

For a passing moment, the idea had some appeal for the reasons Jacob had said. But it was here and gone like one of those fast-flitting, guano-laying bats that flew from the Bernardino caves. This trade, these men, were as much a part of his life as his family. Not as dear, but more plentiful.

The agent's wagon sat by the trough near the well. The two-horse team was peaceful, broken in a way his own horses were not. *Maybe in a way that horses should never be,* Buchanan thought.

The Connecticut-born Jacob had his own thoughts,

too. He liked the rancher, a fellow New Englander. But like most men from the shipping centers in Connecticut, Rhode Island, and Massachusetts, he did not understand men who were deaf to the bass and far-reaching voice of the sea.

"I'm confused, Andy. You grew up in Boston—"

"Just till age fourteen."

"That's growing up. How in the name of Sam Adams did you get dust up your nose?"

Buchanan laughed. "You mean where'd the salt air go? It was never truly there, my friend. I used to make my pa frown so much, my ma was afraid his face would set that way. I used to go on deck with him and my kid brother on the three ships we owned. Little Jonathan? He wanted to be a cabin boy since he was able to stand on his own. There was this mate we used to pal around with, a French-Canadian named Charles, who told incredible stories—most of them probably not true, but we didn't know it then. Jonathan swallowed them whole. He was like some preacher who heard the calling before he could shave. I never had that. But you're right about one thing. That sunset to the west? It was not so proud as it looks from here, but it beckoned me to come to the open country."

"I still don't understand why a man raised on a harbor—one of the *great* harbors—could turn from it so completely. Was it your brother?"

"Of course that affected me, but there was more," Buchanan said. "Even before Little Jon was lost in a storm at sea, the ocean smelled dank, like an open grave. Morning tides were the worst when soaked, rotted wood and dead fish would bump the pilings and swirl around them. Those tides tainted the sunrise and everything its light touched, including our family. My brother's death killed my father; he lived in terror that some tatter of clothing would be among the detritus one day. But he was lost before that, doing the same thing day after day after stinking day. My mother could not wait to sell our boats."

"I'm sorry about that, Andy. Like I said, that's a different world back there, whaling and crossing the Atlantic. Out here, the sea feels new."

"Friend, you don't have to tell me. I smell it when the winds turn east each day, late afternoon. It carries the same salt, the same augury of things I don't want, just from a different direction. Hell, before you set sail, you got a checklist. Once you're underway, the only thing that changes is the weather. One seaman's the same as the next. Every day is the same. No, I got different plans, other things to try."

"You hinted at such. I'm guessing you haven't shared whatever you're thinking with the men?"

"I've told them. They ain't blind. They know we've got troubles with overstock and Dawson."

"All ranchers have those troubles," Jacob said. "Including Dawson, who doesn't make friends the way he conducts business."

The hard times were no secret to anyone. For years Buchanan and the other ranchers in the southwest had moved their herds through Texas up to Kansas and Abilene—most recently, among five million other longhorns. It was a struggle to make the journey and get a fair price. This past year, due to the ongoing overstock—compounded by a two-year boom of drives from Wyoming—ranchers were flooding the market with cut-rate beeves. The larger spreads, like Dick Dawson's Double-D, could take the losses. The AB could not.

"Care to let me in on exactly what you're thinking?" Jacob asked.

"Railroad's a bunch of years out, the way the Southern Pacific is moving anywhere but here. Using existing rail to the east—Double-D and others pay for favors. We don't stand a chance."

"That's why I've been pushing you to change tack. I don't talk to Dick Dawson like this—"

"I hear what you're saying, what you *been* saying"—Buchanan looked toward the San Bernardino range—"but I plan on going south with a mixed herd."

It took a moment for Jacob to grasp his intention. "Mexico?"

"That's right."

"Over the mountains?"

"Not if I can help it, and I think I can."

Jacob shook his head. "Andy . . . that's crazy."

"For a large herd, maybe. Not for us. I've been in contact by telegraphy with folks down there and my men agree. I tell you, Chester, there's opportunity. Been talking to a trade exchange in Hidalgo."

"What does Patsy have to say about that, if you don't mind my asking?"

"She's opposed. But you guessed that or you wouldn't've shown her your oranges first."

Jacob flushed slightly. "I gave her a few to flavor her stew or pie."

"Right kind of you," Buchanan said, his mouth twisting. "I guess I'll hear from her later."

"Honestly, I wish her more luck convincing you than I've had." Jacob put the sack in the seat beside a pair of six-shooters. "Andy, I will say one last time: I urge you to consider what I said."

"I considered it last year when you said 'avocados,' too."

"Sacramento wasn't behind those the way they are oranges."

"Not sure that's a good thing, but, anyhow, I just don't have the patience for it."

Jacob replied, "I think, rather, you have the impatience to ranch."

Buchanan chuckled. "I'm not sure I understand that, but I'll give it a think. You sure you won't stay for a meal?"

"Thanks again, but I want to reach the Widmark office by sundown." He gave his host one last, earnest look. "We'll be shipping oranges from somewhere. Just sorry it won't be from here."

"Again, thank you."

The men shook hands and, with guns and oranges as his companions, Chester Jacob set out, pausing at Griswold's chuck wagon just beyond the barnyard to swap a pair of oranges for jerky and water to complete his journey to Los Angeles.

Buchanan lingered for just a moment, taking measure of his own answers to the man's questions. They sat right, for the most part. And then a deeper feeling came over him, as it did so often—not one of the mind but of the heart. The earth was dry and the big wheels of the buckboard threw off dust. Even that little bit, wafting over, brought contentment to the rancher.

That and the lingering smell of Jacob's team dispelling the tang of orange in the air, an odor he had already grown to dislike. The thought of that everywhere would be unnatural.

The smell of roasting rabbit also pleased him. Even though he would not be sharing a meal with the men, he turned toward the chuck wagon of Buck Griswold. Even temporarily one-armed—his left hand got too friendly with a cauldron the cookie thought had cooled—no one could set snares and catch juicy hares like Buck. Even when they were at the ranch, he cooked over an open fire instead of going to the stove in the lodge where the hands lived, a low-lying lodge beyond the stable. He said he had learned in the Texican revolt to be ready to move in a moment.

"Sachem, wildfire or enemy fire comes off the plains, you gotta have your chuck on the hoof," he once told Buchanan. He used the Indian honorific as a way of separating Buchanan from the lesser men who owned ranches in the territory, notably their nemesis Dick Dawson.

Buchanan did not argue with Griswold when it came to his trade, although it forced him to keep the brush cut back far enough from the spread in case wind or a dust devil scooped flame from the fire pit and carried it about two hundred yards. Not impossible but also not likely.

When Buchanan arrived, Will Fremont was busy arranging the two stewpots on the wooden table while Griswold put out the tin plates. The sixty-year-old cookie looked like a fir stripped of foliage and bent partly forward from countless long, tough slogs on his chuck wagon.

"Y'all yakked for too long; I don't need you now." Griswold spoke without bothering to look up. "You want to be useful, summon the troops."

Buchanan obligingly went to the bell that hung on a freestanding A-frame. He gave the cord a few tugs. It was a ship's bell that had belonged to the *Marie Darling*, a British schooner that had gone down in a hurricane that hit Boston Harbor a quarter century before. The boat had not belonged to his family's small fleet; the bell came with an auction of salvaged goods his father had bought. Buchanan had placed it in the small wagon he drove west—mostly for traction. It was all the rancher needed to remind him of the home he had left.

King responded first to the raucous sound. He emerged running from the ditch a good distance north of where he went in, and without his companion. The men would come from the fields and the stables soon after.

The dog reached Buchanan and pantingly eyed the spitted rabbits.

"Not for you, King," the rancher said, petting him as his gaze returned to the retreating buckboard.

Fremont noticed his boss's look.

"That Jacob is like tumbleweeds when he blows in," Fremont said. The foreman got a pair of ladles from the chuck wagon and pointed one at the retreating agent. "After all these years he should know he can't tangle you up."

"Jacob isn't wrong, Fremont," the rancher said. "We're gonna have trouble from those oranges one way or the other."

"How do you figure? I'm thinking it'll be like the Bellville gold rush of 1853. The boom didn't last."

"The boom wasn't deep enough. Too many people, too little gold. This is different. The state will support the importation of a cash crop that can be et and drunk and don't rot, not like avocados. Oranges'll be eating up grazing land, acre by acre. Moving the herd west will mean a longer trip, thinner cattle. Then ya got San

Diego spreading this way. How long before our need for feed and their need for timber and water clash?"

"I see yer point." Fremont brought Griswold's sourdough biscuits from the wagon to the table. "You worried?"

"Not for this year, maybe not for next. But after that, we got two hundred head going on three hundred. We'll need more pasture for them, not less."

The four cowhands had emerged from the stable and ranch house and went to the well. A fifth man was out in the field with the herd; he spent a good part of the year out there.

The men clustered around the well to wash. Fremont lingered.

"If you're serious about Mexico, we can move the herd south, over to where there's timberland," the foreman said. "That'll give us a head start."

"I talked to Miguel about that. It's all fish and timber, good for a day or two of grazing. We'd starve the cattle just getting to where there's enough grass. Or maybe we can use your French balloons."

"Are you serious?"

"Sure. Or maybe we'll teach the cows to jump over the moon."

Realizing he had been had, Fremont waved dismissively. "Boss, I don't see us surrenderin' to a fruit any more'n we did to the Confederates."

The foreman joined the other men around the bucket. Buchanan turned from the stable and headed to the main house.

Damn Chester Jacob, he thought, angrier at himself than at the shipping agent. Life was easier when there were no decisions.

The Buchanan home was not tall or sprawling like on other spreads, but it was nothing like the sod structure Buchanan had built. That was when he arrived on the flatlands with a horse, two cattle, and a wagon with all of his worldly possessions, including a well-used rifle and a hatchet. Cow punching his way west, he had made temporary homes in Kentucky, Texas, and Arizona before settling here in 1856. Until the war, he sold the cattle he produced locally.

He had learned, from his previous homes, to use only grasses with thickly packed roots to make large, fifty-pound bricks, to cut straight poles made of cedar for support, and to secure enough muslin to suspend beneath the roof. Otherwise the roof made of tightly tied bundles of miscellaneous vegetation would drop dusty particles down on everything inside.

To this day Buchanan could vividly recall the smell and feel of the muddy bricks on his hands. He remembered the fear and excitement of his first drive, with thirty head of cattle and just Fremont to help him. A part of him—an insistent part—would have those days again. Not simply turning over earth to plant groves but challenging that earth in all its forms, whether plain or mountain, dry or soaked, windy or snow-covered.

The old home he had built still stood. It served as a root cellar behind the log home Buchanan built when he and Patsy were wed. A large stone chimney sat on one side. The two windows in the back were covered with greased paper to admit light but to keep out the direct sun and gnats; Buchanan did not see the point of buying glass windows when a good dust storm would smash them to shards.

The now-distant smell of Griswold's rabbit had delighted his nostrils, but a Patsy Buchanan meal filled his soul. Before Chester Jacob rolled in, Patsy had been preparing the two fowl her husband had shot that morning at the creek. The girls, Diedre and Margaret, were busying themselves with freshly baked—now slightly burnt—bread as well as potatoes from their garden.

"Come on, Pa!" eight-year-old Diedre called out when she saw him through the open door. "The bread is *already* on the table!"

"Be right in, honey."

As he reached the shade of the plank-floored porch, Buchanan turned and kicked the back of one heel and then the other against a post. Collected dust puffed from the leather. When he finished, he stood and looked toward Old Greyback. The rancher watched transfixed as the sunlight slowly shifted across the crags till it burst back at him from the snow-white peaks.

A beacon, he thought. But was it calling him forward or, like a lighthouse, warning him of shoals?

Buchanan was not a devout or superstitious man. Not like his wife, a preacher's daughter. In war he saw firsthand how God had better things to do than look after individual soldiers or the families who would be grieving for their terrible losses. He had not fought for the same reason he had come west: to test himself. There were occasions when he felt compelled to *do* something. It was a sense of patriotic duty that had sent him into the Confederate Territory of Arizona to fight alongside the anti-secessionists. He was part of the Timber Squad, so called because they flushed out the enemy by letting themselves be seen and heard, like a falling tree. When the Rebels fired—revealing their positions—the eight Union soldiers had already dropped to the ground, presenting no target and returning fire.

"Pa!"

This time it was Margaret. He turned, considering this new challenge, the one he had set for himself. He felt now the way he had nearly a quarter century earlier when he left Boston. It was something like the feel and smell of raising a sod house. And the time for it was coming fast. April was here and he had to move the cattle within the next two or three weeks, after they'd fatted some on new grass—not June, as usual, when the rivers were swollen and the grasses high.

Just then King reached the door, having made short work of a few scraps of rabbit Griswold had slipped him. His tail vigorously swept the air as he looked up at his master.

"Speaking of getting fatted, old friend, let's go get it!"

The dog barked and wound round him, padding to his place beside the rancher's chair. Patsy was taking the crisp fowl from the hearth and Margaret was using a wooden spoon to press the potatoes in a wooden bowl.

"My arm hurts," the ten-year-old complained. "I kept mashing and mashing so they wouldn't be stiff when you got here."

"Deeply appreciated."

The girls resumed telling their mother about what they had learned in Miss Sally Haven's classroom the day before about earthquakes, about a scientist who used gunpowder to cause sound waves that told him what the earth was made of. The two, along with ten other children, attended class outside of San Bernardino town three days a week. They were brought over by Will Fremont if he had no pressing duties; otherwise, Patsy took the wagon. Fremont did not seem to mind shopping for supplies, getting horses shod, and waiting outside the schoolhouse to bring the girls back.

Buchanan kissed his wife on the cheek. She was a petite woman with straw-colored hair worn on top of her head under a checkered blue kerchief. Her blue eyes spoke eloquently of her Scandinavian heritage.

"Sorry I was delayed. I wanted to hear what Chester had to say."

"You may tell us after grace," Patsy said.

"Yes, ma'am."

"And save your impertinence until after you wash."

"Yes, ma'am."

Patsy's mouth twisted playfully and the girls laughed as their father went to the basin.

Unlike deep yearning, dirt washed away easy.

CHAPTER THREE

GRACE WAS SPOKEN, as always, with Patsy leading. Despite running the kitchen, the household, the garden, and two daughters, she was never too busy to make time for God. Her husband had once said that this was when they should take a photograph or cut a silhouette, she was that still.

Patsy Wallach Buchanan was the daughter of Reverend Tudor Wallach, a Virginia abolitionist and Episcopalian preacher who came west to bring religion to the heathens. Patsy's mother had died giving her birth and Wallach's ways were the only ones she ever knew. The two traveled from church to church and then—farther west and south—from mission to mission. They would preach the word of God and His intentions for the wilderness, both tamed and untamed. Patsy learned to play the organ and accompanied her father's fiery sermons.

Buchanan met the young woman in 1859. The Wallachs were just up from a two-year evangelical passage through Mexico down to Yucatán and had stopped at the Mission San Luis Rey. They were there on the one day a year Buchanan visited the sanctuary to honor the memory of his family—his lost brother in particular—by working beside the Indians and the Mexicans who were planting crops. That was not where his interests lay. He put his back to unearthing tree stumps and moving or breaking rocks. What Jacob had taken as a "sign" was exactly the opposite. Buchanan set himself a task that taxed his arms and back to the utmost as a form of scourging, of penance for having avoided the fate that took Jonathan Buchanan.

After morning services, Patsy was also in the field. She was sunburnt and thin from her arduous travels, but her spirit and eyes were unbowed. The two worked side by side long into the late summer night, falling in love by torchlight. Buchanan stayed the night, which he had not planned to do; after breakfast, it was she who proposed to the strapping rancher.

"God saw fit to place us here, together, like two lights in the dusky firmament," she said. "Who are we, Andrew Buchanan, to deny His will?"

The rancher did not pretend to know the mind of God but he knew inner and outer beauty when he was in their presence. He accepted at once.

As God would have it, the night before, Tudor Wallach had learned from a passing French trapper of a northern race known as "Esquimaux." Wallach had prayed through the night and God told him to go north; Patsy decided not to and asked Buchanan to marry her. Reverend Wallach tearfully officiated before their mutual departures.

The newlyweds rode south on a restless palomino that had never carried more than one rider. Proximity to each other was intoxicating and it took three days for them to reach the Buchanan homestead. The rancher was proud of his sod house but also instantly apologetic.

"It is not the smell of flowers and saintly portraits you may be used to," he said as it rose from the horizon like one of the potatoes they had harvested.

"I have slept in houses that natives constructed in trees," the twenty-year-old informed her husband. "This home, our home, will be a lovely reminder of the dust from which Adam was crafted."

It was the first of many times she tried, mostly without success, to teach her husband to seek God's purpose in everything, from sod to oranges.

Patsy had pinned back the window coverings for their meal, the sun spilling generously across the north side of the room. The table around which the family gathered was made of a light spruce, darkened as if with stigmata where Patsy folded her hands when she said grace. She believed it to be the shadow of the Christ's own hands enveloping hers; Buchanan suspected, but never said, that it was grease from fowl and rabbit, whatever he had caught for supper. The table was made by Joe Deems, a humble work of carpentry to honor the Ultimate Carpenter. The twenty-seven-year-old Oklahoman had been a lusty, womanizing logger up north and was Buchanan's second hire following the war, after Fremont. The native Californian had arrived shortly before Patsy and at once came under her reverent spell. He ended both his wrong-minded ways and salty language. Purchasing a Good Book of his own in Wichita, he became the drive's unofficial preacher and, sometimes, its conscience.

The family received letters from Tudor Wallach on

occasion. The reverend had remained in Alaska and married a converted Indian. The letters came on a Widmark boat and were delivered by Jacob. He did not have one today, which was why he had gone to see Patsy first. He knew she would be hopeful, hearing him arrive.

The last time he had written, seven or eight months previous, the reverend seemed content save for the frigid climate and oddly long or short days—although apparently, he said, God approved of his work, since the Almighty's finger was at times visible in the night sky, draping the heavens with celestial gowns of green and yellow. Wallach was only unhappy about being unable to lay eyes on his granddaughters, and their inability to see him.

"But the Word of God surpasses the desires of men, so I remain in my chapel built of blocks of snow and ice."

He had enclosed a new pencil sketch of the white church, domed with a cross made of seal bone. The drawing, on a cured pelt of some kind, hung framed beside a youthful daguerreotype of the reverend.

Grace ended with an expression of love and prayers for the preacher, followed by silent thanksgiving. Then the eight hands and four paws became active, along with youthful curiosity.

"Stay, King," Patsy ordered. The dog dropped to the ground; the woman's voice was the only one he obeyed.

"What did Mr. Jacob want, Daddy?" Diedre asked.

"Just to tell me about his oranges, kinda bragging."

"You were talking for quite a spell," Margaret said. She was the wise, intuitive one.

Buchanan cut and served the first duck. "Mr. Jacob

had the same business proposition as last time. He wants me to stop raising beef and start growing oranges."

"I don't like the smell of them," Diedre said. "They burn my nose."

"You're not being very practical," the older girl replied. "Oranges are juicy *and* you can eat them."

Diedre's mouth turned down and her nose turned up. "I still don't care for them."

"Don't make faces," Patsy said. She passed the bread basket. "I saw you squeeze the orange Chester showed you, Andrew. You were, I trust, seeing if it was ripe?"

"I was making a point, Patsy."

"I find that words are suitable for that."

It was a gentle rebuke; she was not wrong. Jacob's insistence—again—about orchards and the sea had frustrated him.

"Why did you turn him down, Andrew?"

"Because growing those things . . . it'd be like starting over again."

"'To every thing there is a season, and a time to every purpose under the heaven,'" she said.

"I am not one to say the Bible is in error, but I question whether one season has ended and another begun."

"I like our garden," Margaret said. "I could have helped grow oranges."

"Thanks, Maggie," her father said. "But we couldn't've done what Mr. Jacob suggests without surrendering our stockyard and maybe the corral for the groves and irrigation. Growing oranges—growing anything—would be a commitment to doing only that."

Plates full, the girls had started to eat. Patsy pretended not to notice her husband slipping King a sliver of duck meat. Looking away gave her time to consider her words carefully. "Would that have been so bad?"

"For a *rancher*?"

"For the family."

Buchanan regarded her. "This has been on your mind since Chester first mentioned it at the new year."

"Longer than that, and not this but something *like* it. You've said yourself we may—" She stopped so as not to alarm the girls. "We may have challenges with the size of the herd and their value. And then there's the trip you're considering."

"I've done more than consider," he said.

It seemed as good a time as any to say it. Patsy regarded him with a look he had not seen before, one that was uncustomary for her. It seemed lost.

"Pa, are you going somewhere?" Diedre asked.

"The drive. You know that, honeybunch."

"In April?" Margaret asked.

"Don't speak while you're chewing, girls," Patsy said. She was still looking at her husband. "Might you explain what you mean, Andrew?"

Buchanan tore his bread in half and buttered it. "You remember that gaucho and his hand who came through last month from Hidalgo looking to buy cattle?"

"Of course. You sold him a half dozen."

"He wanted more but he'd already sent his own men back with twenty-odd head and didn't have the manpower to handle extra. He asked if Joe and Miguel could be hired on loan to go back with him, but I needed them here."

Miguel was Buchanan's most recent hire, a newly arrived Mexican skilled with horses and men.

"Was the buyer not intending to return?" Patsy asked.

"He was not. He was turning back to try and breed what he bought. He said that the Mexican government was paying workers more money to become *traqueros*, to build railroads, than to raise cattle. Told me if he couldn't raise a herd himself he'd move his family to Venezuela. It was clear from our talk that Mexico needs meat."

"What about feeding them with the herds that are bunched in Texas?"

"It's a long way to take the kinds of numbers that're stockpiled there. The big ranchers seem content to wait and force the smaller ones into selling out to them. They can take the losses. They can also bribe the men at the rail yards to get their cattle out."

The overproduction of beef had been a problem since the end of the war, when the Union no longer had to provide meat for its troops. The demand for meat in the East was greater than ever, but the three trails to get them to cattle cars—the Chisholm, Goodnight-Loving, and Great Western—were continually bottle-necked.

"You got them through last year," Patsy said.

"Not without skinned knuckles."

She shot him a look. "You never told me."

"It wasn't me so much as the men. Will, Reb in particular. They got fed up being pushed so they pushed back. It'll be worse this time."

Patsy ate in silence for a time. The sound of cutlery on plates called attention to the silence.

"Where in Mexico?" Patsy finally asked.

"Pachuca in Hidalgo."

Her blue eyes widened. "That's a trip of about a thousand miles!"

"It's four or five hundred less than Wichita," Buchanan pointed out.

"As the crow flies." Patsy said. "To Kansas, it flies flat across the plains. That is not so with *el estado libre y soberano de Hidalgo.*"

"The mountains do lie inconveniently between here and there," Buchanan admitted. "But I've been talking to Miguel. He says there's a pass that curves between them. He went through it a few summers back. It's called the Valley of the Ancient Lake on the railroad survey I saw. Miss Sally had the map in a paper-covered little book. I drew it down myself, exact."

"I've heard of that valley. Cabazon, if it's the same, with the Big Salt Creek beyond."

"I saw that name Cabazon on a map, too. Tell me about it."

"I don't have firsthand experience," she said. "My father and I spent time in the mission of La Purísima Concepción de Caborca. We reached it going south through Texas, along the Mexican coast, then turned east. But many travelers who attempted crossings spoke of the hardships."

"What kind of hardships?"

"The ground, for one. Many said it was like quicksand."

"Rains did that on our past drives, turned good trail to mud."

"You're going to have an answer for everything, aren't you?" Patsy said. It sounded more like an accusation. "Then answer this. Miguel may not have realized that, going farther south, the valley runs into the Orocopia Mountains. You must cross them or circle them, but you cannot go south there and ignore them. Then there's the inland sea, which is salt water surrounded by desert."

"Perhaps those other travelers were unprepared."

"It may well be. Even so, none of those I spoke with attempted to make the crossing with nearly three hundred head of cattle. And with a man at your side who has been thinking more and more about matters other than cattle."

"He needs this drive to succeed as much as any man," her husband replied.

She was referring to Fremont and his fancy for Miss Sally. Patsy did not know what cowboys knew: on a drive, home and romance were a separate life, as though they belonged to some other man.

Patsy's voice had risen slightly while she spoke, and Buchanan did not comment further. He had learned to hold his peace while his wife said her piece.

"It would be at best an unforgiving trip," the woman went on. "I do not see the sense of it—not at all."

There was another silence, longer now. In fairness to Patsy, she had never discouraged her husband's ideas or ambitions. She would not be protesting now, he felt, if there were no options.

"You have dismissed the notion of selling the herd and planting oranges," she continued. "I do not understand why. I'm sure the Double-D or the Running S would take the cattle for a fair price. That would give us enough to live on and to pay the hands off until we have a crop for Mr. Jacob."

"Mother," Margaret asked, "does that mean we would never have steak to eat?"

"You will have no supper at all if you interrupt," the woman answered firmly.

The older girl slumped over her plate. Even King retreated a little, on his belly.

"Sit upright," Patsy said.

Margaret obliged and Diedre sat even straighter. Patsy once again fixed her eyes on her husband.

"Mightn't the girls and I tend to the groves? You have spoken of raising horses."

"As a part of raising cattle, not instead of," Buchanan said. "I couldn't afford to keep anyone on, maybe not even Fremont."

The third silence was the last one.

The question of the southward drive went unmentioned for the rest of the afternoon, except in Buchanan's mind. He did not like to worry his wife, especially when she was not wrong about the dangers and he was stubbornly holding a contrary view. It was no different from when he set out from Boston with only a vague idea and a lot of determination as to what he would find and what he would do. That afternoon, after he fed their barn animals and checked on men and cattle, he stood by the trough and gazed northward.

All I have to do is ride after Chester Jacob, agree to his proposal, and then there will be no further strife with Patsy, no danger to myself or the men, no hardships other than whatever nature might hammer down on us—

"And no reason to live past forty, other than to see the girls grow and keep my wife contented," he said.

Dammit.

His afternoon chores done, Buchanan went to the stable and saddled his horse and rode at the mountains. They were too far to reach and barely moved but that did not matter. He wanted to ride, hard. Even his choice of the notoriously spirited mustang was made to challenge himself. The stallion was descended from the original Spanish horses and was among those left to grow wild. Riding him was a challenge, but Buchanan did not want him or his men to be riding a heavily domesticated animal when he tried to change the mind of a stray longhorn who was seven feet from tip to tip.

Just a few weeks from now, he thought. That was when the roundup would begin. And this year, Buchanan decided with finality, the drive would be going to Mexico. No other decision was possible, given all the considerations.

Excitement, not fear, began to build in the rancher.

The day was starting to turn rust-colored by the time Buchanan returned home, but the highest peaks of Old Greyback still gleamed with sunlight. Maybe if he read the Good Book along with his ladies, or paid better attention in church, Buchanan would know whether it was God or the devil who was bidding him, *Approach . . .*

CHAPTER FOUR

THE AB RANCH was run by eight men.

In addition to Buchanan, Fremont, cookie Griswold, and Joe Deems, there was Reb Mitchell, a Floridian who had fought for the wrong side of the Mason-Dixon Line but was forgiven; roper-wrangler Lewis Prescott, a rodeo trick-rider before the war, a Union cavalry officer during it; and stable boy Pete Sloane. Sloane was a dead shot with a long gun and was single-handedly responsible for the many coyote and fox pelts that covered cots in the ranch house. The most recent addition, arriving in time for the previous drive, was Miguel López, a retired revolutionary. The thirty-three-year-old had spent most of his adult life fighting both Spain and the French alongside fellow freedom fighters. Common purpose made allies of farmers and brigands until there was no one to fight but each other. Not wanting to fight his own countrymen—many of them former comrades who had turned to waylaying travelers and raiding villages—he came north.

Reb Mitchell spent most of his time in the high country, in the small cabin at the fringe of the spread nearly a day's ride from the compound. There was too much boundary for wire, and posts had a habit of drawing lightning and burning acres of dry grass, so Mitchell stayed there to watch the outlying members of the herd and to make sure that homesteaders and braves of the Yuma tribe did not make off with beeves. The Indians, who mostly lived and fished on the Colorado River, sometimes had a hankering for adventure or for something with larger bones than bass and trout. It was Mitchell's wild hog–call shouts more than his Springfield rifle that gave them pause. The Rebel was also responsible for moving the herd in case the Mohave River flooded, which happened seasonally and suddenly.

The roundup typically started three or four days before the drive, depending on where and how widely the cattle were grazing. Fremont would go out first to make that determination. Then he, Deems, and Prescott would pack their gear and join Mitchell.

This year Fremont came back with word that they'd need only two days to gather the herd. Preparations to depart for at least four months, and up to six, began in earnest.

For Buchanan, family was one of the two things that had dominated the days before the drive and undertaking it. The first days were mostly two parents trying not to wear their feelings on the outside where it would affect the girls and the work both had to do. Night was the best time to talk, when work was done and the girls were asleep. Diedre and Margaret slept in their own room, Buchanan and Patsy in the living room, their bed close to the hearth. Buchanan also liked to be near the door in case of a fire or varmint that somehow eluded Sloane.

Husband and wife were polite after the girls retired. Buchanan had informed his wife of his decision just days before and nothing more was said; the disappointment that hung in the room like a tester of smoke from a blocked chimney arose from love and not hate. However, both knew that their concerns would get squeezed to the surface—like that orange the man had crushed—the closer it came to the event.

Fueling the smoldering fire like dry brush were the messages communicated by telegraphy from the Western Union office in San Bernardino—a four-hour ride from the ranch—to the government postal service office in Pachuca, Hidalgo. The region had become a semiautonomous state only two years before, when the French were finally driven back across the sea and the Mexican Republic was restored. In none of his messages did Buchanan inform the authorities at the commerce exchange there when he was leaving or arriving or with how many head. Without a European army, López said that the countryside was a breeding ground for bandit gangs and bribed officials.

"Best not to give them notice," the Mexican had warned.

Nonetheless, in several communications, the Comisión Permanente not only informed Buchanan about current prices and established markets, they furnished the names of men to help should he wish to divide the herd short of Hidalgo. Luis Cordero seemed particularly keen to get cattle to the railroad workers laying track north to America. Buchanan both read and spoke enough Spanish to know that the official seemed pleased and eager to have cattle coming south.

THE MORNING THE men began their two-pronged departure was always charged with a prairie fire excitement. All the men were up before the sun and Buchanan would settle them, like he did with horses. He made sure each man knew his duties, since changeable weather, a larger herd, less experienced cowhands, and cowboys who were just older than the year before created a lot of first-time situations. This year, with a new destination and rugged terrain, it was essential that each man be both independent and a functioning part of the team. In a stampede, where nothing was ever predictable, both of those qualities would be needed.

Buchanan was impressed with the job Fremont had done reviewing the details with his men. Against what everyone except Patsy had predicted, the months Fremont had spent with Miss Sally made him a more conscientious and attentive foreman.

"You cannot impress a woman by pretending to be the ideal she cherishes," Patsy had said. "It must be true."

Fremont, Deems, and Prescott had ridden out in high and eager spirits, as memorable a departure as Buchanan could remember.

While they brought in the herd, the rest of the men—and women—packed provisions and supplies that could not be hunted (a water pouch could be stitched from the pelt of a deer), gathered, or cut from a tree (a branch could be fashioned into a new spoke for a wheel to replace a cracked one on Griswold's wagon). If need be, canvas bedrolls ruined by rain or snow could be replaced using the saddle as a pillow with the horse blanket for warmth. Tougher to fix were bones shattered by falls, wounds incurred in skirmishes, or disease that came with the wind and cold weather. Griswold was proficient with cures up to and including minor gunshots, knife cuts, arrow wounds, burns, and snakebites; mud was his preferred cure-all. It absorbed blood, drew out poison, and cooled the heat of broken skin. Nearly impossible to replace were horses, and most times one of the two extras the men brought were impressed into service.

But these were men accustomed to hardship, and Deems was always ready with the appropriate word of God to see them through. It was astonishing to Buchanan how many men became believers in the middle of a dust storm; not nigh as many as in the thunder of battle but more than a few. On the day before the second group rode out to meet the riders and beeves headed southwest for the first time, Griswold had said to Buchanan, "I believe we will come out of this with men who go to church more regular."

The rancher was not so sure. Cowboys had very, very short memories, and those wisps were mostly washed away by the first night's drinking. For his part, even in the midst of a stampede, Buchanan never thought half so much about himself as he did about his family.

Two days later, before Buchanan's own departure with Griswold and López, the night was fragile as a pie crust. A little Spanish, even less French—Buchanan could get by with these. The language he did not speak at all was "Patsy." The word "drive" was not spoken by the woman. Anything that might suggest the group's direction or destination was avoided as though they were pits of vipers. Patsy had no doubt used those words in her head so often, without much liking, that to say them aloud might produce an outburst that was either sad or angry, perhaps both. It was not until the sun had set and they were consigned to being indoors that she broached how she was feeling.

Dinner was done, the table cleared, and the girls abed when Buchanan finally approached his wife. King had gone out to help Griswold clean up the ranch house kitchen, which would not be used for a while. He had only just returned and was settled by the fire.

The next day was school, and Patsy was seated in a rocking chair mending one of her old blouses so Margaret could wear it. A lamp on the small table beside put an orange glow to her brown linen dress. When he spoke, his voice was gentle, like the light.

"I remember when you made the dye for that blouse," Buchanan said, pulling over Diedre's stool and sitting beside her. "Moss and nut hulls. Margaret was so small. And now she's of an age to wear it."

"That's part of it," Patsy said softly.

Buchanan looked at her curiously. "Part of what?"

She stopped her work and looked up. The lamp showed tears in her eyes. "Why I am so upset."

Buchanan rose to hold her. She raised a hand to keep him where he was.

"No. I will say my say."

"All right." Buchanan eased back onto the stool.

"There is never a day I don't fear for your safety. That mad horse you ride, Confederate marauders—danger is fulsome and coarse beyond these grounds. We have a different option now." She held up the garment. "We have different responsibilities."

Buchanan stood. He did not want to have this discussion child-sized.

"When your father left, did you feel the same way?"

"My father had a calling."

"As do I."

"What is it? Tell me. To explore? To test yourself? To be more like your grandfather than your father?"

"A little of all of that, I suppose. Mostly to build something."

"For who?"

"For all of us."

"But without soliciting ideas from any of us. Your calling, what drives you—and please forgive me for speaking frankly—is vanity."

Buchanan smiled. "'A worthless thing.'"

She was momentarily confused, then surprised. "That's right."

"You see? I do listen to Father Abbott's sermons. And forgive *me* for speaking frankly, but you're wrong."

"Have you considered what you do not know about this enterprise? I fear not."

"Every drive is different."

"Like every dust storm, every fire. But at least with those we know generally what to expect. We know what to *do*: seek shelter, water, protect the horses."

Buchanan let that subject drop. "What I feel is not vanity, Patsy. Cattle provide for us—not abundantly but well enough. That is why this trip must be made. We can become one of those large spreads."

"Succeed, and the other men will move in. They've let us be because we are not a threat. Fail, and I will never see you again. I may never even know what happened to you!"

"I won't fail," Buchanan insisted. "Besides, what

value would I be to you or our daughters if I stopped being a man?"

"How is a farmer not a man?"

"It isn't a question of the trade. I have thought about this every day since Chester first suggested the idea. I cannot abide working for someone, in this case Laurence Widmark. He would be our one and only source of transportation. And, working for him, I would once more be involved once again with the sea. And the *sameness* of the sea."

"Security," she said. "It would be the first time we have had that."

"It's a form of death, Patsy. I have not come all this distance, in years and miles, to be back where I started."

"So we are at this same conflicted place still." Patsy picked up her sewing. The tears were now streaming from her eyes.

Buchanan looked down at her, helpless. Her sadness was a veil he could not penetrate. He could only remove it by taking it on himself.

"You mentioned my grandfather. You know some but not all of how I came to be here."

Her eyes moved to his. Now she seemed hurt. "You have kept something from me, Andrew?"

"Not any facts, only a few truths."

"I don't understand the distinction."

"It was something . . . something I didn't understand myself, not fully, until this whole thing arose."

"Go on," she said.

He knelt beside the rocker and placed a hand on hers. "When my brother died, my father's grief was as bottomless as the sea that took the boy. Before that black time he used to enjoy visiting his ships, talking to the sailors, arguing with others of his profession. Afterward, he left the house only when he had to, and then with no joy in his step. I had been apprenticed to him and took over as many duties as I could. My mother had to quiet her own sorrow around him so that he could be persuaded to eat, sleep, take the pipe he had once enjoyed.

"Uncle Bernard, the haberdasher from New York, came for a memorial. Not long after entering our home, he took me for a walk. It was a cold winter's day, as befit our loss, and he encouraged me to leave that place or be dragged down by it. He did not just mean our home.

"'There is a pall over the waters,' he told me as we strolled the commons. He said that he had felt it himself as a child, which is why he learned a trade and left. Men never beat it, you know. The sea. At best, we are tolerated by the waters, by its swells and storms, lured by its superficial calm into the throes of its deep unrest. His parting words to me were 'Get away, Andy. Find your own self where there is something to push against . . . not just swallow you whole.'

"I took his advice," Buchanan said. "I'm not sure how much my father noticed about anything by then, but my mother encouraged my going."

"Are you suggesting that I should do the same? Encourage you to 'push against' land that is as unforgiving as the ocean you just described?"

He thought for a moment. "I suppose I am."

"Do you know what your mother was doing, Andrew? She was giving up her joy, the only strong man in her life, her only surviving son, to give you freedom. She knew what unhappiness lay ahead. I am not so courageous. My father once told me—and this *I* have not shared—that it was God who sent you west so that we might meet at the mission. God's will. That helped to ease the concerns I had about the peril you faced every day. But not now."

The woman looked down at the blouse, her tears staining the fabric. King's head rose but he remained spread beside the fire. Buchanan suddenly felt as though his hand were intruding. He removed it but remained kneeling by her side.

He did not agree with much of what Patsy had said, but there was one truth he could not avoid. He saw now, through her eyes, that his mother, Rachel Jackson Buchanan, *had* sacrificed herself to save him. It gave rise to a hard, sudden realization:

What is a man, farmer or rancher, who will not do that for his family?

Buchanan stood and turned his back to the woman. He did not want to see any further disappointment in her eyes, in her sweet face. He considered the question he had just asked himself, weighing not the muscles in his arms but the strength in his heart. After a long moment he turned back to her.

"What you call this pride of mine," he said, "it's strong and at times ungovernable. But I am prepared to make you a promise, if you will have it. Two promises, in fact. The first is that once we are underway, if it appears we cannot succeed, I will turn back. The second is that, whether we reach Hidalgo or not, when I return, the AB Ranch will become an orchard."

She hesitated long enough to make sure she had heard what he had said. Then her damp eyes rose to meet his. There was a flicker of life in them. "You mean this?"

"If my mortal and venial sins be the work of the devil, they will all be gone."

Tears came again, this time with happiness. "Thank you, Andrew."

"Chester Jacob will no doubt pass through in our absence. Please inform him of our decision and find out what he needs from the Buchanan family to solemnize the arrangement."

The woman set her work on the floor and put her arms around her husband's neck.

The change in her had been swift, but even as Buchanan kissed her neck, he knew that he had committed to two courses of action that went against his very nature. The orchards—he could find a way to endure that. Most of the men would leave, but those who stayed could, as Patsy suggested, help him break horses for other ranches in the territory. As for Widmark, Buchanan would find a way to transport his oranges by sea and land. And maybe, as he had jokingly suggested to Jacob, he would figure out how to send them east. There was something to the idea of returning to Boston a conquering orange king, thinking of ways it could be served with the bass and flounder that populated the harbor.

Of course, Buchanan's other promise had made a mockery of his wife's relief, because he knew it was a lie. Once he set out, he knew that even if he ultimately reached Hidalgo with one cow—or did not reach it at all—there was nothing that would turn him back from completing what would be his last drive. . . .

CHAPTER FIVE

THE DAY BEGAN as most days, with the rancher dressing and making a trip to the privy. It was the last solid structure he would inhabit for quite some time. His wife woke with him, also as she did every morning, but there was no talk of the day ahead. Only the sound of preparation filled their home, the rancher checking the essentials while his wife made sure he had personal items like their picture, his journal, and at least three pencils. When that was done, Buchanan went to the porch while his wife roused the girls. With his bag over his shoulder, his boots clunking, and his spurs ringing on the boards, he inhaled the clean morning air, freshened by the night's ocean winds, There were scratching sounds in the eave above, varmints that came out from the thatching before the hunting birds did.

Buchanan was wearing his Colts from the war; a Spencer repeating rifle leaned against a post. They were proficient weapons and he was proficient *with* them. He hoped that nothing warranted their overuse. There had never been a drive where they were not needed for hunting, protecting, or signaling; there had never been a drive when the weapons were more than a short reach away. The only one who was more capable with a firearm was Pete Sloane. That was the main reason he was selected to stayed behind.

The other item Buchanan kept handy, worn in a loop on his belt, was a spyglass that his father had used for over a score of years to watch the seas. The maritime glass was a compactible eighteen inches of brass and was as fine an instrument as Boston lens makers could craft.

Patsy followed her husband out. Despite his assurances, he was still undertaking a drive of which she disapproved. Still, she would never show him her back or fail to appear at all. She would wait until he was out of sight before preparing to take their daughters to school. The sleepy girls stood beside their mother, still in their nightdresses, waiting for their final hugs. King pushed between them and came forward.

"Goodbye for now, boy," Buchanan said, scratching him behind the ears and taking a good licking in return. "You keep guard over the trenches, stop the varmints from getting too close to the house."

Rising, he wrapped his arms around both daughters. "Help your ma in all ways," he said into their ears. "Make me proud."

"We will," they promised as one.

Then he moved on to Patsy, who was standing behind the door lantern she had lit. She wore an encouraging smile that stopped short of her eyes.

"You have your maps, your journal, your notes."

"I do," he said, kissing her forehead.

"God be with you," she said as her husband hugged her tightly.

"And with you," he replied.

Buchanan turned, picked up the rifle and, with a wave, walked toward the corral and the first sage-purple hint of the rising sun. Miguel López and Buck Griswold were finishing their preparations. Griswold would have been up most of the night provisioning his wagon while Pete Sloane readied the two-horse team and made sure the two extra horses in back were secure. Like the animals in front, these were pintos; they could be frisky, but Griswold wanted that energy. They were different from riderless mustangs, which were not to be trusted. The animals were packed with bundles of supplies, including extra hatchets, picks, and shovels, in case they were needed. Funerals on a drive were not unknown.

Sloane had been hired three years previous. At twenty-four years of age, he was a veteran of the war, having fought with the volunteer 104th Ohio Infantry. Sloane was mature in a way that combat made a man and he had no desire to test himself on the trail, like the others, nor ambition to be a rancher. His only wish, even four years on, was for honest work by day and quiet at night. War did that, too, to many men. Sloane was someone Buchanan knew would be happy to raise horses.

López took care of the horses that he and Buchanan would ride. The Mexican was proud of the animals he called "*mis bellezas salvajes,*" "my wild beauties." For most of his Mexican campaigns López had ridden burros or gone on foot.

The air was already warm and as dry as it had been for the past week. As they prepared to mount, the rancher took Sloane aside.

"Fill the cisterns and watch the horizon for lightning. If it's night, smell for smoke. Wildfires come on fast."

"I will do that, Mr. Buchanan."

"Also, I think we got field mice up top over the porch, filching tomatoes again. If you wouldn't mind checking . . . ?"

"They'll be food for the hawks this morning, early."

"And you remember the hornet's nests we had in the chimney a couple months ago . . ."

"Smoke pots will be ready below in case they return." The square-jawed young man smiled. "You will have enough to occupy you, sir. I will see to your family above all."

"Thank you, Pete. See you late summer. We'll have things to talk about when I get back."

"Yes, sir. And, Mr. Buchanan? Don't worry."

Buchanan hesitated. "There's one more thing. We're leaving better'n a month before the other ranches hit the trail. When word gets out, when they learn where we've headed, they may come by, try to find out where and why. You can tell 'em you don't know but they won't believe that from Patsy."

"She'll tell them it's none of their damn business, or words close enough to impart her meaning," Sloane said. "If I see anyone coming, I'll let her know what you said."

"Good man. Thank you."

"Good luck," the young man said before making a final check of the two palominos, a pair of tame riding horses that stayed easygoing when the herd or the weather wasn't.

Buchanan, López, and Griswold rode out with the sun, headed southeast to rendezvous with the herd.

With 283 head at last count, Buchanan had two things going for him. The number of steers was smaller than most cattle drives by more than half, and he had more men by that same percentage to handle the job. As soon as they linked up with Fremont's group, Buchanan, as trail boss, would ride point. He would take a half-mile lead on the herd, more than twice the normal distance, so he could watch for any problem spots.

The three men were silent as they rode, each contemplating the task that lay ahead. With all that he knew was to come—and likely more that he had not considered—Buchanan felt excitement, not dread. Even the dangers posed by bandits and Indians did not concern him unduly. There were always renegades. At least they would not have to deal with the Jayhawkers. Those men had been abolitionist Kansas guerrillas before the war, marksmen with Sharps rifles during the hostilities, and then feared rustlers after. The AB drive had only encountered small bands twice over the years, and both times the Jayhawkers were satisfied to accept no more than a meal. Perhaps they recognized a kinship with the struggling rancher. There was something melancholy about the aging warriors, and Buchanan made a commitment to himself that, raising oranges or horses, he would not let himself become like them in twenty or thirty years.

Lighting a cigarette he had rolled before leaving, López pulled down the brim of his hat to block the sun rising square in the direction they were headed.

Buchanan set a modest pace to reach the expected late afternoon union with the herd. He had allowed time for Griswold to settle the team. They objected to pulling a wagon laden for a long run, as this was, plus two extra horses.

López was riding between the wagon and Buchanan. When the three men had settled into a predictable pace, Griswold leaned toward López and shouted over the clatter of his hanging utensils.

"How d'you feel going home, amigo?"

López shrugged. "In Mexico, there was nothing for me. I have no family except cousins I don't like very much, and most of my close compadres are under wooden crosses which may not even be standing anymore. At the ranch is I am home."

"I guess I feel the same," Griswold said, "though I might feel that sense a mite more powerful if I had a little hut and a woman instead of the six of you for bunkmates."

"I think I will have both when I get back."

"Oh? You gonna ask Maria?"

"I think so. It will be a long time before we are together again and I miss her already."

"I seen those Mexicano girls at the laundry and you got yourself a princess, Miguel."

"*Sí.* I tell her mother to marry off her two older sisters first so she will wait for me."

"Why didn't you tie the knot before you left?" Buchanan asked.

"It is not fair to a bride to show her what love is and then go away. I have seen this problem in the past. To wait for the first time is expected. To wait for the second is not so easy. It is a way to—what do you say?—*vientos malos,* the bad winds."

"You're not wrong," Buchanan laughed. But it was not a knowing laugh. He had never been one for dance hall entertainment. He was saving money for cattle. Patsy had been right about his grandfather. Mathias Buchanan was a harpooner who, in the five years young Andrew Buchanan had been privileged to know him, loved telling stories not of the sea but of how he turned skill and ambition into owning his own ship. Buchanan was inspired by the man's gruff, clear-eyed certainty in his own abilities. Andrew's father, Jeremiah, did not quite match that spirit, that virility.

The young man had never wanted to be tied to a family while he was journeying west. Patsy had been a miracle, and after they met, there had been no question about her fidelity. She would turn to Jesus before she would seek comfort from any other man. As for him, he would rather be on his horse doing something that mattered.

Though you did tell her your first lie, the one about turning back, he thought. Maybe that was worse than unfaithfulness.

López pinched out the tip of his cigarette and tucked the remainder in the pocket of his leather vest. During his years as a rebel, he had mastered the art of half sleeping in the saddle, making up for a night spent reconnoitering or running. He did that now, his horse dumbly, obediently moving with the others.

Fremont had once described the plains here as having a "dead-possum sameness," still and brownish, with rolling rises here and there. He was not wrong. The trail they blazed went more or less straight through low ripples of hills and gullies. Occasional grasses and scrub, some hardy cactuses, and a few thirsty oaks were the only growth. Vegetation had been spotty for several springs, first from his cattle grazing and then from drought. A year before, a series of lightning strikes that could be seen, heard, and felt at the ranch started fires that burned away the underbrush, leaving only charred curls that mostly blew off, snagged on rocks, and hid large patches of the straw-colored dirt beneath.

"Larger herds'd die tryin' to cross here, Sachem," Griswold said.

"I see what looks like light bouncing off water ahead," Buchanan said.

"I noticed it, too. I was talking about starving, not dyin' of thirst. We need a name for this place, like 'the Buchanan Deadlands.'"

"When we get to higher elevations, we may wish for plains so flat," López said.

By early afternoon they reached a creek that was part of a tributary of the Mohave River. There they were able to water the thirsty horses and refill their own canteens.

The mountains to the south looked even more impressive here. They were slightly nearer and there were no trees to speak of concealing the foothills. The ribbon of water winding toward them seemed small and insignificant.

The morning brown hawks and golden eagles had already hunted, and the smaller meadowlarks and other grassland birds were out picking at insects and scrub and adding song to the stop.

"Thought there'd be more civilization out here," Griswold said.

"Cucamonga is north, Temecula south," Buchanan said. "After I made my map, I was looking for other surveyors' documents in San Bernardino to see where they agreed and disagreed."

"Doesn't exactly fill a man with confidence, you sayin' that."

"Like newspapers, facts don't tell the whole story. I got talking to an old-timer there who told me there was a flood of settlers when the republic became a possession of the United States in 1848. A lot of 'em gave up when the gold boom went bust and either there was too little water or too little good soil for farming. That left this whole middle section open."

"But not uninhabited," López said, pointing at marks along the creek. "Somebody dragged a canoe out of the water."

"Most likely Pechanga," Buchanan said. "I was told they're peaceable enough."

"Shoulda brought stuff to trade," Griswold said as they prepared to set out again.

"It'll be all right," Buchanan said. "They don't want to fight any more'n we do."

"Hey, Sachem, you remember when Jacob stopped by a few weeks back?"

"I do," Buchanan replied. "Hold on." The rancher turned and rode back behind the chuck wagon; the extra horses needed extra coaxing after a rest. Then he went back up front. "You were saying about Jacob?"

"Well, I was thinking that orange seeds mighta been good wampum for the planting tribes. I was also thinkin', on a trip like this, it would be something to have food and water in one small container like those oranges he carried. Tastier, too."

"The strings get caught in the teeth," López pointed out.

"I'd serve 'em with fish," Griswold said. "Then you could use the little bones to dig it out."

They splashed across the creek, Buchanan somewhat amused at how the cookie's thinking aligned with his.

The creek marked a dramatic boundary between the flatlands and the terrain that loomed not far beyond. Buchanan imagined that the slope of the land had driven floods westward, to their rear, for as long as the river that fed them had existed. Those waters had both irrigated and leveled that region. Almost at once, stretching well north and south, were low bluffs following the course of the Mohave. They were topped with low grasses; with their roots dug deep, the hearty blades managed to survive on groundwater despite being sunburnt. It looked to Buchanan as though at some time in the past the earth to the east had just fallen away, perhaps weakened by water and dropped by quakes like the one they had experienced at the ranch.

The men turned south. According to the map, they would come to where the Mohave River running north and south met the Santa Ana River running crosswise. From the bluffs, they saw the river coming nearer.

"All we have to do is follow it into the valley," Buchanan said. "It forks into two creeks, one of which cuts through a small valley and meets up with the Santa Ana. That's where we meet the herd."

"I think I like these drives without beeves," López said. "Much easier."

There was a superstition about easy beginnings to a drive presaging a hard finish, but Buchanan did not believe fancies like that. To him, all that sighting the Mohave meant was there lay about ten miles behind them with some eight or nine miles to go to the rendezvous. They would just reach the spot by dusk. Fremont and the cattle should already be there.

The small party was still on the bluff, and Buchanan rode ahead to find a spot they could traverse to get to the river. Riding close to the edge, he was looking not just for a gentle slope but one that looked solid enough to support a horse and the chuck wagon. He was glad, just then, that Griswold insisted on keeping the washing water inside instead of outside. The cookie did it for a smoother ride, the weight of the large barrel centering the wagon. It also meant the men doing some of his work for him: instead of just dumping their plates, cups, and utensils in an empty basin, they had to bring them inside where they belonged.

He was still within shouting distance when he found a spot he thought was suitable. The land had fallen from some winter rain, no doubt, given the rivulets that had been baked in by the sun. He motioned the others over, then started down.

The ground crumbled under the hooves of Buchanan's mustang, which struggled to keep his footing. Afraid of tumbling down on his larger horse, López pulled back on the reins as he descended. Its back legs bent, front legs doing the work, the animal was able to slide the twenty feet to the ground. The incline was more charitable to Griswold's wheels, which slid as much as they turned. The ruts actually kept the wagon from tipping to one side or the other as it descended.

Whooping and grinning, Griswold seemed to enjoy the ride.

"You got a strange idea of fun," López said when the wagon reached bottom.

Convened at the base of the bluff, the party continued south along the Mohave River until the northern wall of the valley came into view. Buchanan stopped them and took out his spyglass. He scanned the terrain to the southeast. Fremont had agreed to light a large campfire upon reaching his goal, assuming dry weather, but Buchanan saw no smoke. He inched the telescope north, looking for the dust of hooves in motion. He did not see those either.

"Don't look like you spotted 'em, Sachem," Griswold remarked.

"I have not. They could be farther east, behind some of those hills. Or the wind may just be blowing in the wrong direction. We'll move on. I'm sure we'll see some sign of them soon."

The men continued along the western bank of the river. The herd would have been traveling on the eastern side. Their course took them across low rocky hills toward the main headwaters of the tributary at Mill Creek, where the meeting had been arranged.

The mountains to the southwest had swallowed the sun early, so the men made camp in preparation for the late-morning push through the stone-covered hills that opened into the valley. Griswold welcomed the layover to tie down his canvas, which had jostled loose during the journey. He declined assistance from López .

"When it comes to my wagon, there's some things I do better one-armed than other folks do with two."

"You can sew your name on it too, *mi amigo*, as long as we get sourdough and whiskey beans first," López replied.

"I'll secure the wagon first, Miguel. Or don't you feel a wind threatening?"

"Griz is right," Buchanan said. "The ocean winds'll get this far at least."

The rancher smiled. It reminded him of the comment he had made to Jacob about floating beef. God help him, he could not stop imagining potentialities—just as he could not help drawing out the spyglass and looking for the herd.

* * *

THE NIGHT WAS windy and loud, the grasses and spotty trees rustling and groaning as the easterlies blew over. Tumbleweeds rolled constantly, and blown bits of grass bit as they stung the face. Griswold slept through it inside the wagon, the back panel up and the heavy curtains that opened to the driver's seat pulled shut, and the other two took shelter with their bedrolls behind their saddles, lodged next to the wagon wheels.

They finally fell asleep for a few hours before dawn broke calm, cloudy, and colder than they had anticipated.

"The cattle won't like this," López remarked as they saddled up. "Once we meet up, we should maybe push south, where it's warmer, and then west."

"That'll add days and higher elevations," Buchanan said. "It'll be colder than whatever we find on the ground. We'll stick to the route as planned."

The rancher's comments were practical, not critical, and López took them as such. Buchanan had always welcomed ideas from his men, especially men like López who had lived in other places and knew different things from him.

The elevation actually lowered as they neared the valley, in a way the map did not indicate. But then a different kind of chill settled on Buchanan. The nearer they came to the tributary, and as the morning progressed, the more the rancher's soul began to dampen. He did not need to check his map to know that they were nearly in sight of the meeting spot. Even though the herd was coming from a different direction, through a cut in the valley that lay ahead, they should have seen or heard something. Moving cattle causes birds to scatter, men to shout and sometimes to fire their weapons. Dismounting and placing an ear to the ground, Buchanan should have heard the sound of their hooves or felt the vibration.

There was no sign of a cattle drive anywhere nearby. The rancher stood and once again took out the spyglass.

"Maybe they came down farther east for some reason?"

"That's about a two-day rounding outside the valley. I can't think of what would make them take it. And Fremont would've sent a rider ahead to let us know."

"You want me to ride north?" López offered.

"No." Buchanan collapsed the telescope and tucked it in his belt. "I want you and Griz to continue through the valley to the creek and wait there. I'm going to cut to the northeast."

"You want jerky?" Griswold asked. "You didn't eat much last night."

"I'm not hungry," Buchanan said as he turned his mustang toward the north. He reined hard—a warning lest the horse think to give him any trouble.

"Señor Boss, do not kill yourself or the horse."

"Miguel, something ain't right. I intend to find my herd."

The rancher kicked the mustang with both heels and rode out, possessed of a sudden sense that it was not just his wife who disapproved of his adventure but perhaps God Himself.

CHAPTER SIX

FOR THE COWHANDS and foreman of the AB, the first days of the roundup had passed without trial or incident. The day before their arrival, Mitchell had been able to bring most of the herd in. The cattle had been unusually cooperative, perhaps because he went easy on them; they had a longer journey ahead—men and cattle alike—and he knew they would all have to husband their resources.

By the time the others arrived, there were mainly just strays to be rounded up. Mitchell handled that as well while Fremont, Deems, and Prescott got the herd moving south.

The terrain was hospitable enough, with ample grass for the cattle. At some points the Mohave River dried into a muddy sludge, as the water traveled mostly underground, but there was enough for the herd. Fremont was in good spirits the night before the final push to Mill Creek. Camping around a generous fire on a cool night, the men had the herd gathered against a high, steep hill. Prescott had shot a few mountain quail that had strayed too far from the foothills, and Deems had made a firepit to roast them.

"Long as you ain't in a hurry, they taste better cooked in the earth," he said.

The men did not need to make haste. They would bed down for the night and in the morning Prescott would go ahead to scout for Buchanan and the others. There were just two miles or so remaining to the headwaters and they would be there by noon.

The sun was setting, and with business done, Mitchell was eager for some of Griswold's sourdough, which he had been without for too long. Fremont got the flat, paper-wrapped biscuits from a canvas sack strung from his saddle. They were a flour-and-water concoction that, while hard on the outside, were soft inside because of the way Griswold baked them with bacon fat. The men slept well after their long trek and well-deserved feast.

The morning was overcast with more than just clouds. Deems was already gone when the three remaining men rose with daybreak. They splashed canteen water on their faces and ate the remaining biscuits. The men could have used coffee to wash them down but were traveling light and had to settle for water.

Prescott checked on the cattle, looking for those that might have taken a leg injury the men might have missed or were showing any kind of discharge from eyes or mouth. Illness was not uncommon, given the unfamiliar grass, water, and climate, and sick cattle had to be cut from the herd and destroyed. The animals seemed as fine as a cursory look could reveal. Prescott reported such to Fremont.

The cowboys had just finished saddling the horses when there was a stirring among the cattle. Wolf packs hunted only at night, and his first thought was that a rattler nesting in the hillside had come out and was moving among the cattle. But then he heard a horse snort from somewhere around the hill. It was not the sound of one of their smaller trail horses but a larger saddle horse—the kind used to range over rugged terrain.

"Bar Double-D riders," Fremont said. "Has to be. No one else within twenty miles."

"Their cattle range to the north, not south," Mitchell said. "I brought a few of them back couple of weeks ago."

"They got no business down here unless they're lookin' for wild horses," Prescott said.

Fremont leaned toward the sound, listened. "Three . . . four . . . five sets of hooves, I count. *Could* be trackin' ponies."

The foreman walked to where his Springfield lay against a rock. Following Fremont's lead, Mitchell stepped over to the tree where he had leaned his Enfield. Prescott stayed with the herd to keep them calm. Neither man picked his weapon up. They did not want to appear belligerent or provoke gunfire. But of all the ranches in the territory, they trusted Dick Dawson's operation the least. Dawson himself was generally cordial with Andy Buchanan, but he hired men who liked to dirty their hands. That was especially true of his foreman, an unrepentant Rebel named Yancy St. Jacques from Louisiana. It was not unusual for the men to encounter one another in town or on the trail, usually from a distance. These were the same folks they tangled with on the last drive when they tried to keep the AB beef from buyers.

Fremont and Prescott were waiting as five cowboys rode into camp, St. Jacques at their head. All of the men save the foreman were wearing gun belts, and each had a rifle in his scabbard. St. Jacques carried a Bowie knife in a sheath on his hip. The way each man held his reins, low near his thighs, he could draw and fire before Fremont or Prescott would be able to get off a shot.

St. Jacques sat on a black horse with an ornately worked saddle. He had on a white wide-brim hat with an eagle feather in the band and set at a jaunty angle to the right. It was a contrast to the buckskins demanded by his trade, if not his personality. His smile showed a lot of teeth; like the hat, they suggested the genteel ways of a vanished society.

"Good morning, gentlemen," said St. Jacques, his voice as smooth as buttermilk. "May we join you for a spell?"

"As long as it's a short spell," Fremont replied. "We have business to see to."

"Thank you."

St. Jacques had stopped but the Double-D men had separated into a line, like a hungry eagle spreading its wings.

"Uncommon early for you boys to be so far from home, ain't it?" Fremont asked.

"I might say the same about you," St. Jacques replied. "In our case, an uncommon purpose demands it."

"What might that purpose be?" Fremont asked.

"Mr. Dawson did not want us to miss you."

"For what reason?"

"Business." St. Jacques was looking at where the horses were corralled. "I do not see Mr. Buchanan's mustang."

"You see correctly. He ain't here."

"I thought we spotted him on the flatlands. Or at least our tracker did. Were we mistaken?"

"This bodes longer than a 'short spell,' Yancy. Would you mind tellin' me what business we have?"

"Blunt as a whip handle, as always." St. Jacques's eyes settled back on Fremont. "All right, then, sir. We're here because Mr. Dawson is set on buying this herd."

Not just the statement but the confidence with which it was spoken chilled the AB foreman like snow blown sideways. "I can't help you there, friend."

"They are for sale, are they not . . . friend?"

"You know the answer to that and you also know I am not authorized to sell to other than the receiver named by my employer, not by yours. You know, too, I think, that if Mr. Dawson had wanted to confer with Mr. Buchanan about this, he would have fared better doin' so at the ranch."

"As a matter of fact, Mr. Dawson had thought to do just that before your drive. Your early departure prevented that. It was late May last year and the year before, wasn't it?"

"You and your cowboys know the answer to that."

"How would they know?" St. Jacques asked.

"Because I was standin' in the sales office in Abilene, right next to the calendar, when yer point rider threatened to put my head through it."

"I'm sorry, Mr. Fremont. You know how men get frayed after driving a thousand head of cattle. Or . . . don't you know?"

"Brass and sass," Fremont said. "That's what we used to call braggarts at the lumber camp. We gotta go."

The AB trail boss started to turn to his men.

"Not just yet," St. Jacques said.

Fremont looked back. "Why not?"

"Our conversation is not quite concluded. You see, we are here because we heard rumors, something a shipping agent told a farmer who told a sheepherder who told one of my hands. He said that you were looking to sell somewhere else. To the south."

"Given where you found us, that's obviously so."

"To Mexico?"

"You're familiar, Mr. St. Jacques, with all the meat markets in this region."

"There aren't any."

"Exactly. There's your answer."

"Ah, some brass and sass," St. Jacques laughed. "Your time with Sally Haven has not been wasted, Mr. Fremont. You are quite the interlocutor."

"Uh-huh." It galled Fremont hearing her name come from that white-tooth mouth. He let it pass and turned to the two men. "Let's get the herd movin'—"

"Not just yet." The Double-D foreman made a soft chucking sound in his cheek and rode his horse forward a few paces. "To be frank, sir, Mr. Dawson does not think it's a good idea to start selling beef to the Mexicans."

Fremont turned back fully to face St. Jacques. "I will be happy to relay that concern to Mr. Buchanan and you can tell him your reasons when we're—"

"I will tell *you*, Mr. Fremont. I will tell you now, and you can explain to your employer why you sold the cattle. Mr. Dawson believes that if you bring food to Mexico, then Mexican workers will have no reason to come here. Coming here, they provide labor that otherwise engages cowboys or draws freed slaves."

"None of what you just said is our problem, sir."

"How unneighborly. Money and manpower—compliant manpower, eager manpower with many bambinos to feed—is everyone's problem."

Fremont's eyes went to George Haywood, a former slave who was as far from St. Jacques as he could be. The black man was the tracker St. Jacques had mentioned. He sat as still as a statue and expressionless on his stallion.

"You're the only one allowed to break your own rules, I guess," Fremont said.

"If you mean Mr. Haywood, his work keeps him out under the stars. Finding you, for example."

"I will not ask if he is permitted to lay at the ranch house when he is not in the field."

St. Jacques's smile thinned. "I am pleased, sir, that you do not wade into a matter that is not your concern. Especially given your tendency to talk the liver out of a man."

Fremont smirked. "I will not do that now, since, again, we have work to do."

Once more Fremont turned to go. His back to the Double-D men, he reached for his rifle. Once more St. Jacques stopped him.

"Leave the Springfield, Mr. Fremont, and stop being obstinate."

As the AB men watched, four sets of hands drew six-shooters and rifles. The long barrels were pointed up, the others were leveled at the three cowboys.

"I will ask one last time that you sell us your cattle." St. Jacques reached into his saddlebag and withdrew two stacks of bills. He shook them. "There's eight hundred dollars in gold banknotes here, a fair price for your herd. Instead of making a dangerous drive with unknown perils in front and known perils behind, you sign the bill of sale I'm carrying and you all get to go home. And for those who prefer to work and earn some cash, I am authorized to offer employment to any who wish to ride back with me and join our drive in three weeks." St. Jacques's alert eyes went from Prescott to Mitchell. "I am sure neither of you men wants to wage a losing battle. Mr. Mitchell, you and I have had enough of that, haven't we?"

Prescott spit. Mitchell—with respect for the speaker's aristocratic Southern roots—did and said nothing.

"Cut to what's your 'or else'?" Fremont said. "You gonna shoot us? Steal the herd?"

St. Jacques laughed. "Those actions would be illegal, and Mr. Dawson is a law-abiding citizen, as are we."

"Yeah. I felt your law abidance in Abilene."

"I'm told Mr. Prescott struck first—"

"That's a lie!" Prescott snapped.

"—but no matter. Should you decline our offer, we will stampede your herd. And when you've rounded them up, we will stampede them again. And we will follow you until it makes no good sense to herd them again and deliver beeves showing bone to the Mexicans."

Fremont weighed his options. His job, as described in the document to which he had affixed his name, was to protect and preserve the herd at any cost short of the loss of life. But coming out of this encounter bent and ashamed—before his men and before Miss Sally—was a darker prospect than not coming out of it at all.

"Don't do it." St. Jacques nodded toward the Springfield. "It's temptation in Eden. We will defend ourselves. Just take the money and ride off."

"Or," said a firm, familiar voice from behind one of the horses, "you folks can go back to the Double-D and tender my regards *and* my regrets to Mr. Dawson."

Fremont and his men, St. Jacques and his men, all turned toward the speaker. Buchanan's Spencer rifle was aimed at a point just above St. Jacques's saddle, at the man's right hip. Now it was the Double-D foreman who was considering options.

"Don't," Buchanan warned him. Without changing his aim, he faced the line of Double-D men. "Don't none of you do anything hasty either."

St. Jacques chuckled. "Good morning, Mr. Buchanan. Am I supposed to raise my hands?"

"Standard for outlaws, but snakes don't have hands. Tell your men to put aside their guns."

"They will take no such action because you will not fire, sir. You have a family—"

"Mention them again and you will bleed on your fancy saddle."

"You mistake my intention. I do not threaten women and children. You Yankees left that much of a gentleman still standing. I meant that this course of action will end badly for you, your men, and your drive. Even now you have not thought this through. Shoot me, and your cattle are just as likely to trample you in a panic."

"Then we go down together."

"There is no need for anyone to 'go down.' Instead, I repeat what I said to your foreman. Mr. Dawson wishes to buy your herd."

"Yeah, I heard some of that along with your threats. The answer is no."

"Then I appeal to your ability to count, Mr. Buchanan. You are still outgunned."

"Wasn't it just you who said that killing's illegal?"

"So it is. But self-defense is not. Lower your Spencer, take the money, and go home."

Buchanan came from behind the horse without removing his hand from the trigger. "You got the others?"

St. Jacques and his men seemed perplexed.

"I got 'em all," said a voice from behind a group of cactuses behind the men.

There was a stout oak behind Buchanan, and Joe Deems seemed to sprout from behind it. His Colts in both hands, held hip high and angled up, he maneuvered behind the line of cowboys.

"Keep facing front," Buchanan warned. "You said yourself that a shooting would be self-defense. Don't make it so."

"In the back?" St. Jacques asked.

"Be kinda stupid if we let four armed men turn and draw on one."

The Double-D foreman hesitated only a moment before ordering his men to holster their weapons.

"I want the guns in the dirt," Buchanan said.

St. Jacques glared at him. "Don't push me."

"Says the man who rode in barking orders at my men and me. Next time I speak it'll be to apologize for shooting your horse. I got enough gold to buy as many as I'm forced to kill—for dead-horse prices, of course."

Not just the eyes of St. Jacques but also those of his men were on Buchanan.

Another moment passed before St. Jacques told his men to toss the weapons down. Spitting and cursing, their movements stiff with anger, the men obliged. The guns thumped on the ground, leaving their owners enraged but without menace.

"We'll keep 'em safe in the chuck wagon and make sure you get 'em back," Buchanan said. "I want to make sure you only got rocks to throw if you give chase."

St. Jacques indicated for the men to head off to the north. He turned his own mount, then stopped and looked back. "That was foolish, Mr. Buchanan."

"Wasn't a first for me; won't be the last."

"You may be wrong about one of those," St. Jacques said. The Double-D foreman spurred his stallion forward, surprising the horses of his men. The cowboys had to struggle to contain them as they fell in behind him.

As the dust clouds of the retreating cowboys simultaneously rose and shrank, Will Fremont went to collect the Double-D guns.

"Sorry, boss," the trail boss said as he scooped them up.

"No need. From what I heard, you did the right thing."

"To that point, mebbe. I honestly don't know what I would've done next."

"You would have sold him the cattle to protect your men, same as me."

"That was not the last thought I had when you two showed up." Fremont looked over at the other cowhand. "Thank you, Joe."

"God will punish them," Deems said.

Fremont was not convinced of that, or whether he would have done what his boss had said: surrendered. The foreman's blood was still raging and he hugged the guns as if he meant to crush them. Fremont had served as a sergeant with the 1st Delaware Volunteer Cavalry Regiment. Though a slave state, Delaware had sided with the Union. Fremont had been a lumberjack and an abolitionist, and, in addition to everything else, St. Jacques's comments had fired up all the old tensions and resentments.

Buchanan relaxed for the first time since he had arrived. He turned to Fremont, who had not relaxed. "You did fine, Fremont."

"I shoulda had one of us watching. That was careless."

"It wouldn't've changed anything."

"It was still stupid of me," Fremont said. "Let me just find places for these arms so we can move out." He paused beside his boss. "Say, how'd you happen to be here?"

"Didn't see any signs of your approach this morning. That caused some worry, so I rode out. A lucky encounter with Joe got me here pronto."

"Praise God for that," Deems said. Before joining Prescott and Mitchell, who were setting the herd in motion, Deems turned from the others to offer a silent prayer of thanksgiving.

Fremont walked to his horse, his heart still unsettled as he sought the canvas bag that had held their food. It was just large enough to hold the sidearms. He used his lariat to tie the rifles into two bundles. Winding the rope around the pommel of his saddle, he let the rifles hang on either side of his horse.

Buchanan looked at the small black specks that had, just minutes before, been a menace to them. Deems had been earnest in his supplication to the Lord, but Buchanan wondered again if God was against him for some reason—not vanity but maybe something older; maybe what Patsy had said about leaving his mother when she needed him.

He would not learn the answer by thinking about it, so he stopped. With that undecided, Buchanan shouldered his rifle and started back to where he had left his horse concealed behind the herd.

CHAPTER SEVEN

Buck Griswold and Miguel López had spent the morning watching a creek flow. Griswold had determined that there were no fish worth catching and López had not seen any game large enough to make a meal.

Now the Mexican was getting restless, getting on and off the buckboard every few minutes. Griswold was inside preparing the salted meat he had brought.

"Miguel, you look like a man who's thinking about going after the man who went after the cattle."

Miguel López had been considering doing just that, although he did not say so to Griswold.

"I don't need a nursemaid, if that's what's holdin' you back," Griswold went on.

"Boss told us to wait, so I'm waiting."

"Wait till the cows come home," Griswold chuckled.

The men had settled the chuck wagon on the highest spot above the creek, a small rise with a view of the mouth of the valley beyond. López had unhitched the horses front and back and tied them to a boulder at the creek so they could drink. The cowhand sat or stood or walked with an ear turned to the valley, thinking he would hear the lowing of the herd before he saw it. He hoped the drive was merely held due to a few wandering head or a rockslide and that Buchanan had met them and was already headed back.

"Ya want to go out and see if you can bag a deer, that's okay, too," Griswold said. "This kinda timberland, they gotta be out there somewhere."

"Gracias, but this is not the hour that deer are about."

"Maybe not, but you'll see some scenery."

"No. I should rest while I can."

"That is sensible, I guess. Me? I never knew all this was out here."

"I thought you traveled here. Sachem said you knew the area."

"From maps and from the south side, *sí*."

"Fightin'? Always fightin'?"

"It had to be done. What did you do during your war?"

"Same as now, actually. I made my home in Texas during the war. I refused to take the loyalty oath to the Confederacy, which everyone else including my wife and son and brother swore to. So I left one of the biggest spreads in Houston, the Honeysuckle, and ran out of food, and horse, at the AB."

"Why did you not go back when the war was over?"

"I tried. I wrote, but my wife didn't want me. She said our boy and my brother got kilt in the Trans-Mississippi fightin', so there was nothing to go back to. Told me I shoulda died alongside 'em." He shrugged, although a sadness had settled upon him. "I don't think about it too much. I don't sit around wishin' I'd stayed. I growed up on my great-grandpap's stories about fightin' the Redcoats in two wars. Like you fightin' invaders, that made some sense. But to fight each other? If there is a Lord God, then He did not intend this to be so."

López looked at his companion. "I am a little ashamed, my friend."

"Why's that?"

"I never knew any of that about you. The others, they talk. I talk. Lewis, he even showed me how to twirl a gun. Only you and Mr. Buchanan, you do not talk. Well, he's the boss, like the captain of a ship. He cannot be your amigo. But you . . . you are always alone with your pots or out picking this mushroom or that berry."

"I learnt that keepin' busy helps me not to think about what I done, right or wrong or just plain ridiculous."

López rolled and lit one of his cigarettes, thought again of the heroic fighters he had known. He thought, too, about what a long and unpredictable journey it had been for him, from his boyhood in the seaside village of Guaymas to fighting in the war against the French to working as a cowboy here.

"I suppose it makes no sense because we all get planted soon enough. Why should we rush it? We must do useful things while we can."

As his melancholy seemed to grow, Griswold's watery eyes fixed on a spot along the water. "I think I see some duck potatoes growin' out there. Reckon I'll do something and gather 'em."

"You want help?"

"I can manage," he said. "My arm is stiff, not broke."

Easing from the cart and stretching his injured arm when he had the room, the spindly cook picked up a stick and ambled through the grasses, pushing them aside so he would not accidentally set foot on anything that might sting or bite. Back at the ranch, scorpions no bigger than a thumbnail could enter a man's boot while he slept and give him a crippling sting in the morning.

López followed the cookie as he walked.

I know you, Señor Griswold. You on guard against the one man who will ask if you left Texas because you were afraid. Yourself.

López had seen that look in the eyes of many men in many villages. Those sad *oveja*, those sheep, turned their heads to the ground or glanced another way or simply walked off when he and his fellow *revolucionarios* came seeking food or shelter, recruits or repairs. Firearms were particularly hard-hit. They were third-hand to begin with, the elements were rough on the ammunition, and more often than not the rebels went without them. Knives, whips, machetes, and captured swords of *oficiales* made up the bulk of their arms. Those men they encountered were not loyal to the oppressors any more than Griswold could swear allegiance to the Stars and Bars. They were simply afraid.

And they were afraid still. Those men who had fought could not find a welcome or peace in those same villages, so they lived in the foothills, off the land, off the villagers, off travelers. It was a sad end to a glorious victory.

López looked out at the creek and the valley and up at the gray clouds. He leaned back, his head resting against one of the bonnet ribs of the wagon, shut his eyes, and the next thing he knew he was awakened by cattle bellowing from afar. He looked out in time to see the herd emerging from the valley like a sea of brown with whitecaps rising as cattle raised their heads here and there. There was a stirring quality to seeing the herd arrive unlike coming upon it already here.

The cowboy launched himself from the driver's seat and made for the spectacle of steers, horses, and riders. He passed Griswold, who stood there watching, his arms full of the pulled greens with their thick, white veins. There was no time to put the saddle on. López grabbed his riata from around the horn, pulled his kerchief over his face nearly to the eyes, grabbed the mane of his palomino, and swung onto the animal's back.

Whooping with excitement, López galloped ahead. He could see Fremont and Buchanan maneuvering the lead cow so the herd would follow him around the southwest turn of the creek.

Fremont saw the Mexican riding in and motioned him broadly, a signal to go to the tail position. López acknowledged with an excited sweep of his hat. Holding on to the palomino tightly with his thighs, he turned into the dust cloud and slowed by half. With vision obscured by a tawny haze, he did not want to risk running into cattle or riders.

López joined Mitchell in back. The tail rider had been stitching from side to side, keeping the cattle moving. López fell in, crisscrossing in the opposite direction. The passage was completed quickly and the men helped the cattle find spots along the river to drink or feed. While they dismounted and washed the dirt of the drive from hands and faces, Buchanan and Fremont walked toward the chuck wagon.

Still at the river, López welcomed Mitchell back to

the fold. Although the two men came from entirely dissimilar backgrounds, they had both been "rebels" for different causes and were both outsiders here. Soon the other hands stopped by the creek to wash off the trail dust. That was where López learned what had happened back on the plains.

"It has come to this," he said to Mitchell. "The heroes die in war and the villains are set free."

"No one to keep the order, that's a fact, Miguel."

"I heard Dawson was a man of decency."

"That may be. He *did* offer to pay for the steer over the barrels of five rifles."

Prescott wandered over, shaking his hands dry. "Boss played his poker smart. I'm not sure Fremont was gonna fold."

"That woulda been okay with me. I was ready to shoot the varmints," Mitchell admitted.

While the men debated tactics, Buchanan was preoccupied with what came next. He pulled Fremont aside to discuss it by the chuck wagon. Griswold had hurried back, stuffed his leaves in an empty sack, and grabbed a can from the shelf. This was where the two men came to plan in private and the hands all knew to let them be. Griswold knew to give them coffee.

"We're gonna have to watch our back goin' and our front coming back," Fremont said with grim conviction.

"They do mean to stop us," Buchanan agreed.

"All they have to do is cripple our drive," Fremont said. "Only way we prevent them is by killing. Do you trust what St. Jacques said about Patsy and the girls?"

"I don't think he'll hurt 'em, if that's what you're asking. Scare 'em? He might try, but Sloane'll see through that."

Griswold poured his strong brew and the men sipped it gratefully. The rancher thought briefly of the promise he should not have made to Patsy.

"Right now, we got about two hours of daylight left," Buchanan said. "The more distance we can put between us and them, the better. Let's get the herd back on the hoof as soon as possible."

"I'll let the men know," Fremont said, returning his cup to Griswold.

Buchanan finished the coffee then accepted another pour from Griswold while he thought it through. A plan—at least the beginning of one—came to mind.

"Hey, Will?"

The foreman turned. "Yeah?"

"Tell ya what. You take point and lead the cattle on till dark. I'll bring up the rear with Griz. I may fall back a spell to watch and listen. We'll have another look at things when we make camp."

"Sounds good." Fremont smiled. "By the way, I been thinking. I do believe St. Jacques and Dawson will stay away from your family. I spend more time with town folk than you do. Sheriff Lipcan in San Bernardino, the cowhands at the Running S, Fred Gold the retired marshal who works at the saloon—they wouldn't stand for anything like that. Dawson and even that puffed-up foreman don't want that kind of trouble."

"You're probably right, Will. I certainly hope you are."

Fremont smiled again then went to inform the riders that they were moving on. Buchanan declined more coffee and Griswold, pleased with his previous harvest, went to gather more garnish before the sunlight faded completely. Then he went to gather up the Dawson guns he'd taken—which he'd lashed here and there to the saddles of the men—and moved them to the chuck box in back of Griswold's wagon.

Alone for the first time since leaving the ranch, Buchanan quietly cursed Dawson for having added these political complications to the anticipated physical hardships. But as he returned to his men, the rancher was resolved more than ever to make it to Hidalgo and back. That, not with fear and violence, was the way to respond to the hostile designs of the Double-D.

CHAPTER EIGHT

When the drive resumed, it followed the gentle curves of the Mohave River. The fast-moving waters led them through a stony plain that ran past a wall of red rock. Small caves pocked the floor of the cliff. Fremont suspected the rocks and the caves had a common origin: a river that once flowed much higher through this region. He had seen similar formations in his logging days. None of the caves showed signs of current human habitation.

It was just before sunset that the drive completed a crossing at a shallow point in the river and entered a region thickly populated with fir and juniper. The last of the light revealed a vista that was both expansive and towering.

When they got the last of the herd across, the clouds had broken and sun covered the land. The sight caused Mitchell to slow without realizing it.

"What's wrong?" López asked.

"I grew up beside Florida marshland that was rank and rotted," he told López. "It is difficult to comprehend that the same God created that . . . and this."

"And the desert full of cactuses where I grew up," López said. "Maybe the Lord hammers us on an anvil before He gives us paradise?"

"Could be," Mitchell said. "Makes me kinda itchy to see what lies beyond. I never been up close to mountains."

"Amigo, I can tell you now how you will feel. Very, very small."

The ground was deep with wood chips close to the river, the work of beavers. The pulpy carpet had absorbed and held rain to provide a soft passage. There weren't even gnats circling the cowboys, a twilight bane in most southwestern places. Mitchell suspected it was the river spray combined with a soft sweep of wind from the mountains that kept them from gathering. That same wind also sharpened the rich scent of the trees. The combination not only cleared the dust from his nostrils—it was almost intoxicating.

The men organized the herd into a line that that was two cattle wide in order to make it through the trees. Still in the lead on point, Fremont found a clearing created by mountain runoff; that same water, soaking into porous earth, had created a region that was thick with grass.

"Settle the cattle in there and we do things same as on the prairie," Fremont told the men. "I want two men on watch tonight. Joe and Lewis, you take first shift north and south. Remember, stay sharp and keep your fires big 'n' bright. There'll be wolves and great cats hunting, and they likely ain't seen beeves out this way."

"And Dawsons?" Prescott asked.

"I said wolves, didn't I?" Fremont answered.

The joke did not change the fact that the real danger *was* wolves. On flatland trails, wolf packs in particular looked for stragglers while the drive was in motion, pulling them down and away in woodlands or gullies. Cowboys were often too busy calming the survivors to give chase to what was already behind them and done.

"How do we handle 'em if they come?" Prescott asked. "We can't shoot and panic the herd."

"Build two fires, point and tail, make torches, and keep your horses near," Fremont said. "Wave the brands if you see their eyes. That's how we used to protect the wounded during the war."

As the two perimeter fires and one campfire were lit, Fremont went to the southern edge of the forest and watched for Buchanan. The rancher had been just within sight for most of the journey but they lost him as the sun went behind the mountains. The treetops stayed bright against the reddening sky, with darkness swallowing them from the bottom in tiny, gliding bites. Below them was different. A purple, then brown, then dead-black shadow fell over the river and its surroundings. It was a strange sensation, being in night but looking up and still seeing day.

Fremont knew that his boss would be able to hear and smell the herd, however far back he was. Seeing them was another matter. The foreman fished his stubby fingers into his shirt pocket where a half-smoked cheroot had stayed mostly dry during the river crossing. He lit it using the lantern that hung from the chuck wagon, where Griswold was well along with dinner preparations

"Griz, I'm gonna double back a way and watch for the boss," Fremont said.

"If he's still on the other side of the river, he'll likely bed down there."

"That's what I'm worried about."

"Huh? Oh, I see," Griswold said. "You're thinkin' o' them Double-D hardcases. You gonna camp out?"

"Don't know. Depends on what makes sense."

"You got yer Indian blanket? Gets cold in the mountains."

"When were you ever in mountains?"

"We all crossed country to git here in the first place, Will."

"That's true."

"If you do stay out there, I'll take yer watch."

"Thanks. If I stay, I'll be countin' on the morning birds to have me up before sunup. If I ain't back, tell Mitchell to get the herd moving."

"I'll do that. Pay attention to the night birds, too. They go silent, hide. You said yourself, we don't know what or who is out there."

"I been in those situations before," Fremont said.

The trail boss had not bothered unsaddling his horse, having had it in mind to go back out since they arrived without Buchanan. With a few quick motions, he made sure his rifle slid easy in and out of the scabbard—the sun sometimes shrunk the leather—and, for good measure, he took one of the Double-D revolvers. Setting out, he stayed on the narrow riverbank, since the grasses there were even higher than at Mill Creek and likely as not to conceal predators of all kinds and sizes.

Fremont passed an area where beavers had built a lodge. He had not noticed the structure when the herd rode by, and he was considerably impressed by the community the animals had built. They used not only trees but also mud and rocks. Safe from most predators because they were freestanding in the water, providing shelter from the elements, and constructed close to the vegetation that made up the beaver diet, the lodge was a perfect little fort.

Fremont had been out about ten minutes when the horse shied and the rider saw a small pack of coyotes. Four in number, they crouched low as they made their way through the tall grass, their eyes flashing like fireflies through the stalks. The blades barely stirred with their passage, and the beasts were as silent as they were nearly invisible.

"Easy, boy, they ain't gonna bother us," Fremont said, patting the animal's neck. "Looks like they're hunting for food, not a fight."

In Fremont's experience, coyotes were loath to attack a full-grown, healthy horse unless they were starving. From what he had seen of acorn husks underfoot, squirrels were plentiful, though probably in their tree hollows by now; more likely the coyotes were after rabbits or wild turkey, which he had also spotted when they rode in.

When they were past the pack, the horse continued to buck its head from side to side, dancing as it fought the direction Fremont wanted him to go.

"What is it, boy? More of 'em ahead?"

It was only when the foreman heard the low, guttural sound from the grasses that he realized there were no more coyotes and that they had likely been moving *from* something—something that was still there.

"Whoa," Fremont said quietly, reining the horse to a stop.

Griswold had been right. Save for the rushing water, the night was strangely still. The river was to the left, but it was deeper and rushing faster than a sensible man would try to cross. Fremont gave the horse a gentle heel poke in the ribs and simultaneously walked him farther across the bank to water's edge. He drew on his cigar to bring the flame back to life. With his reins in his left hand, the rider lay his right hand on his Springfield.

Horse and rider were about four feet from the edge of the grass when they came to a spot that caused the horse to rear. When it came down, Fremont saw that they were in an area where the grass was crushed flat and there was a dark shape within them. The form was hunched, with the contours of a bell. And it had the smell of wet fur. Fremont knew at once it was a large grizzly just seated there, its eyes tracking the two as they walked past.

A very low, guttural sound came from the animal. Fremont had heard enough wildlife to know when he was being warned, like now, instead of being actually menaced.

The foreman leaned close to the horse and low, on its side facing the bear. That had the dual purpose of being able to soothe the animal and block its vision.

"Steady," he whispered as the steed edged sideways until it was splashing along the river in awkward, uncertain steps.

Never taking his eyes from the dark shape reposing in the grass, and ready to spur his horse if the shape moved, Fremont suddenly noticed another shape pressed against it: there was a cub, silent and unmoving.

"I didn't think that was your den," he said quietly. He spoke in a way he had heard Miss Sally address rambunctious boys and girls in her class. It was his intention that his soft voice would continue to calm the horse and also assure the bear of his peaceful intentions. "You come from those caves we saw across the river, yeah?"

The bear growled again, still low but less threatening now. It sounded almost mournful to Fremont.

"Yer little one didn't fall or get attacked; there ain't no blood. It drowned comin' over, I suspect. I'm sorry, mama bear."

The grizzly could not have understood his words but Fremont believed, like a horse, like a dog, like any warm-blooded creature, it recognized his tone.

The rider guided the horse forward, his left hand still tight on the reins. He no longer felt he was in danger; the bear was simply protecting its cub from scavengers, as the coyotes must have discovered.

Fremont moved on, the horse steadying to a spirited but less irregular pace. Even the treetops were dark now. A chorus of night creatures began in earnest, along with evening breezes that caused the trees to creak. The man whoa'd to a stop and listened. All he heard to his left was the rush of the river. He knew that unless Buchanan made a sound, he would not know whether or not the man was there.

"I think we're gonna remain here tonight," he said to the horse. "Boss'll see the campfire if he's out there. We'll bed down away from the fire in case anyone else sees it and decides to take a shot at us."

Fremont walked along the river a little farther until he began to feel not just stones but branches underfoot, pushed ashore by a turn in the river that he could not see. Dismounting, he gathered sticks as he led the horse ahead. When he had a fat armful, he dropped the kindling to the ground, felt for the driest piece, then built the others into a teepee shape. The one he selected still had bark and it had spent at least a day in the direct sun. He bent a piece back and held it to the tip of his cheroot, drawing smoke to make the flame grow. Fremont had done this hundreds of times since he was a boy—using his father's and grandfather's discarded stogies when they came west—but that only guaranteed know-how, not success.

It took nearly till the end of the used-up cigar before the bark finally did more than smolder. He set the ignited end down as he added the stick to the pile. Cupping his hand to protect the tiny flame, the fire climbed up, caused several others to smoke, and finally released a choking plume that erupted in fire. With that first light Fremont quickly gathered other twigs and branches and pressed them to the base of his tiny pyre. The fire grew and warmed him, not just with heat but security. Animals out here would not have seen many campfires, only wildfires. They would know to stay away.

Tying the palomino to a bush outside the circle of light, Fremont removed the saddle and placed it by the trunk of a tree to block the wind while he slept. Then he collected larger branches from among the trees. These were not for the fire but to build a perimeter around himself. The horse would only let him know if it felt threatened; the crack of the sticks would let Fremont know if anyone or anything was approaching him from another side. Taking one final look across the river, he briefly considered calling out. He dismissed that notion. If Double-D men were out there, they might not know Buchanan was watching for them. They would see him and come this way to investigate.

Settling his head on the comfortable leather, bathed in the familiar warmth and smell of the campfire, he woke only when the popping got quiet and the kindling needed refreshing. He looked up before going back to sleep; in the small hours of the night, when even the predators were asleep—save for a pair of owls that gave an occasional hoot—the landscape was dominated by stars and a half-moon. They were all clearer and more numerous than in the dusty plains. Fremont felt as though he had come to a place where the world was new, where rest came not just to the body but to the spirit.

Griswold was right. Even in this Eden, in this private corner sheltered from the wind, nocturnal cold effortlessly found him. It settled slowly as the brilliant stars emerged—so slowly it was hardly noticed. He was glad he had the fire and the blanket.

When the new day arrived the cold renewed its acquaintance. The first hints of dawn stirred the air like a chill caressed the skin. Fremont shivered awake, the fire having expired some short time before. He glanced ahead, at the river, where the earliest rays of dawn would fall. As a crescent of light began to shine over the eastern hills, they lightened the caves they had passed the day before—and, in front of one of them Fremont saw Buchanan's horse. The animal was tied to a tree, positioned so that it blocked the mouth of the cave.

After performing his morning duties and washing his face in the river, Fremont replaced the saddle and rode across. The horse seemed happy to be away from that side of the river and also, perhaps, he recognized the horse ahead. The mustang across the way raised his head several times, snorting in welcome.

Peering ahead, Fremont was surprised that their coming had not roused Buchanan. The horse clomped onto the bank and galloped the two hundred or so yards to the cave. There, Fremont swung from the saddle and was surprised to find the cave empty. Nor were there any signs of habitation: no fire, no bedroll, no Buchanan.

Confused and concerned, Fremont went back outside and looked around. He stopped and smiled—first with surprise, then with relief.

The rancher was standing outside, his back to the river, a Colt in each hand. He holstered them quickly and walked over.

"Good morning, Will."

"Did ya think someone shanghaied my horse to pretend they was me?"

"Be a good way to draw me out."

"How'd ya do that, go from cave to cave?" Fremont asked. "Is there another way out?"

"No, I slept back there." Buchanan jerked his thumb to his left, toward a cave farther south.

"Sensible precaution."

"It's more than that. Did you know all those men who were with St. Jacques?"

"I recognized the Swede Oland, that thug Kent, and I heard about George Haywood, the freed slave."

"Escaped," Buchanan corrected him. "Did you know he was a tracker during the war?"

"I did."

"I encountered him a few times in Arizona," Buchanan said. "Noticed him in church a couple of times, too, sittin' in the back, ignorin' the stares of folks who was still uneasy with emancipation."

"A God-fearing rustler?"

"He may be a contradiction, but he looked a special kind of unhappy to be riding with that gang, and then again turning tail. If the Double-D does not intend for those cattle to reach Mexico, they would've dispatched him pronto to follow us."

Fremont looked back along the trail. "Was there any sign of him?"

"No, and I did not expect there to be unless he caught up. That's kinda why I'm glad you followed."

"Glad? Why?"

"Because if Haywood's out there, he may have mistook you for me or else thought we were moving together on the opposite side of the Mohave River."

"He would've hung back," Fremont realized.

"Most likely." Buchanan started toward the cave he had slept in to get his gear. "You go ahead. If he's back here, that will bring him out. He won't have a gun, so don't worry about bein' shot."

Fremont grinned with self-satisfaction. "Right. We got those."

Buchanan stopped, looked back. "Say, Will, thanks for the night watch, old friend."

"It was either that or poker." He smiled. "And a man gets tired of losing."

The rancher waved and Fremont, after looking upriver for any sign of Haywood, climbed back in the saddle and recrossed the river. As he did, he turned his face upward so the rising sun could warm him. Gazing out at the slightly higher ground, he noticed that the bear and her cub were gone. In their place was crushed brush, a hole in the graceful flow of things.

It struck him as being as poignant as some of the human death he had witnessed, and Will Fremont said a silent prayer for the mother and cub as he passed.

CHAPTER NINE

MEN AND CATTLE were already in motion when Fremont returned, which was not the same thing as the drive having resumed.

Griswold was the first to meet him. He was sitting at his wagon, ready to go but with nowhere to move.

"We got up, we ate, and then they realized they was tryin' to wrangle crows, not cattle," Griswold said.

"What're you talkin' about, Griz?"

"They're nestin'!" he answered, pointing ahead.

"Aw, rats," Fremont said, and rode toward the herd.

The cattle were uncooperative about leaving, not because they liked where they were, although Fremont knew that cattle could be stubborn that way. The problem was the way the herd had come apart during the night, forming little pockets of steer—nests, they called them.

A drive began with a herd moving not as one but in pieces. After several days the herd behind the lead steer was supposed to move when he did. But to get around the trees required them to be busted into tiny groups, none of which had their own lead cow. So they just meandered.

Assessing the situation, Fremont gave each man his instructions before riding into the trail boss position.

"We're gonna have to move 'em like we did on the river, two by two, till we get through the trees," he said. "Soon as they're lined up that way, we can work 'em through."

Fremont assigned Deems and Prescott as swing riders at the sides, López and Mitchell on flank well behind them. Because Fremont was on point until Buchanan returned, Griswold temporarily took the place of tail rider. That meant, in effect, that there would be two men for each of the two nests in the center, one man for the nest in front, one for the nest in back.

The strident and inexorable racket from the chuck wagon helped keep the back end of the herd going forward. When Fremont got bunched up because of slower steers—some aged, some weak from the trek, a few newly overfed and disinclined to move—he would shout through a tin horn he carried to alert one of the flank riders.

The drive had left the Mohave River behind, north of the valley. The plan was to reorganize the herd and regain the waterway to the south, on the western side of the forest, and follow it southwest. According to Buchanan's hand-drawn map, that would enable them to pass through the San Bernardino and San Gabriel mountain ranges. The route added some twenty miles to the drive but saved them from having to push the herd into higher elevations.

Without a precise idea where exactly the river was—the maps did not have that level of detail—Fremont decided to break from the herd and get up as high as he could. He galloped to a rise east of the trees. Fremont saw at once that the woods were of considerable breadth and length. He also saw something that concerned him deeply.

When they moved cattle across the flatlands, the rising sun would reveal crevasses and gopher holes. Out here, it revealed larger, more dramatic structures and impediments in the terrain. Unfortunately, between the shadows of the trees, what Fremont saw were fallen pines—not a few but years of them knocked over by the spring runoff from melted mountain snows.

"It's impassable," he said with resignation, then looked ahead. To the west, the trees climbed thickly into the foothills. There was no way through those pines. The path around the woods—the one they would have to take—lay to the east, a series of hills like the one he was on, each reaching anywhere from three hundred to four hundred feet. Water from the mountains had prevented trees from taking root there. Moss-covered boulders at the foot of the rise suggested that the incline Fremont was on had been created, like so many other formations, by the volatile earth years before. Maybe that was what knocked some trees down; he did not know and it did not matter.

Fremont considered the problem. They had driven cattle over rises of one hundred feet or so in the past, but nothing like this. Still, it was the best option.

He went back to confer with his riders, calling them over as he descended to the floor of the forest.

"That clearing we had back there?" he said. "That

was the work of beavers on the river, cartin' off the trees toppled by runoff. Up ahead the trees are too far from water, so there ain't no beavers. That means if we try to cross, we're gonna run into a passel of uprooted and rotted trees. Acres of them."

"Gettin' over humps like that are gonna cause a lot of busted legs, and that's *if* the cattle agree to be driven," Prescott said.

"They won't," Mitchell said. "We'll probably have to rope and pull each steer over to get them to move. Between you an' me, doin' two cattle at a time—"

"We'll be at it for days," Prescott said. "We'd also have to pull grass to feed cattle that have logs to their front and back."

"I know, which is why we're going to have to go around to the east," Fremont said. "We can take them up the slope I was just on. Leads to a plateau about two hundred feet to above the tree line."

"Where's the boss?" Deems asked. It was a question, not a criticism of Fremont's plan.

"Boss is watching our tail for those Double-D mudsills, but I believe this is the decision he would make. Anyway, that's how we'll handle this."

The men murmured assent and resumed their positions with the goal of winding the double line of cattle from the forest to the grassy ledge.

"We're gonna get us some exercise," he said to himself. The only option was to turn back, and no one suggested or wanted that.

Turning to take his place at point, Fremont began the arduous task of leading two lines of cattle through thick woods to a passage that a more generous God would have made a bit wider. . . .

* * *

EVEN IF HE had not seen and heard Will Fremont the night before, Andrew Buchanan would have smelled the fire of someone on his own side of the river. And that was a good thing. In the dark, the smell of a wood fire was as reliable a compass as actually seeing something, especially with winds blowing gently north as they had the night before. Smells had a way of pooling in a cave, probably because of the natural flues they possessed in deep, unseen recesses.

Now, with the sun risen, Buchanan took the time to make entries in his journal—his "ship's log," as his wife teased, and not without reason. That was where he got the idea. Buchanan had a book for each drive and looked back on them with some regularity. The tally of lost cattle and depleted supplies was most useful in planning each new trek. But what he learned rereading the diaries was that events were rarely as he remembered them. Details like passing encounters, illness, detours due to flooding or fire—a lot of that was forgotten under the pressure of just getting a job done.

He wrote down the events since he had left the camp to come here, then stood by a section of the rock wall and chewed on beef jerky while he considered the situation.

The rancher yearned to be with his herd. It was a pull he felt stronger than ever because of the stakes. But he knew that if George Haywood was tracking him, the man would follow that smoke scent starting at sunup. He hoped so: Haywood would pin it to the spot across the river, which was southeast of his own position. The way the sun made its crossing, Buchanan chose a spot to wait that would be in shadow till noon. Not only was the Double-D hand not likely to see him against the cliff, the tracker would be too busy splashing across the river to hear his horse, which the rancher had relocated inside the cave.

The major dilemma—for Haywood and Buchanan both—involved firearms. Despite his conversation with Fremont, it was possible that, riding hard, Haywood could have gone back for a gun. The tracker would have picked up the cattle trail easy, in which case Buchanan would be sitting here another day, waiting for an armed man.

But that did not seem likely, he told himself.

The tracker's orders would likely be to follow, not engage. And nothing he had ever seen or heard about Haywood suggested he was a violent man. Not like the other Double-D crew. He would probably leave a trail of some kind, something the others could follow while they went back for weapons.

The other problem involved what to do with Haywood if he showed up unarmed. Buchanan did not want to have to shoot an unarmed man, and he did not want to shoot *that* man. It was only fate, not malice, that had put them on opposite sides.

The sunny, still morning was a marked change from the dreary, wind-whipped afternoon of the previous day, so much so that Buchanan could even hear, muted and distant, the cattle complaining about having to move on and the coaxing sounds of the riders. He was grateful for the quality of the men he had assembled. They respected Fremont enough to accept his leadership without question—even Griswold. The man could have made his life easier by riding ahead with the trail boss, as most cookies did, and by minding his rolling domain, nothing more. Instead, he unfailingly pitched in as needed.

Even with a bad arm, Buchanan thought.

The quiet climate did not, however, give Buchanan an opportunity to take things easy. He was doing what Haywood would be doing if he was out there: smelling and listening without distraction. He even considered the possibility that Haywood might come on him from above, for a larger view of the terrain. But he would still have to come down, and the detour would take time.

It was not long before the rancher learned that the tracker had not gone back to the ranch but had set out after the AB herd unarmed.

Curiously, there was nothing concealed about Haywood's approach. The lone rider clopped along the stones of the riverbank. The sounds were quick, suggesting either a man in flight or a man with a destination. There was also a fifth sound, lighter than the hoofbeats and also less regular.

Buchanan smiled. *It's Haywood, and he's leaving a trail of stones.*

The herd had cut a path even a schoolboy could have followed, but Buchanan knew Haywood was doing more than that. He would have seen the threatening clouds the day before and chosen speed over stealth. In the event of the marks being washed away by rain, he was leaving a trail the others could follow. Smooth stones being the norm on the banks, he would have picked up jagged ones to drop among them.

Leaving his horse tethered to a rock in the cave, Buchanan pressed his back to the cliff until he was flat against it. The river was about thirty feet away. Following his nose, the tracker would be looking ahead, not to the west where Buchanan was standing. Buchanan was not cocky, however. He did not believe that St. Jacques would have given over his Bowie knife, not with open country to cross and no other defense. Besides, Buchanan did not recall Haywood being handy at knife-throwing. But the cowboy was good on horseback and he would likely have a stone in his hand. He could throw the rock, get low behind his mount, and cover thirty feet in seconds. If the target of such a man were to miss what might be his only shot, he would get trampled. Even an injury to the rancher would doom the herd. With Buchanan's horse and his guns, and a kerchief across his face, Haywood could get close enough to be mistaken for him . . . and pick off enough riders to end the drive.

Like it or not, Buchanan thought, *I have to be prepared to issue a command and then fire if it is not obeyed.* Now that the moment was upon him, he decided what that order should be. It was reasonable. He hoped that Haywood would be, too.

The cowboy's black saddle horse came into view around the edge of the cliff. He was moving rapidly, his rifle scabbard full of stones, his eyes ahead. The rider was bent low behind the neck of his horse, his focus on the spot where Fremont had been camped—

"Stop there, Mr. Haywood!"

Buchanan stepped from the cliff and was looking at the tracker over the barrel of his gun. The rider changed up like this was a cavalry drill. He redirected the charge into a quarter turn so he was facing whoever had spoken. His eyes moved the same way, pivoting and fixing on Buchanan. If Haywood was annoyed at being ambushed, he did not show it.

"Good morning," Buchanan said.

The rider did not reply. He just looked at the other man with an unchanged expression.

George Haywood was a big man. His loose, ivory-colored slicker made him seem even more thickly muscled than he was. His dark eyes were more intimidating than his size, and Buchanan suspected that most people looked away. Haywood also had large, scarred hands. One of those hands held the reins. Another held a large piece of quartz. There was a sack of the rock slung from his saddle.

"Your being here presents us both with some hard choices," Buchanan went on.

"You got a gun. Seems the choices are yours."

"I don't want it to be that way but I can't abide having you at my back."

"You can't *abide*? We both fought a war, Mr. Buchanan, one that guarantees me the same right as you to be where I am. Besides, you got property that was stolen from me. If you intend to take my horse, too, that one's a hangin' offense."

Buchanan wondered if the man had been running those words through his head. Alone out here the mind could not help doing that.

"You can put the prairie lawyering back on the shelf," Buchanan said. "I learnt some, too, in my time. I would never be caught with a stolen horse. You charged, I fired at the animal. Did that in the war, rather than killing men. The result is the same: You're on foot, waiting for your comrades. Also, a fall like that—you could be hurt." Still aiming at Haywood, Buchanan took a few steps forward. "Instead of all this talk, I got a better idea."

Haywood did not ask what it was. He just waited.

"Come to work for me, at least for the rest of the drive.

Give me your word you'll execute faithfully, by which I mean not interfering, and I will take that as a contract."

"Thank you for that courtesy, but you are asking me to betray my present employer and Yancy St. Jacques. Dawson, at least, ain't given me a reason to do that."

"I'm askin' you to stay on the right side of the law. And to thank me for saving you from a rope."

"A rope? How do you figure?"

"My foreman wouldn't've taken the Double-D money or given up the cattle. You would've had to kill him. Rustlin' and murder also end in a noose."

Haywood was silent.

"Or wouldn't you have returned fire?" Buchanan asked. "I'm betting you are better than that."

"Mr. Buchanan, I didn't want what happened back there. We were promised it wouldn't come to that."

"I believe you, yet here we are. And it's bound to get uglier. What do you think will happen when your friends catch up to us, especially if they wait till we cross the border where the laws of Mexico don't exist for any practical application? Dawson won't let the cattle reach market in Mexico, not from what I heard. So St. Jacques comes back with more men and arms to kill us and our herd and blame it on banditos. Maybe you skirt justice, maybe you don't. How's that gonna sit with you inside?"

Haywood's expression was still unchanged but he seemed to be considering what Buchanan had said. At least, he did not spit or make some other show of rejection the way the others had done on the previous day.

"May I dismount?" Haywood asked. "Been riding awhile."

"Sure. Just step back and toward the river where you can't swat his rump."

Haywood's eyes showed some life; he seemed, to Buchanan, amused or impressed by the man's caution, maybe both. He was experienced enough to know that even a wildly bucking animal was a threat, not just its hooves but by offering a man cover if he decided to run at his opponent or make for the river. A cornered man might think it was worth trying in order to dash to the midpoint of the water, hoping that it was deep enough to offer concealment and escape.

The cowboy raised his hands and slid easily from the saddle. Then he walked several paces, just out of arm's reach of the stallion.

"You can lower your arms," the rancher said. "Like I indicated, I trust ya."

Haywood eased them down. He faced Buchanan, not defiant but unbowed.

"Tell me something, Mr. Buchanan, if you don't mind."

"If I can, and if it's short."

"Why don't you accept the offer? You do that, St. Jacques will forget about what happened up north."

"Will he, now?"

"Dawson will make sure of it, and that's no small thing. Yancy's a Southern gentleman—or was. They hold grudges like they hold a whip. Tight."

"The promise to curb a feral dog is no reason to *do* a thing, Mr. Haywood. He shouldn't've been loose in the first place. What would *you* do? Would you give in?"

"Dunno. I never had that kind of money to give or take. It's attractive."

"How attractive is submission to Dick Dawson? Should I take an offer that puts me on my knees—not just now but next time, when he wants my horses and my land? How attractive is servitude?"

The question had a point and that point found its target.

Haywood inhaled and continued. "I say again, this is not something I want but here are the facts, Mr. Buchanan. The Double-D men, more men than before, will follow me this far, and if I'm not here, they will continue on their own. Goin' forward, they'll hear you, smell you, see you, and eventually they will catch up."

"And there will be needless bloodshed on both sides. We will find high ground and wait for you. We will set fires behind us. We will do everything we can, including see our cattle starve, before we do what St. Jacques ordered. Now, Mr. Haywood, what is your answer?"

Once again, the tracker became thoughtful.

"If I do what you ask, I will have to stay in Mexico. Or at least leave this territory."

"You'd have a job with me."

"That's not my meaning. Somehow, somewhere, St. Jacques and the others will come for me. A rope or a bullet, maybe a beating–you've seen them use their fists."

"My men have."

"Like you just said, the result of any of them is the same."

"I'm sorry for that, but I cannot let you drop more stones and make this easier for them. The choice for you is settin' here a day or two, horseless–I *will* be forced to shoot him–and then doing one thing you say you're against, or doing something else that goes against your nature: joining us, at least for the present, and giving me your word you won't try anything."

For the first time, Haywood smiled. "You're sincere. That's a real offer."

"As real as the bear tracks to my back."

Haywood renewed his smile. "I was wondering if you'd believe me if I said there's a bear behind you."

"The grizzly I heard and smelt ain't close enough to worry me. And you and I both know my horse woulda let me know if it was. So what'll it be, Mr. Haywood? You can keep the horse but not the rocks. We can talk about your concerns as we head south."

This time there was no hesitation. "I'll ride with you."

"My men may not trust you."

"Won't be the first time I've been alone. You're a good man and I won't break my word. I will do nothing to slow you down or signal the Double-D."

Buchanan lowered the rifle and turned toward his mustang. "Mount up, Mr. Haywood. We got some catching up to do."

CHAPTER TEN

THE MEN OF the AB Ranch had undergone a swift and unpleasant change. They were no longer supplicants at the altar of the San Bernardino range or its lush foothills. The forests were no longer columns on which the vault of heaven rested; they were a crown of thorns. What had been majestic beauty below was humbling now for another reason entirely. The recent spring thaw that had swollen the rivers with melted snow now conspired to make their ascent into the foothills a brutal one.

The slope was as gentle up close as it was from a distance. And it was grassy. Fremont would not have hesitated to climb it with Miss Sally on his arm. To the west, on their right, it fell away gradually to the green-robed rocks and trees; to the east it rose more sharply toward the mountains; ahead, according to what Fremont had been able to see, it was nothing but open country leading flatly to the west, to mountains to the east. Southwest was where they wanted to go, which made it an ideal route.

But it proved to be far from that. The earth beneath the animals' hooves and the wagon wheels was soft, creating a slow, uneven march from the start. Steer ran into steer, the horses whinnied as a leg would be swallowed nearly to the knee, and Griswold was working his pintos hard to keep the chuck wagon or its trailing extra horses from getting stuck. Traveling across the already-trod ground, the four sets of hooves and four chuck wagon wheels were constantly getting stuck in the soft earth. While the panicked horses tied behind wanted to race ahead, the chuck wagon slid from side to side as the procession got underway. Griswold quickly fell behind, then far behind, as the wheels continually became stuck. It was then a matter of the cookie climbing down, steadying all four animals, and starting over—at an angle and without traction. Griswold's own boots were muddy nearly to the knees. López frequently fell back to help lest they leave the chuck wagon behind.

"D'ya ever have a situation like this in Mexico?" Griswold asked, standing beside the cowboy and pulling hard.

"*Sí*," the Mexican replied. "We had a cannon for one battle."

"What didja do?"

López replied, "What we cannot do here. Pulled it as far as we could and then fired."

The nine horses and six riders tired quickly, but to rest on the hill meant a slow, unhappy retreat over ground already covered.

Buchanan and his companion had no trouble catching up to the herd. Riding into the forest, the rancher was surprised to see them on the slope. He went in among the trees to see how far they had gone and how much they had left to cover. The front of the drive still had most of the hill to go before reaching what looked like a plain on top. Buchanan and Haywood turned back and started up the incline.

Griswold was several wagon lengths back, focused on coaxing his forward horses along and hoping his rearward horses remained steady. He was using his bad arm more than he should and shouting more than usual.

"I do not intend to become buzzard feed up here!" he was yelling when Buchanan passed on the east side of the wagon. The cookie's face lit up like a July Fourth sparkler. "Boss! Welcome to Soft Clay City."

"What happened out there?" Buchanan asked, gesturing to the west.

"Fallen trees, a lot of 'em! I hear they was more like mush than—"

There was an audible clap of Griswold's mouth when he saw George Haywood ride up beside Buchanan. "Eh?"

"Buck Griswold, George Haywood," Buchanan said, making introductions as he looked ahead.

"I seen you in town," Griswold said. "Ain't you Double-D?"

"Mr. Haywood will be riding with us," Buchanan said, excusing himself and driving his mustang toward the herd. He left a thick, unhappy silence in his wake.

"If you brake, I'll rig some help," Haywood said.

Griswold dumbly reached out and pulled the wooden handle toward him, causing the wagon to skid to a stop. Haywood dismounted and moved closer to the side of the chuck wagon and settled beside the horse on the left.

"Was recent events misrepresented to me?" the cookie asked.

Haywood did not answer. He walked his horse in front of the others, doing so slowly so as not to excite them, then grabbed his rope and tied it to his saddle. Then he ran it between the pintos to the tongue under the front of the wagon.

"Start 'em up again," Haywood ordered, swinging back onto his horse.

"Yes, sir, at once," Griswold grumbled. "I always take orders from men I don't know and until a few breaths ago I was told not to trust."

"We live in changing times," Haywood said. "Don't forget to release the brake."

"I know my rig," Griswold protested, though not loudly.

The cookie did as he was instructed and the tracker urged his horse forward with a loud "Gyah!" Initially, all the big horse did was pull. The pintos were daunted by the larger animal and by hooves that were stuck in the ground. Behind them, the chuck wagon shuddered from the effort. The old joints of the weather-beaten cart groaned, the pans shook, and kegs of water knocked against each other as the lids rocked up and down. In back, the two spare horses had hunkered down like mules, afraid of the wood-and-metal monster roaring before them.

"Whoa, whoa—we're comin' apart!" Griswold yelled fearfully, but he did not stop the wagon.

Haywood appeared not to hear him. He kicked the animal hard. The stallion whinnied and reared, then came down with a short forward leap. The entire rig moved forward with a rattling jerk, nudging the pintos ahead and dragging the animals behind forward. The chuck wagon was rolling again and Haywood kept his horse moving. The tracker's mount closed the gap between the tail rider and the herd, and Griswold only stopped when it was about to run directly into a wall of cattle. This time, and each time thereafter, the experienced cookie left them enough space to give Haywood's horse room to tuck into the next pull.

In front of the chuck wagon the drive was having a difficult, chaotic time. The passage of nearly three hundred steers and the back-and-forth movement of the cowboys had turned the surface of the slop into suctioning mud. This left the herd in disarray. While the animals in front moved with some efficiency, those behind became stuck. The steers ended up at angles to the way forward and to one another, causing disarray among the beeves that came next. The drive quickly formed a bottle shape with a neck of forward-moving cattle up front and a bulge of crowded, unhappy animals behind.

Buchanan had ridden, in turn, to López and Mitchell on the east and west flanks, cutting through the crowded herd to reach them. Then he rode forward to Deems and Prescott on swing, and finally to Fremont. He had given them all the same instructions:

"The cattle are just sliding into each other, side to side and back to front, so keep about a hundred of 'em back until there's room to move. That means wait for about two acres of ground between your lead cattle and the group in front before moving."

It was not a neat solution, since each smaller herd still became mired in the pulped ground. But it prevented the kind of jams that caused backsliding. It was only the adhesion of the muck that prevented injury, since no cow moved fast enough or slid back far enough to harm another cow. Buchanan remained with Fremont on point, turning back whenever one of the other riders needed assistance moving his smaller herd.

"You want I should be with Griz on tail?" Fremont had asked. "He was strugglin'."

"George Haywood is there, helpin' out," Buchanan informed him.

Fremont looked as though he'd been kicked in the skull, but there were more pressing matters than having his puzzlement cleared up. Amid grunts of disapproval from the mired cattle and snorts from the horses, Fremont went back to guiding the herd forward.

Over the course of the morning and into the late afternoon, the three groups managed to negotiate the slope. Toward the end, they were pushing so much mud backward that Griswold had to move the extra horses to the sides to give him extra pull. He relied on their panic and unhappiness to keep them moving forward.

Fremont was focused the entire time and continued to keep his feelings roped tight until the three groups plus Griswold and Haywood had reached the top. There was, in fact, a long, wide-open plateau, and Buchanan told Prescott, Mitchell, and Fremont to get the cattle into a bunch and then make camp.

While the cookie made supper, Haywood found a spot to nap. The tracker lay down off to the eastern side, where a plain continued with a very slight incline into the foothills. When the roundup was finished, Buchanan had gone back down the slope, the surface of it all but destroyed by their passage. Deems and López had ridden down to see about freeing the handful of cattle that had been left behind.

The herd above settled, Fremont rode down.

"Good job getting them up this mess," Buchanan said.

"What the hell happened back at the Mohave?"

Buchanan looked at his trail boss briefly before turning his eyes back down the slope. "You talkin' about George Haywood? The man who just got Griz up the slope?"

"Yeah, that man. The one who wanted to snatch our herd—him and his dry-gulch pardners."

"It was either leave Haywood to be picked up by the Double-D riders, shoot him, or take him with us. What would you have done?"

"Not brought him here! A day ago that hombre was ready to *shoot us*. You took him right to where his guns is!"

"He gave me his word not to move against us. I believe him."

Fremont was dumbfounded. "His word? Did you consider makin' a deal that *didn't* give him free run of the place, like tyin' him to his horse? Hell, the Double-D riders don't even need him now. I left a trail a schoolboy could follow."

"Don't go runnin' yourself down—"

"I *ain't*. Did you look over the side?"

"I did—"

"Then you saw that we wouldn't've gotten through below, but that ain't my point. You could've cut a deal that had him lie. You could've, I dunno, took his horse and offered to give it back if he told St. Jacques we continued west around the San Gabriels before turning south."

"You would've trusted him but only to lie?"

"That's what varmints do: They lie, cheat and steal. I *know* those Dawsons!"

Buchanan watched as Deems and López struggled up with a pair of steers. The two cattle were roped around the horns, the two cowboys' horses fighting for footing.

"Will, it's been a really tough day, for you especially. Why don't you see if Prescott's organized enough to lend these boys a hand, then get yourself some coffee?"

"Boss?"

Buchanan turned to his old friend. "Look, if I tried to tie him to anything, he would've resisted and I would've had to shoot him. Self-defense against an unarmed man? That would've been the end of me. Besides, I knew him in the war. And if you look past all the air in your lungs, you know he's not like the others."

"I have to take your say-so on that."

"Will you?"

Fremont went silent.

"I don't blame you for bein' mad," Buchanan said. "I truly do not. But we are where we are, so I'm asking you to let it rest."

Fremont looked at his boss. He still felt betrayed but swallowed that along with anything else he thought to say. Reining his horse around, he cantered back to the plateau proper and sent Prescott back.

Buchanan did not blame his foreman for being incensed, even outraged. Fremont was the one who had taken the brunt of the threats and humiliation, not him. Except for Prescott, the men who were there would have their own beefs, and rightly so. Buchanan would have to have a talk with them as soon as things were settled. One thing the rancher could not afford to do was to doubt his own decisions or show indecision to the men. Not this early and with the roughest parts of the drive still to come.

Prescott arrived and Buchanan joined him lower on the slope. Between the four of them the cowboys managed to save all but one of the cattle, whose struggles to go forward had caused him to slide back and to the side of the slope. He tumbled down into the woods, on his side, still alive when he struck the ground. López went to the edge and put a rifle bullet in his head.

There were still two hours of daylight left and the men used it to check the condition of as many cattle as they could get to. There seemed to be no major injuries and, mercifully, the ground was solid there, away from the course of the runoff.

With Haywood still asleep, Buchanan waited while the men situated the herd. That meant placing the largest head on all sides, at the perimeter. Nighttime stampedes were not common. Predators caused local unrest among the herd. But nearby thunder or gunfire could send them running. If that happened, cowboys would run with the herd and fire guns at the feet of the big steer to get them to run in the other direction. The big animals in front would create a wall for the swelling, surging herd behind them, causing all the cattle to come to a quick, ugly stop. If there were no further noisemaking, the herd would stay where it was. If the cattle had not gone far, they could be moved back. If not, that meant the men would get no further sleep, instead watching to make sure the herd stayed put.

When the stockade area was established, Buchanan went over to talk to the men. There was resentment in the air, as real as the smoke of the campfire. Cowboys on a drive did not have secrets; there was never the time or energy to craft, tell, and remember lies. The truth always came out.

The trail boss had already heard most of what Buchanan had to say, and while the rancher spoke, Fremont remained silent behind a fresh cigar—although the frequency of his smoke signals communicated lingering unhappiness.

When the explanation was done, no one spoke until after the trail boss did. It took him a few puffs and then some more to gather his word.

"There isn't a man here who, in the same situation, woulda pointed a gun at a Double-D man. Not one. But back on the last drive, the one where we ended up pushing some faces in, Haywood stayed out of it. I don't think it was because he was afraid but because he knew they was wrong." Fremont looked over to where the tracker was resting, silhouetted against the setting sun. "I don't like what he did to us, but he's here and it's best to make peace with that."

"I saw him help Griz up the hill," Deems said. "Far as I'm concerned, that's penance of some kind."

"I didn't even ask him to; he just did it," Griswold remarked. "I'd still be back there or worse if he hadn't."

"And it's not like we can't use another good man," Prescott said.

"As long as he don't try and get his guns," Mitchell said. "That could be why he agreed to ride with us."

"I've got 'em in the chuck box, behind the tools," Fremont said. "Whoever's riding tail will be watching for him."

"You're gonna trust him," Mitchell said. It was not a question.

"Any reason not to, other than that he's a Dawson?" Buchanan asked.

Mitchell hesitated. He was not like St. Jacques, one of those Southerners who was still fighting for a different end to the war. Whatever ideas he dragged with him from the past had not affected anyone—so far. The man spent most of his time living in the field, alone in the cabin; he was the hand everyone knew least.

"I guess not, sir," Mitchell said. "No objections, not if the boss an' everyone else is okay."

"You sure?" Fremont pressed. "I don't want my men distracted because of an outsider."

"I'm sure, Will. I'm sure."

"Like that time we had a cowgirl with us, remember? The one Sloane was gonna marry?"

"She *was* good," Griswold said. "When they busted up, we kept the wrong one."

Prescott shook his head. "But horns and rattles, I did hate ridin' behind her."

There was soft laughter and a few campfire comments. Whether it was intentional or not, Prescott's reminder lightened the mood and any objections. Fremont regarded Mitchell.

Before the sun had set, Haywood was invited to join them for a meal. He brought his own jerky so as not to burden the supplies, but there was a general acceptance of his being there.

For the moment, that was good enough for Andrew Buchanan.

CHAPTER ELEVEN

BUCHANAN WAS SLEEPING more or less the way he had the night before. He was on the ground in his bedroll, handmade by himself before the previous drive so it was relatively fresh. Six feet long and wide enough to be doubled over, the roll was made of waterproof canvas that kept a man dry on the ground or could serve as a makeshift tent in the rain. Leather straps made it easy to bundle up and store behind the saddle.

The waterproofing was accomplished with a mixture of beeswax and linseed oil. Since he had bought his first bedroll from an old cowhand two score years before, that smell put him into a restful mind for slumber. Buchanan could not grab shut-eye in the saddle the way López could, a talent envied by every man on the ranch. But the familiar scent was the next best thing.

Warm inside the bedroll, Buchanan, like the others,

rested his head on his jacket. Had they not contained the Double-D guns, Fremont would have taken that sack he carried and stuffed it with leaves or earth, having first filtered the large pebbles and worms through his fingers.

Although the process was the same as the previous night, Buchanan always felt a strong sense of home when he bedded down with the men and horses. It had the familiar sounds and smells of a home, and there was the familiar comfort of the campfire. While the scent of each was different depending on the kind of wood being burned, a campfire was basically the same. It was like Griz's meals: sometimes a little dull when he got low on some ingredient, sometimes fancy—like tonight, flavored with the leaves he had gathered—but there was no mistaking who made them. Buchanan had once tried to explain to his wife how he endured the months away from his family. Lying with her husband on a bearskin rug before their hearth, she did not understand how a campfire could be anything like the home fire.

"Random rocks and sticks don't have the memories of love and family," she had said. "They don't come with shelter, of comfort in a storm. Of the birth of our children."

"It's different," Buchanan had agreed. He had relied on his lack of inflection to weaken the word "different" to mean "lesser" as opposed to "a home away from home." She and her father had traveled widely, but in a covered wagon with overnight stays mostly at missions or rectories. She would not understand how a sense of home could be transportable and re-created each night with a group of men, seven-by-fourteen-foot canvas sheets, a circle of rocks around burning sticks, and—most of all—a shared sense of purpose.

Most of which Buchanan had been lacking the night before. That, plus exhaustion from a day's work well done, was what allowed cowboys to sleep better under the stars than under their own roofs.

At least writing in his journal helped him to sleep wherever he was. Something about doing that before bed, in dim campfire or moonlight, made his eyes want to shut.

Then there was the sea of cattle, a wall of meat and hide, hooves and horns, all of it dressed in a brand he had designed himself. It was something else Patsy seemed incapable of understanding, not that he tried hard to explain it. But he took a pride in their raising and feeding that he did not believe he could ever get from an orange. There had not been a lot of time to think about groves, but just the thought of them filled him with a kind of sickness; he could never have done to a cow what he did to Jacob's orange. There was something about pitting his will against a calf or a grown steer or a herd of them that watering and picking could not equal . . . or replace. The idea frightened him. It scared him more than a rattler shaded by a rock.

Finally, he had lain down with a deep sense of pride in his men, in himself. They had overcome an unexpected obstacle, he had dealt fairly with an enemy—Patsy would approve of that act of Christian charity—and he had allowed his men to have their say in it. A drive was not democracy, but he had read the parts of the U.S. Constitution that applied: free speech and the right to bear arms. He had applied the ideas of the late Mr. Lincoln by showing malice toward none—to George

Haywood, anyway. Buchanan felt patriotic by his conduct.

Which was why, even though there was danger ahead and also now behind, this first night with the herd, with his hands, brought a kind of comfort Buchanan had sorely needed. It also strengthened the resolve he felt to persevere.

Deems was on watch, and it was at some point after Buchanan had fallen asleep that the cowboy bent close.

"There's movement by the wagon."

Buchanan was fully awake and easing from the bedroll as Deems moved off. The rancher had his gun belt across his saddle; he drew the gun nearest to him as he rose. He followed Deems. The campfire had died down but Buchanan was quickly able to orient himself. Despite the urgency—any unexpected noise could stampede the cattle—the two men moved as quietly as possible. If there was no cause for concern, it did not pay to deprive the other hands of sleep.

The wagon was at the north end of the camp, away from the cattle. It was dark but they could hear Griswold snoring inside and followed the sound. Buchanan heard the gentle ruckus now as well. The chuck wagon was situated between the camp and the slope, all four horses tethered to a stunted juniper to the east. The sound was coming from behind the wagon. It sounded just the right size to be a raccoon.

Stepping lightly but swiftly, Buchanan took the lead from Deems. The horses were corralled there, not just Griswold's but the others. They were quiet, which argued against a scavenger. Buchanan wished that were not so.

Ideally, the men would have separated and come at

the wagon from both sides. But the prospect of accidentally shooting each other was a real possibility, especially in the dark. Because he was on watch, the cowboy was carrying his rifle; that was also not the most effective weapon at close range.

It was cold enough to see his breath, and Buchanan forced himself to relax so as not to shiver. When they were just a few steps away, the sound behind the wagon stopped.

The men stopped as well.

"Whoever's there, don't shoot!" a deep voice whispered.

It was George Haywood. Buchanan came around, his Colt held waist-high. The tracker was standing at the chuck box. The doors were open and he was feeling inside.

"You shoulda had biscuits when they were offered," Buchanan said. "Or is there something else you're after?"

"I'm looking for matches," Haywood said, withdrawing the box and holding it up.

"Matches, sir? Why?"

"Back by the herd, I heard dry pine cones snapping and the bleat of what I think was a mountain goat. Thought to light a torch, scare him off."

"A goat," Deems said. "At night."

"Kids wander off, get lost, cry for their ma. That can spook a herd. You want to take that chance?"

Buchanan considered the explanation. It was a much shorter walk to get a match here than to go where Deems and the campfire had been.

"All right, show me where you heard it," Buchanan said.

Fremont joined them just then, rifle in hand, sleep

still in his eyes. The men started in the direction Haywood indicated. Except for Griswold, all the men were now awake, and armed. More alert now, Fremont quietly told the cowboys to be ready to steady the herd in case there was shooting. That was all he said; it was basically all he knew, although he had his suspicions.

Buchanan, Haywood, and Deems walked softly. They could not see much in the deep evening blackness. They passed the sleeping area, where Haywood's saddle and horse were, near but apart from the others. The herd was nearby, in an area bounded by large boulders on the east and south sides, some larger than the largest cattle. The boulders mounted up, piled higher and higher and making their way to the mountains. To the south was open country; to the west, a churned-up stretch of ground that led back to the slope. The dark shapes of trees, tall and stout, rose up in the area around the boulders.

Haywood was between the men, Buchanan in front. The tracker stopped to pick up a branch, then tapped the rancher on the shoulder and pointed to the area between them and the nearest pines.

"You smell that?"

Buchanan inhaled through his nose. He picked up the rich, nutty earth scent.

"Pine cones."

"No. Under that, a different musk," Haywood said. "I'm going out in front to do what I was planning. Don't nobody move."

"Go ahead," Buchanan told him.

The tracker crouched, felt around, and picked up a brittle pine cone about the size of a man's foot. He forced it onto the stick he was carrying, then popped a wooden match from the box. He struck the tip on his leather belt. It sparked and he touched the flame to the pine cone. The seed scales flared and quickly ignited, burning fast, falling away as curled ash, but also setting light to the dry tinder beneath them. With a small but competent flame, Haywood rose and moved forward.

The circle of light revealed more pine cones along with tree limbs that had fallen from somewhere above, all of them lying on or among a field of small rocks. Whatever had been making the sound was no longer moving, but Haywood still felt its presence. He stopped and raised the torch higher.

There was not much wind, and the flame flickered just enough to catch the feet of the goat he had heard. It was lying with its small hooves facing him.

"Must've fell," Deems said.

"Uh-uh," Haywood replied. He raised the light very slowly.

The fire finally illuminated more than the goat that Haywood had heard. It was small, a kid as he had suspected, and it was dead. The cougar sitting on top of its prey, the one Haywood had smelled, was very much alive. The cat hissed and showed bloody teeth. Neither Haywood nor anyone behind him moved closer.

"He caught it behind the neck; goat probably never knew what killed it," Haywood said. He continued to hold the torch on the mountain lion but he did not approach. "We're gonna have to do something about this fella. Those rocks behind it are probably also inhabited."

"A mate?"

"Likely as not, and if there are cubs, more feral than this one."

Buchanan was angry that he had not thought of any

of that. The eastern trails tended to be flat, with relatively few places for a predator to hide, even at night. As Patsy had tried to warn him, he did not have an instinct for this place.

"What do you suggest?" As soon as it was spoken, Buchanan regretted asking the question. The men heard him. They heard him, still early in a dangerous drive, not making a decision but asking a Double-D man to do that. It did not matter that his concern was for the safety of the men and the herd above all. He added quickly exactly what he was thinking: "Letting the critter be seems the best thing to do.

"Doesn't seem sensible, but that's right," Haywood replied. "I'm going to stay here between the cat and the herd. While I keep the light between us, you all make more torches. We'll stick them in the ground. Won't chase the cat off, but it'll discourage him from coming any lower. He'll probably drag the thing back to his den."

Buchanan turned to his trail boss. "Get 'em made, Will."

Without taking his eyes off the cat, Haywood said, "You can use pine cones, but they'll burn longer with dead grass mashed with soil. Look to the roots of the good growth. Doesn't appear as if there's been a fire here for a lotta years."

With a disapproving look—which rolled from Haywood to Buchanan—Fremont rallied the others. Buchanan had an unexpected sense of unease just then; he felt that he could as easily have been on a ship in a storm, asked the first mate for advice, and dodged a mutiny. Had he fled so many years, so many miles, to end up going nowhere?

The trail boss relayed the order to the men clustered

with arms at the ready. He instructed Deems to see if Griswold had any horse patties, which he had collected on the ranch and kept bagged in the wagon. It was necessary for fuel when wood was damp from rain.

The cat had tensed slightly when the men arrived; it relaxed now that the bulk of them had dispersed. Its mirror-slick eyes were orange-white, reflecting the fire. Moving very slowly, Haywood found a small, flat stone and sat on it, keeping the torch high and in front of him.

Buchanan stepped up behind him, standing a few paces back so as not to alarm the cat. It continued to display its teeth but nothing more.

"You understand why I questioned you back at the chuck wagon," Buchanan said

"I do and I don't resent it, if that's what you're asking. I heard what Fremont said before, that the guns're there. I most likely would have doubted me, too." Without taking his eyes from the mountain lion, he asked the rancher, "How do you know I *didn't* take my weapons back?"

Once again Buchanan felt as if he were caught short by the Double-D man. "I don't."

"Truth be said, I considered running. I truly did. I knew I could arm myself and make my way down that slope better, faster, than any of you. Figured I'd go back to meet the man I work for. I mean, a man's word wrung out of me the way you did—that doesn't hold much coffee."

"Why didn't you get away?"

"Not sure. I may still."

Buchanan was touched by the man's truthfulness, even resting as it did on dishonesty. He considered distributing the Dawson guns among the men when this was over.

The men had begun returning with branches wrapped in a variety of kindling on branches of various shapes and lengths. To conserve matches, they lit the torches from Haywood's torch and stuck them in the ground. It reminded Buchanan of a picket line Captain Dundee had once set to frighten enemy horses. It turned a charge into a chaotic route, and Dundee's front line was able to capture several good steeds.

When everything was arranged, and the cat seemed content that it was safe, it proceeded to do as Haywood had predicted. His teeth locking on the limp, bloody neck of the animal, the mountain lion backed off, dragging it behind. In the farthest reaches of the light the men saw the predator reach the rocks; a second cat emerged to help pull the goat up and into the darkness. Only when the animals had returned to their den and the night birds returned did Buchanan realize how quiet it had been.

"No crickets out here either," Haywood said.

"I was just noticing."

"That surprised me, too, scouting in the Black Hills during the war. On the plains, if that sound goes away, you hear it and you wake up. Likely the winds. Flatlands—insects ride them. If they came here, they'd ride up and down, cold to heat, probably die."

"You know how to write?"

Haywood shook his head. His expression seemed to move in the flickering light. It had not. The man was as serious as a sharpened hatchet.

"I saw before that you keep a journal," the former slave said. "Maybe you're thinking I should do the same."

"You've got a lot of wisdom to record."

"Well, I never learned writing. No opportunity. I try and speak well by imitating what I hear, so I can show people I am no less than they." He tapped his temple. "I keep my travels up here and also on my back. Every scar is something I said or did or tried, someone I helped when I shouldn't've, like a house slave giving birth or a white girl who stumbled while she was chasing butterflies through the field. All of it branded into my flesh. Funny thing is, I still wrestle with what's right as against what's right to *survive*."

"I reckon there's too much of the mountain lion and too little of the angels in most of us."

"Angels." Haywood pushed his torch into the ground and stood. Buchanan rose as well. "You asked why I didn't run. Truth is, I seen you and your ladies in church a few times. If this drive ends with a widow and two girls having no father, no wherewithal . . ." His voice trailed off. "We don't need to bring the mark of Cain out here, to a new Eden. I don't want to be a part of that. As long as you and your man there, Fremont, don't give me cause, I want to see this through."

"'Want to'?"

"It's a struggle. Things have happened kind of sudden. I'm still thinking about it."

He turned back toward the horses corralled near the chuck wagon, then stopped. "Make a note of this in your journal, because I wasn't truthful with you about my intentions. I did take them—the guns. It was easier and quieter feeling for my familiar belongings in the dark than hunting for a box of matches." He flipped the box to Buchanan. "You can have these back, though."

The rancher caught them and watched the tracker as he went back to his solitary spot.

"Why are you telling me now?" Buchanan asked.

"Because I don't have to worry about anyone trying to take them. I can track, I can ride, and I'm a real good shot. Learned during the war; best training there is."

Skills, experience, and gold, Buchanan thought. Those three were what he expected to gain on the drive. The words were inscribed in his journal. He had not inscribed "wisdom," which, ironically, underscored how much he did not yet possess. The reason for that was he knew and understood his men. Through López, he grasped what was important to Mexicans. He had not expected to meet, let alone travel with, someone like Haywood. Part of him was humbled, part of him frustrated, but mostly he was grateful.

Somehow he would have to explain that feeling to the rest of the hands. Otherwise, resentment, like weeds, would foul the drive and poison the aftermath.

I want to choose how my life flows, not have it forced on me, he thought as he returned to his bedroll.

CHAPTER TWELVE

THE MEN WOKE in a crawling mist. It was cold, clinging, and thick, blinding them for more than a few feet before them. Buchanan and Fremont approached Prescott, who had been on watch the past two hours.

"It started comin' down from the mountain just before sunup like it was something alive," Prescott said. "I didn't like rippling heat on the plains, but I liked it better'n this."

"Map's not gonna help us here," Fremont said. "Dammit, we're in new terrain. I should've set out flags last night."

"Don't whip yourself. We're getting smarter by the day," Buchanan said. The rancher walked into what had been plateau the day before and was cloud now. "We know where the western fall-off is and we know generally where the rocks are. If we have two point riders and move slowly, we should be all right."

"We had about two miles of ground ahead," Fremont said. "Hopefully, this'll lift by then."

"Until it does we'll take point together," Buchanan said. "Double length in front."

AFTER A QUICK breakfast around the chuck wagon—with Mitchell eating by himself, acting "prickly," as Griswold put it—Fremont and Buchanan prepared to take point with everyone else in the same positions as before. No one said anything to or about George Haywood. He fell in with Griswold as he had the previous day. The cookie had removed his sling during the night and was taking advantage of the slow pace to roll his arm, wincing whenever it hit a sore spot.

"We're like those rhymes for kids," Griswold said. "Y'know, a strange fit like Bessy Bell and Mary Gray or Robin Hood and Little John."

"I'm guessing, cookie, that you say these things when there's nobody else here. Am I right?"

"There's horses. I know they listen, I can see their ears move."

"I suppose it's possible," Haywood said. "Trees listen to the wind, so why not?"

Griswold chuckled. "You sounded like a Paiute just then. Met an old one last autumn while I was headed to San Bernardino for supplies. He had—if you can believe this—he was out in the plains with his horse and he had this mat covered with food his tribe had growed. He was swappin' for things they needed, like canteens, utensils, eyeglasses."

"How did he do?"

"I never saw him again, so either he got everything

he wanted or he didn't get spit. I wonder about that every time I take that trail."

The two men continued to talk while the herd got underway. This time the pace was slow, without the lurching and stopping that had rattled Griswold and his animals the previous day.

"Kinda like heaven must be when you first get there," Griswold said as they proceeded. "Mebbe not as cold, though."

"Or noisy," Haywood pointed out.

Griswold listened. "Yer right. Everything sounds louder. I wonder why. Prob'ly because you can't see anything, so you listen harder."

Haywood moved in front of the chuck wagon team. He wanted to try and see the cattle. In the mist, with the sound spread out, it was difficult to tell whether he and Griswold were staying in a line or going astray—whether they were right on top of the herd or a ways distant.

There was a whinny from somewhere just ahead. Haywood moved forward cautiously.

"Who's back there?" Reb Mitchell asked.

"It's Haywood."

"You need something?"

"Just keeping Griswold near to the herd."

"I'll shout if I stop hearin' the wagon," Mitchell said. "Horse don't like a rider this close to our back."

"Him or you?"

"Don't bother me, mister. I got work to do."

"Cattle're moving fine on their own. I asked whether it was the horse or you who don't like it?"

"Your meanin' was clear. So was mine, I thought. Go back where you belong."

"On tail?"

It took a moment for Mitchell to realize what he was being asked. "On tail."

"I was listening when you all decided to let me stay," Haywood went on. "You didn't want me here."

"You're a Dawson man."

"I got you out of a jam last night, freed the chuck wagon the day before."

"I looked in the chuck box when I had my coffee," Mitchell said. "Thought I'd heard the picks and shovels rattlin' more than before. You also took your guns."

"Suspicious man."

"Of a man who put a gun on me? Yeah. I'd shoot you for that here and now if your acts was mine to judge."

"Why don't you?"

"I'm not sure Fremont or the boss'd believe my reasons."

Mitchell rode ahead a bit, and Haywood stopped to let the man and the herd move on. "I wondered where your ultimate loyalties lay."

"Now ya do," Mitchell said, his voice fading as he himself was gone with the mist.

The chuck wagon rattled up a few moments later and Haywood fell in beside Griswold.

"I guess we're purty close," he said. "I could hear ya talkin'."

"Talk. It's like overlapping trails. Does nothing but confuse you."

Griswold smiled. "I like that," he said. The smile was fleeting as he looked ahead at the gauzy white expanse, heard the clops and moos and occasional quiet voices of the hands. "Y'ever get tired of it?" Griswold asked. "Havin' a twister inside, whippin' things up?"

"I think I'm thirty years old, and I cannot recall a time when there was quiet. But, yeah, I'm tired. Tired of men like St. Jacques and Reb Mitchell wearing their hate in their eyes."

"Friend, their world got ripped up at the seams. You hold that against them, you're no better than they are."

Haywood dismissed the thought but did not say so. It would not be possible to explain to this man what the fall of that civilization meant to a vast population of souls in bondage, without dignity or hope.

The tracker returned to the front of the wagon. Behind him, Griswold sat merrily composing rhymes about flies and foxes, clouds and ponds, any mismatched combination he could think of. Whether the horses enjoyed them or not, they were less agitated than they had been the day before.

It was late morning when the mist began to break. There was relief—and surprise—as the men were able to get their bearings.

They were still on a plateau but before afternoon it would come to an end. The edges, from what they could see, suggested it stopped in a sheer drop. There was, however, a slope that turned to the east, up the mountain.

Buchanan and Fremont rode ahead to confirm what they had seen. Finally able to kiss the ground, the warming sun had caused a nest of baby rattlesnakes to become active; Buchanan heard and then saw the vipers, swerving his horse at the last moment.

Reaching the ridgeline, the men rode right to the edge and looked down. Below was a wooded area like the one they had left. It went on for miles. Between it and the herd was a straight drop of several hundred feet. It struck Buchanan like one of the cakes Patsy baked for birthdays. The rock wall looked like a knife had come down and sliced away a huge wedge of rock. Even if they could get down to the forest floor, it presented the same problems as the landscape they had left behind. That left only one way out: the slope to the east, rising into the peaks of the San Bernardino Mountains. It was girded by a narrow ledge that disappeared behind an intervening mountain.

"Goddammit," Fremont said. "We can't even turn back, not with that sludge we dug getting up here."

Buchanan took out his glass and eyed the ledge. "I'm gonna ride over and have a look. You tell 'em to stop the herd."

"Boss, that is a *very* narrow pass—"

"Like you said, the only way to move the herd. It's likely solid, though."

"—and we don't know where it ends."

Buchanan removed the map from his saddlebag and unfolded it against the neck of his horse. He traced the path of the San Bernardino Mountains with a finger, then closed one eye and used that finger to sketch the same path on the peaks ahead.

"We go southeast, up that ledge, we will likely find a way into the valley."

"Maybe," Fremont said. "And once you start out in that direction, there ain't enough room to turn around."

"We don't try, the herd dies here."

Haywood rode up just then. Buchanan did not see the man's rifle or six-shooters. He had left his bedroll behind, most likely stowed in the chuck wagon.

"I saw where you were pointing," Haywood said. "Okay if I ride ahead and scout it out?"

"Depends," Fremont said. "You gonna report fair or tell us we gotta sit tight, mebbe to sell to yer boss?"

"I don't have to ride up a mountain to see what the smart play is—"

"Will, let it be! And you, Mr. Haywood," Buchanan said, "you go too far! Your efforts here have been appreciated but your misdeeds toward my men are open wounds. You go salting them and, by God, you will be without that horse and walking away from our camp."

Fremont's lips were pressed tight and quivering but the tracker seemed impervious to the assault. Haywood lifted his eyes toward the rock ridge.

"Give me an hour. I'll see if the path is clear."

"All right."

"Borrow your spyglass?"

Without hesitation, Buchanan pulled it from its sling and handed it over. Haywood held on to it as he left the men at a good clip.

"I'm sorry, boss," Fremont said.

"We're just starting out, Will. We nurse resentments this way, we won't make it till the end."

"I know. I'll do my best."

As he was speaking, Fremont slapped his neck suddenly and, pinching himself with two fingers, pulled out a tick. He flicked it to the ground and rubbed the spot.

"I guess my problem is me," Fremont said. "Haywood ain't got tact, but what if he's right?"

Buchanan folded away the map. "He ain't, and you know he ain't. We knew this'd be tough and new and that we were up to it. Besides, I'll take your instincts and stubborn backbone over some other man's know-how any day."

Fremont grinned.

"Besides, Haywood ain't such a curly wolf," the rancher said when he was sure the tracker was out of earshot. "Walked smack into our ambush, didn't he?"

Fremont smiled, grateful for Buchanan's graciousness including him.

"Enough woolgathering," the rancher said. "Whatever's up there, that's the way we'll be going."

CHAPTER THIRTEEN

WHILE HAYWOOD WAS gone, Buchanan sat on a flat rock beneath a brilliant expanse of noon sky. He invested the time making notes in his journal relating to points on the map that coincided with the journey and the conditions they had found. He did not expect to be making this trip again, but someone might; he liked the idea that, given to the San Bernardino town clerk or even to Miss Sally for her library, his words might help someone who wanted to cross this territory or another like it.

When that was done, Buchanan and Fremont conferred on tactics as they walked to the chuck wagon. That was where the other men were gathered for a short meal. Griswold was beside the wagon, under an open flap where he was setting out the last of the prepared biscuits from a fold-down platform.

Fremont informed them that the riders would be tracking only the western side of the herd, since there was nowhere for the cattle to go to the east.

"We can probably run 'em a little quick, since they won't be happy pinned where they are," Buchanan added. "Definitely keep 'em moving, since we don't want to be up there at night if that can be helped. And keep your horses eyes left so they don't see the fall-off."

"Maybe Prescott can show us some o' his trick-ridin'!" Griswold said.

"You'll be too busy keeping your own rig safe," Prescott said. "I was looking up there before, saw a turn that's gonna take some care."

"I can drive this buggy two-wheeled if I have to," Griswold boasted.

"With one horse danglin' over the side?" Prescott asked.

Buchanan put away his journal and looked from the ledge to the herd. Darkness, not night, was going to fall awfully fast that low on the mountain.

"López, Deems, gather up the torches we used on the cougar in case we have to take it slower than we want. Griz, gather some dry pine cones, grass, and horse patties to light 'em?"

"Sure, I got time," Griswold said. "I plan to be waitin' here to see if you make it 'cross that . . . that pig ramp."

"You'll be on tail, not sittin' still," Fremont informed him.

"I had a feelin' you'd say that. Just expressin' my desire is all. This is still a free state, right?"

"Griz—"

"I know, I know. But, hey, you thought about breathin' as we go higher?"

"We won't be above a half mile," Fremont said. "We'll be fine."

"You let the cattle know? The horses? They got more to carry."

"They got four legs t'do it!" Mitchell said.

Griswold shook his head. "Yassir, we're gonna have quite a little adventure. Once met a man who took cattle across the Rockies. He and his men ate 'em and was wearing their hides before he got down."

"That'll be enough," Buchanan said sternly. "There's no snow here and this is a short passage." He had spoken for the benefit of the men, not Griswold.

For all his bellyaching, Griswold went to work quickly and efficiently. He grabbed a canvas bag and spade and moved to where the horses had spent the night. He was inhaling deeply, intending to hold his breath while he gathered whatever droppings had sufficiently dried before the sun rose.

On point, Buchanan and Fremont were organizing the herd into a single line by the time Haywood returned. Handing the rancher his spyglass, the tracker made a point of addressing only him and not Fremont. The trail boss was glad for that. Punching Double-D men instead of cattle would come after the drive.

"It's about ten foot wide in most spots," Haywood reported. "The cattle and chuck wagon'll be fine, though there's one sharp turn where we may have to break some rock."

"How much?"

"Can't say. It's about two hours' ride from here and the shadow's not deep enough yet. Steepest part of the ledge is what you can see. After that, it levels as far as I was able to see. I didn't spot any breaks in the surface, but there are some turns I couldn't see past. Saw some crows and hawks, none of 'em mountain birds. Probably comes down like you said, into a valley."

"Valley of the Ancient Lake, according to the map," Buchanan said.

"There's just one thing. Sundown's gonna come real early out there, based on the shadows of the peaks I can see. You might want to wait till morning to start this."

"That'd mean starting in fog."

"We had enough visibility here for a slow passage. Same may be true up there. Certainly safer than darkness. Once you begin this—"

"It's been pointed out we can only move forward. I'd rather be up there than down here."

Buchanan did not have to explain why. The thought of giving St. Jacques time to close the distance and trap them here also made that idea unacceptable. Buchanan turned to Fremont.

"I need my best man on tail to keep an eye on the extra horses and the chuck wagon."

The way Buchanan said it, Fremont understood that was not all he would be watching for.

"I'll keep 'em moving," he said. "Let's fandango!" he shouted, and rode to the back of the herd.

"Where do you want me?" Haywood asked.

"In the lead, ahead of me. You're the tracker. You got the best eyes."

Haywood nodded once. If he suspected any other reason for being situated where Buchanan could see him, he said nothing. But after a day of truce there was renewed tension between himself and the rancher. Haywood was glad he had his guns. It was not Buchanan so much as his top hand and that Reb Mitchell who chafed him. Will Fremont was not his trail boss, not his master. The next time he or any man pushed, Haywood would shove back.

Before they moved out, Buchanan saw what he had not seen earlier in the fog: that they had made changes in this pristine land. Large swatches had been chewed down to the dirt and the wind had not been sufficient enough to dispel the stink of beast and man. That was different on well-worn trails where the land was already rugged if not tortured. The plains were vast and absorbed the passage. It was different here and as he rode to the front of the line Buchanan cast a look at the rocks where the mountain cat had disappeared. How much different would their world be for the next few days, perhaps weeks, with prey that had been frightened away by the herd.

Like the skies blackened by the railroads, like the creeks dammed for irrigation, human expansion was not without a price. He wondered if he was starting something that would lead to settlements, logging on the Mohave River, and more.

First you have to get to Hidalgo, he reminded himself.

Every man was feeling the effects of the challenge ahead, their movements sharp and careful as they took evenly spaced positions along the herd and started the cattle forward. It was not easy keeping the animals in a line on the plain, since they were not being crowded on the sides by other cattle moving in the same direction. All it took was for one steer to turn slightly, cause a kink in the line, and have to be straightened. But the half mile of plateau was instructional to men who were going to have to deal with those same problems ahead.

Buchanan fell in behind Haywood as they reached the pass. The forward man went ahead, looking back to measure the speed of the herd as the cattle started along the pass. Haywood set his own pace accordingly, appearing to be the portrait of cooperation itself. Buchanan wanted to trust him. He wanted to like him as he did all men, even Chester Jacob with his heartfelt pestering. But he could not even trust Haywood, and that added a needless burden to every moment of the drive.

Buchanan looked back so often, he let the mustang handle the passage. The cliffside to their left amplified the sound of every step taken by horse or cattle; it sounded to Buchanan like steady rain on a tin roof. The ledge itself was wide enough for passage, and the incline was not so severe that any of the cattle had difficulty. The riders did what he had suggested, continually reining their horses gently toward the cattle. Even if the animals were not spooked by the drop, there were loose rocks and patches of scrub. One step too far to the right and horse and rider could go over.

The drive moved at a good pace. After a short climb, the pass leveled, with more and more of the ledge ahead coming into view. It went almost due south, something they had not been able to see from the plateau because of an intervening peak. A strong breeze trapped and running through the peaks created a small challenge whenever it blew dead grass in their direction. Hat brims pulled low and heads half turned kept most of the debris at bay.

Haywood glanced back. "When I reconnoitered, I went a little farther than where we are now," he said, then pointed. "The ledge slopes down; the haze has lifted and you can see it there, making a T with the horizon."

Buchanan looked where he was pointing. He saw the T, which was the ledge making a gentle incline that would bring them to the valley. When he had looked at that spot on the map, it had seemed farther away. It seemed a perfect place to camp. The play of the sun on the lush ground was inviting, but he did not see light sparkling on water, nor had the map shown any rivers or lakes there. He would take a more thorough look when they got closer.

The turn Haywood had mentioned before they started out was nearing, and it was sharper than the men had thought. Haywood had gone ahead. The tracker had stopped and dismounted when Buchanan caught up.

The ledge beyond the spot where they were standing turned from southeast to south at such an angle that the cattle would have to turn to follow that ledge two at a time and the horses could not move beside them. The problem for the chuck wagon was graver: It would not be able to make the turn and keep all four wheels on solid ground.

The rancher turned and yelled back. "Hold the herd! We got an elbow turn here!"

"Hard bend—stop!" Mitchell turned, passing the word down but continuing forward.

His message was repeated down the line, followed by a general bellowing and scuffling of hooves. The animals had to be stopped from back to front to keep from colliding.

While the herd eased to a halt, Buchanan dismounted and led his horse ahead. Haywood was looking up the cliff. It went some five or six hundred feet straight toward the blue canopy above.

"We can build a plank bridge from the chuck wagon," Haywood said. "That'd be the fastest action."

The rancher looked down at the sheer drop. "I'm not sure it'd hold up."

"Maybe not for the entire herd, but that's the risk."

Buchanan was neither frightened nor rattled. As a

boy and a man, he had faced the plains, the elements, the Rebels, and come through it. This was another challenge, that was all. He removed his buckskin glove with his teeth and placed a bare hand on the rock.

Haywood watched him curiously. The rancher seemed to be communing with the mountain, like a pilgrim adoring the statue of a saint.

"I like your first idea better, the one from back at camp," the rancher said, moving from the wall. "Mind holding my horse?"

Buchanan handed the reins to Haywood and headed purposefully back along the ledge. Mitchell had moved forward and was at the head of the herd. There was no room to go around him or the cattle.

Buchanan stopped a few feet in front of him. "Who's next in line, Reb?"

"Deems."

Buchanan cupped his hands around his mouth. "Joseph!"

"Yessir?"

"Who else can hear me?"

Prescott and López answered in turn. López was the farthest in clear earshot.

"Miguel! Call back to Griz! I want the picks passed forward from the wagon! We gotta chop some rock up here! Each man will have to leave his horses and walk 'em to the next man."

"*Sí*, I understand!" López shouted.

Buchanan returned to the bend in the ledge. He was surprised to see the usually expressionless Haywood wearing a half smile.

"Something tickling you?" Buchanan asked.

"This whole thing," Haywood confessed. "Reminds

me of the war. Men would dress as women to draw Rebels over or use rabbit blood to look wounded. It was like a stage comedy, but with death."

"We don't have time for campfire stories," Buchanan said. "If you'll give it, I'm gonna need your help to widen the turn."

"I'll help," he said. "There's a cluster of shrubs on the other side. I'll tie the horses there. It's far enough so flying chips won't hit them."

Buchanan nodded once, deeply—it was both an "Okay" and "Thanks." Then he went back to the herd to wait for the tools. Haywood returned to the bend with the canteens and lay them well along on the western side, where they would not be pushed over or dented by falling rock. Buchanan had also realized that it was not only a matter of paying attention to what was before them but also what was behind them. In the heat of activity, one of them could easily step too far back and plunge to his death.

Mitchell had dismounted and one by one the two picks were passed along the side of his horse. The former Confederate bundled them in one arm.

"Stay where you are," Buchanan said. "I'll come get them. Also . . . Miguel?"

"¿Si?"

"Have Griz pass the torches up as well, and the matches. Each man keeps one torch, one match, passes the rest. No way we are gonna clear this ledge by dark."

"I'll tell him!"

A moment later the line heard Griswold complaining, but his words, if not the tone, were swallowed up by distance.

Mitchell faced Buchanan although his eyes were on

the tracker. "You watch yourself, boss. We can't afford to lose you."

"I'll try not to swing too wide," the rancher said.

"I don't just mean stepping off: There'll be falling rocks. I was on a Union chain gang. There'll be sparks that sting."

"I'll watch out," Buchanan said as he walked off with the picks.

Buchanan and Haywood took up positions on opposite sides of the bend, the tracker with his back facing south. The sun was slightly to the west, lighting the rock wall and suggesting nooks where they could begin. To minimize flying shards, they agreed to chop but then pry as much as possible, pulling away the rocks in chunks.

The first swings caused a ripple among the animals, rolling from front to back as the sound rang out. The sparks were lively, as Mitchell had warned. They shot out with every blow, and the clanging itself penetrated deep inside each man's skull. The initial uneven tempo gave way to a rhythm that broke only when each man determined how hard he had to swing and whether overhand or sidearm. Chunks fell without needing to be pried, although the men realized they had to keep careful watch of the rock above them. If any sizable piece came loose its falling could knock either man to his death.

Except for the ringing of metal on stone, and the occasional sounds of cattle and crumbling rock, the air was silent. There had been birds before, hawks below and eagles above; they were gone know, chased by the strange movement and sound from the mountainside. Every man was aware of the arc of the sun across the peaks, none more so than Buchanan and Haywood. Every few minutes the shifting shadows revealed fresh angles of attack, fractures or outcrops where the picks could tear down more of the wall. The work was slowed only when the men needed to drink or to push rocks over the side. Some stones hit the ledge and tumbled off; others had to be moved lest they pile up and block the herd.

Mitchell relieved Buchanan twice during the afternoon, both times so that the rancher could walk up and down the line to see how the hands were doing, and also to collect torches for himself and Haywood.

It was during the second trip, when he had nearly reached the halfway point of the line, when Mitchell suddenly shouted, "*Get back!*"

Buchanan turned and started in that direction, saw that Mitchell's iron had apparently struck an ancient fissure, causing a rock nearly half his size to slide onto rocks below it; the shelf gave way, one rock after the other, finally causing the big chunk to drop.

Mitchell and then Haywood had dropped their picks and lunged in opposite directions as the massive piece fell and then tumbled down the elbow of the ridge. Mitchell had reached the wall and pressed against it; Haywood had flung himself to the ground and landed facedown in the opposite direction.

The rock kicked up a cloud of dirt as it went over, leaving a trail of crushing, crashing sounds as it fell. When it was silent, Mitchell pushed off the cliff and waved his hand so he could see. Haywood rose and turned.

The men on the line could see none of this because of the dust.

"Everyone all right?" Buchanan shouted.

"Yeah," Mitchell said. "Not sure about the ledge, though. Rock might've taken part of it down or loosened it some"

"Stay where you are," Haywood told him. "I'll check."

While the air was still thick with dust, Haywood got on his hands and knees and crawled along the edge. He felt his way, pressing down with his palms and then leaning into them.

The men were as silent as a graveyard as they waited. Buchanan knew, as they all did, that if that ridge was gone, there was nowhere and no way to move the herd.

"Doesn't seem like there's any damage," Haywood said after what seemed like a very long time. He rose to his knees. "Lost some of the overhang, but that was too weak to—"

There was a sharp cracking sound as a smaller piece, higher up, became dislodged and fell. Once again Mitchell pushed himself back against the cliff while Haywood pivoted on one knee and rolled away several turns. The stone went straight down like a plumb line, less than a foot behind the tracker, gouging the cliff before going over and straight into the field far below.

Once again Haywood went forward to inspect the damage.

"Still solid, but it cut a rut the wagon will have to go over slowly."

Mitchell was looking up the cliff. "Looks like everything that means to fall fell," he reported.

Buchanan did not realize he had been holding his breath until he exhaled. A moment later, with the ledge still obscured, they heard the *chunk, chunk, chunk* of the picks resuming their anvil beat. Taking a moment to reflect on their good fortune, the rancher continued down the line.

The hands were quiet both times Buchanan came through. It was not their usual exhaustion during a drive but something else. The second time he came to the end of the line, he asked Fremont what he thought it was.

"I can only say what's on my mind, but it's a fair guess the others are thinkin', it too," he said. "Part of it is the things we didn't know but should've. We knew there'd be water, grass. But we've all looked out at Old Greyback. How did we not think about low clouds slowing us to a crawl?"

"The lower elevations of Old Greyback are blocked, Will—"

"We've never seen mountain mist? Ever? We were just so eager, like kids at Christmas. We're prepared for wolves on the flatlands. The mountain lion shouldn't've bushwhacked us like that. Those rocks just now—it's a *mountain* we're choppin' at, fer God's sake. An' lookin' back, why *wouldn't* the Double-D try to bury us once and for all out in God's country?"

"All true, Will—every word—and I was stupid not to talk to Patsy more about some of that. She's been through this territory."

"That's probably why she didn't want us to go."

"Did she say something to you?"

"Not with words but with her looks. She hasn't been joyful since you first came up with this plan. I ain't blamin' you, boss. I wanted this, to trailblaze. Always something I hoped to do to see what I was made of. It's just . . . we ain't as practical as women, most of the time."

The sound of the picks got louder as the dust settled

and the efforts seemed to grow. The sinking sun was on everyone's mind.

"We're not gettin' out of here by sundown," Fremont said.

"No. We either move by torchlight or we stay put."

"Staying here is a bad idea," Fremont cautioned. "Settling in, we can't watch all the cattle, which means if they get restless, we lose some number of 'em over the side."

"I agree. So we move out regardless. But we also don't want to light the torches too early. We ain't got the wherewithal to make extras."

Fremont agreed, and Buchanan resolved to get back and at least get the pass widened before the sun went down and the steers—and riders—lost their bearings.

The excavation was much larger than when Buchanan had left, not all of it due to the collapse. Whatever Haywood's leanings, he was putting his big arms and shoulders into the task. He hollowed out enough so that he could come over and assist Buchanan when the rancher returned. They struck the cliff on alternate strokes, tearing off rocks that range, from the size of a man's first to that of a cow's skull. Except for sidestepping each one and then bending to push it over the side, the men did not stop until the ledge was wide enough to move the chuck wagon through. Internal erosion from ages of spring thaw assisted them in taking down the rock. Such would never have occurred to Buchanan however much thinking and planning and talking-to he had done.

The work of widening the ledge was completed shortly before the men lost light where they were.

Haywood gathered up the empty canteens, brought

the horses over, and paused to kick over the last of the rubble.

"Thank you," Buchanan said.

Haywood heard but did not react. He cocked his head to the east as he handed Buchanan the pick. "I'll go ahead, make sure there are no other traps." He lit his torch with the match he had been given. "If there's a problem, I should have enough room to come back and let you know. If not, I'll just wave 'er back and forth and you'll have to come down."

Haywood climbed into the saddle—slower than usual, worn-out from the pickaxing—and was gone without further conversation. Buchanan understood that this had to be tough for him; it had to remind him of the days when he was in bondage. The rancher still did not like the man, still did not entirely trust him, yet was reminded again how they might have been stuck now three times without him.

CHAPTER FOURTEEN

JOE DEEMS EXPERIENCED an unexpected sense of euphoria as the drive proceeded along the ledge. With Mitchell and Buchanan ahead of him, and Haywood in the distance; with the night breeze carrying distant, aromatic scents and silence from all but the occasional night bird below—with the stars blocked by the cliff to the north and a peak to the south—he had the sense of being an ancient pilgrim on a journey to some sacred place. The destination was not necessarily a physical spot. His soul seemed to be on a journey as well. In any event, out here he felt as connected to God as ever in his spiritual life. He felt that if he were to die here, he would be that much closer to heaven. Strengthening that view was the mystical sight ahead and behind: a long line of indistinct shapes, slow-moving and shifting under spots of flickering torchlight. They could be pilgrims on a journey or souls bound for heaven or hell. Deems felt closer than ever to the Bible in his saddlebag as a sense of the vastness outside of creation came near to overcoming him.

None of the other cowboys had anything on his mind but surviving the passage and bedding down. Whether they were filled with faith or hope, no man could afford to let his attention lapse. Every step brought with it a sound of small stones crunching, sliding, or being kicked forward. Those had a sameness after a time. What they listened for was a crack like the one they had heard when the wall came down. It was less likely to be the cliff than the ground below them, unaccustomed to the weight of cattle and weakened after each one had gone past.

Griswold was the most anxious of them all, riding tail. He had lashed his torch to the side bar of the seat so it wouldn't burn the canvas. His arm was good enough so that he did not need the sling, and it kept getting burned by grass ashes that fell from the fire. He was as vocal as ever about his discontent.

"They got me between four horses, an' none of 'em wants to be on a cliff in the dark," the cookie muttered. "An' I'm far back enough so I'm the only one who *can't* hear orders from up front. I can imagine the folks, though. 'Old Griz can handle things on his own, don't worry.' I'm tired o' bein' so reliable. It ages a man. Plus these pebbles are makin' everything ring like the dang earthquake did. I feel like I'm inside a spittoon."

There was buzzing conversation making its way along the line.

"What is it, Miguel?" Griswold demanded.

"Hush!"

"Hush? I need to know!"

"If you stay quiet, then perhaps *I* can hear!"

Griswold turned down the muttering to mumbling just long enough for Miguel to inform him that the ledge was beginning a downward slope.

"It's not bad, they tell me."

"'Not bad' to a horse ain't the same as 'not bad' to a wagon." Holding the reins in his right hand, Griswold rested his healed hand on the brake. "'Not bad' could be if I went over the ledge but left the food behind."

Griswold saw something he had not noticed before: the torches were showing less and less of the cliff in their light.

"Looks to me like the torches are gettin' closer!"

"They are," López informed him. "I'm getting instructions."

"From a guardian angel, I hope."

The herd was more stretched out now and it was taking longer than before to relay information from Buchanan. When López finally had it all, he turned back to Griswold.

"They are not sure the wagon will fit!"

"Well, there's a stick in the wheel! What am I s'posed to do, put it on my *back*?"

"When you get closer to where the point is now, we may have to carry what we can and push it over the side! Otherwise we cannot get the back horses through!"

"Of all the balled-up plannin'! Tell them to chop away more of the mountain! Knock the whole thing down so it doesn't bother innocent travelers ever again."

"I don't think they want to hold up the cattle any longer. And it's AB property, amigo. I am sure the boss is less happy than you."

The cookie fell silent as the drive picked its way

through the blackness. When the chuck wagon neared the spot where Haywood had been, Griswold removed his torch from the post, raised it, and moved it slowly back and forth.

"Miguel? You tell Buchanan I can *make* this!"

"They just told me he is waiting for the cattle to pass: Stay where you are until he can see for himself. And, Griz?"

"Yeah?"

"Bundle yourself in something. It's going to get cold, they say!"

"Tell 'em I survived more'n half a century before any o' them came along," he said.

It was another hour before most of the herd was on flat ground and Buchanan was able to come back. He walked up, Fremont at his side. Both men were carrying torches replenished by underbrush from below. Buchanan was also holding a lasso. López was gone leaving only the three men and four horses.

"We been talking and there may be a solution," Buchanan said. He walked to the endangered side of the wagon and began knotting his rope to the seat bar. "We're gonna tie the torches to the bar on the outside. That'll let you watch the outside edge of the ridge."

"Watch it for what?"

"Will and I are gonna be in the wagon, adding weight to it cliffside. We figure as long as the wheels don't go completely off the side, and as long as the horses are creating pull on both sides, it'll stay planted on the ledge."

Griswold looked at the men as they went about their work.

"Part o' me wants to say that's a good idea," the cookie said, "but the grown-up part says it's nuts."

"Yeah, we're both of the same mind," Buchanan agreed. "If you'd rather get out and lead the horses . . ."

"Hell, no! This plan o' yours has got my full attention. If it works, we're all gonna have a story to tell!"

"You'll lie anyway, say it took place in the clouds during a thunderstorm," Fremont said as he made sure his torch was secure.

"God's always listenin' for ideas," Griswold rebuked him. "I'd stop there if I was you."

Neither Fremont nor Buchanan was superstitious, but the cookie had a point. After everything that had happened, the trail boss was glad that Griswold had not mentioned an avalanche, earthquake, or mountain lion.

The two men went around back and retied the horses so that they were bunched together on the cliffside. It was a question not only of added weight there but of the animals not seeing or hearing the fall that was possible to the south. When they were secure, Fremont and then Buchanan stepped up under the canvas. They cleared a spot on the cliffside of the wagon where they could plant their feet. Then they turned so their backs were against that side, their fingers wrapped around the tops of the wooden ribs.

"I hope we know what we're doin'," Fremont said.

"I'm so tired, I'm not sure any o' this is happenin'," Griswold said.

"It's happening," Buchanan assured him. "You ready?"

"Scootin' over to my right. No point in all this rigamarole if I can't see."

Buchanan felt just that shift in the distribution of the weight. He was glad it was dark inside. He did not want Fremont to see how uncertain he was. No man on a cattle drive had the time or temperament to be truly scared. But the rancher had time to think, and that was the hatching place of fear.

Griswold started the team forward, the hooves scraping on dry earth, the insides of the wagon rattling from everything that was hung or had been hurriedly stacked to make room for the men.

Buchanan leaned closer to Fremont. "You feel us start to lose our grip on the ledge, you get out."

"In a cow's arse I will." He chuckled nervously. "I owe you a small apology."

"Oh?"

"This is not something we could have planned for sittin' around the ranch house table with maps." The wagon hopped slightly as it hit a dip made by the passage of the herd in softer dirt. "That journal o' yours—we live to get it back, future generations will be grateful."

"We'll live," Buchanan said. "I won't pretend to know the mind of God, but He did not set our feet on this path with no purpose."

"Now he's gone devout," Griswold said. "The end is definitely comin'."

The chuck wagon continued to rattle but the horses in front and behind created stability. They never swerved and turned only when Griswold followed the gentle curve of the stone face. He always let the men in back know when something unexpected was coming so they were not alarmed.

It was after taking one such curve that the wagon sloped slightly to the front right, off-center; Griswold whoa'd and reined the team to a hard stop even as the earth and stone beneath the front right wheel gave way.

"Lost some lip on the ledge!" Griswold said. "Just fell away!"

Fremont swore and both he and Buchanan pressed themselves harder against the ribs of the wagon.

"Griz, get off and cut the team free!" Buchanan yelled.

The cookie was unnaturally silent.

"Griz?" Buchanan yelled.

"You hold your horses an' I'll hold mine. I'm leanin' to see! Can't very well slide to that side, can I?"

The driver had a point. The only sounds were the neighing of the horse on that side and the trickle of pebbles bouncing down the lower cliff.

"Front wheel is clear off!" Griswold said. "I'd say about four inches straight'll put it back on solid ground."

"If not?"

"It will," he assured the passengers. "Only question is whether the back ledge gives and both wheels go over. It hasn't while we been stopped on it, so it likely won't."

"You sound confident!" Fremont said.

"What d'ya want me to do, sob like a baby? Hold on—I'm gonna move myself full to the left to add weight. Then I'll try to get us back on!"

The wagon shuddered slightly as Griswold shifted toward the cliff; the wagon dipped further as several clods of earth fell away.

"Come on, wagon . . . we been through too many years for ya to give up on me now!"

The wagon was unsympathetic to Griswold's plea. It settled down where it was. Griswold peered at the edge of the trail in the flickering light.

"No roots up here holdin' this together," he said. "Don't ferget to put that in your journal."

Buchanan did not reply; his mouth was pressed tightly shut, every muscle tensed toward the left side of the wagon. He wished he could hoist the ribs onto his shoulders and raise them, as Atlas did the vault of the heavens.

"Here I go!"

The men heard Griswold say *"Gyah!"* to the horses and they made a futile attempt to move forward. When the wheel bumped against the ledge, they stopped. Griswold had a horsewhip in a holder near the brake. He retrieved it.

"Hold on back there! I gotta give the boys some coaxin'!"

Griswold simultaneously whipped the reins hard and cracked the whip in the air between the pintos. The snap got their attention and they tried to go forward a second time. The men inside felt a bump as, once again, the wheel hit the ledge but did not clear it. It started to settle back but Griswold used the whip again, this time striking the animal on the right. It nickered and pulled forward, this time succeeding in getting solid ground beneath the wheel. The rear wheel showed signs of wanting to eat through the ledge, but Griswold did not allow the weight of the cart to come to rest on it. He whipped the animal on the left, then on the right again, keeping them interested in moving ahead. In the rear, the two horses moved forward in their cliff-hugging line, adding an extra push forward.

The first wheel had enough traction and forward momentum now so that the three grounded corners immediately pulled the fourth along when it briefly left solid ground. It rolled easily back onto the ledge of the downward-sloping trail.

After a few heart-stopping moments, all four wheels were on solid ground and following the horses down.

"*Wahoo!* I actually have to put on the brakes now!" Griswold cheered.

The chuck wagon slowed but did not stop as the driver moved back to the center of the seat and kept careful watch on the ledge. Inside, Buchanan and Fremont moved from the ribs. They steadied themselves on the two water barrels—which were a godsend, adding needed weight to the wagon bed. They stepped on the one bare spot in the wagon, where Griswold usually slept. Surrounding them left and right were the low cabinets full of vegetables for stew and tins of condiments and coffee, sacks of flour, medical supplies, and other necessities, including a bundle of dry kindling in the event of rain, as well as the boards that usually hung on the ribs, where the cookie kept his utensils, pans, and pots.

No one other than Griswold spoke. Buchanan and Fremont were nearly too worn-out to remain upright, let alone have a conversation.

There was applause from López, who was waiting for Griswold. The Mexican was the only man who stayed behind to meet him. The others were in the mouth of the valley, torches stuck in the ground as they settled the herd in for the night.

Buchanan climbed from the back of the wagon, followed by Fremont. They looked out at the herd. In the limited firelight they saw a stream and rich grasses, and the cattle mooed contentedly at both.

"Soon as they're set, let's douse the fires," Buchanan said. "If St. Jacques is out there, we don't need to give him any help spotting us."

Just then the rancher noticed Haywood standing by the herd. He wanted to thank the man again for his help on the ledge, although he knew that Haywood had most likely done it for himself—whatever his personal reasons were. If the man wanted to be alone, Buchanan would give him that. He was too hungry and too tired to think about it any deeper than that.

Griswold had settled the chuck wagon in an arbor of pine and dogwood, which was where the horses had been corralled. Buchanan could see the glow of a lantern through the canvas, heard him rattling around inside. The rancher walked over, climbed onto the seat, and looked in. Griswold's back was to him as he poked through his gear.

"That passage made a real mess o' things," he muttered. "Reb needs liniment for sore arms and it'll have to be beans for supper; that's all I got time for. Mebbe some carrots."

"I think the men will be happy for anything. I know *I* am. I'm also proud of what you did up there, Griz."

"Aw, it's just like the scales I love watchin' at the apothecary. Gotta balance. Ya get unlucky, then lucky. Long as the first one don't kill ya, it works out."

"You need good people, and I've got 'em. You were a hero up there."

Griswold turned then. Tears had cut clean tracks in his dirty cheeks.

"Griz? What is it?"

"No need to worry yourself, Sachem—I'll be fine—but I was mighty afeared up there. Mighty. My wife, Abi, she used to say it was cussedness, not courage, that made me brave. I think she was right. My heart was beatin' so hard up there, I thought it'd hop out my mouth and dance a jig."

"We were *all* frightened."

"Yeah, well, y'all been to war, you and Fremont. You learned how to face it like men. I just whoop and holler like a boy with a slingshot facin' a bear."

"You're the one who got us back safe. *You* did that, not me and not Will."

"I didn't know what I was *doin'*! When I whipped them horses . . . for all I know, they mighta run off the cliff. I got lucky. I got the good turn on the scales."

"I don't see it that way, and, besides, the fact that we're here to talk about this is all thanks to you. I suggest you listen to me, to the men, not to Abi when we pat your shoulder and praise your bones to the stars."

Griswold sniffled back his upset. "Thank ya, Sachem. Thank ya."

"You earned it. Now—get some beans warming, unless you want a rebellion out there."

"Them? They're almost too tired to walk, let alone fight."

"You ever know a fight they wasn't too tired for?"

The cookie smiled and shook his head, then went back to gathering his utensils and muttering about how there was no rest for him, ever, anywhere.

Buchanan went out, grateful to be there, with these men. Now he had to rally his own energies so he could inform the arm-weary Mitchell—whose turn it was to take first watch—that he would swap nights.

CHAPTER FIFTEEN

"WAY I FIGURE it, the Double-D riders will be close enough to smell you sometime late tomorrow."

Buchanan was standing with one foot on a boulder, the rest of him leaning across it, his rifle over the same knee. He did not chew tobacco as a rule, but he did so now to help himself not just stay awake but alert. He did not have a good mental picture of his surroundings, having seen them only from afar, and after that by short-lived torchlight. He could hear the stream but had no good idea how wide it was. And he stood back from the fire he had lit with the last of the torches. He did not think St. Jacques would be out there—not yet. But not finding Haywood or their tracks, he might have sent riders ahead in several directions, looking to pick up the trail. If so, he did not want to be a target.

Not that a gunshot would necessarily be directed at a man. Stampeding the cattle in the dark could be even more deadly, which was why Buchanan had the men bed down on a small rise to the west. Like floodwaters, raging steer chose the path that was easiest.

The rancher was surprised when, shortly after the men had settled in, with all but a few of them asleep and snoring, George Haywood walked up to him. The tracker had stayed to himself after the drive had reached the valley, eating his own jerky and making his own small campfire with a flint from his saddlebag. He had worked harder than any man during the mountain crossing; if he was tired, his solidly planted footsteps and erect posture showed none of it.

The man's appearance here was unexpected. What he had to say was not.

"My thinking took a similar path," Buchanan said. "Figured he might even send an advance party."

Haywood shook his head. "Man's eager but not hasty. Whatever force St. Jacques has, he'll want 'em together. He'll figure you dropped a man or two behind to try and skirmish. Pick his riders off, retreat, repeat."

"I thought about doing that myself. But I can't spare the men and I wouldn't risk 'em like that."

"His man Flynn is a good tracker. He'll pick us up and then they'll make tracks. I was actually going to suggest waiting and taking down some of the ledge, but I don't think he'll come that way."

"No, Dawson's got maps, too. Without cattle, St. Jacques'll come through the woods we couldn't cross. Lets him out about a mile north of here, close enough to trail us and wait for us to be jammed in the bottleneck at the end of the valley."

"What's out there?"

"The desert and sea of the Inland Empire." Buchanan's bent leg was stiffening and he stood to stretch it. "Anyway, I just want to say again how much I deeply appreciate what you've done for us."

"I did it for me," Haywood said.

"You've made that blue sky clear every time I brought up my gratitude. That's fine. You being stubborn won't change me any."

Haywood stood still in the darkness.

"You come over to tell me you're considering rejoining him?" Buchanan asked.

"If I don't go back . . . well, it's like I said before. I'm throwing my life away. At least, the life I want."

"What's that?"

"My own spread. Dawson has said he'll set me up long as I sell to him."

"I did that when I started. Ain't a bad way to go about it."

"Except that I don't like serving anyone but me. But running from him because I crossed his purpose—that's a lifetime sentence. If and when you get back, you'll find that out."

"Maybe, but Dawson ain't the same as St. Jacques. Oh, he wants what he wants. But what he wants most is not just to be the biggest cattleman in the Southwest but to be the only one. I can help give him that by getting out of his way."

"Oranges?"

"And horses. Maybe a man has to change things when his life is at a halfway point."

"Then . . . what would've been the point of all this?"

"You gotta prove you can do something before deciding not to. A part of me still wants to open the market in Mexico. But maybe my wife's right. That's a man just being a man. What's been growing more is the need to show your bosses they can't push smaller spreads around. More power he gets, the more he'll need to be reminded of having lost one." Buchanan put his leg back where it had been and leaned on it. He was tired down to the marrow.

Haywood came nearer. "This has been new for me, too. What was 'right' was always what put more miles between who I was—*what* I was—and where I want to be. I was born a slave. Got my name from the first two tasks set before me: feeding horses and chopping wood. Took my first name from the first president, since by escape or some other means I intended to be the first free man on the plantation. I had no right to grow or discover anything, except a faster way to a whipping. Not even love. Just catching the eyes of a woman was a moment of hope and humanity, but it was gone like one of those yellow butterflies I watched in the field. I envied them, Mr. Buchanan. By my soul I did. Now I'm free and for the first time in my life I am facing an honest-to-God *choice*."

"I'm sorry to be the cause of that. Mr. Haywood. I truly am."

"You know something else? You're the first man I've met who ever called me *Mister* Haywood. That doesn't make this easy."

"'This' meaning your leaving, or 'this' meaning . . . what, a Judas kiss?"

Haywood was silent again but his eyes gleamed in the campfire. "I mean I'm going to ask again, sir. You got a lot to lose out here—almost did, without even making a Confederate cent. I'm leaving. Any chance I can carry word to St. Jacques that you'll at least talk with him?"

Buchanan was quiet. "Tell ya my problem, friend. My tired brain's for doing what you say, but my rancher's heart is against it. I'll have to go with the heart on that one."

"That's your final answer? If I wait a spell—"

"I gotta be able to look at my men and at my own refection in Big Salt Creek. That's my answer."

"I understand."

"But thanks for asking."

"Don't move, Haywood!"

The barked command came from behind Buchanan and he spun, rifle in hand. The voice had been low, twisted, angry to the point where he had not recognized it as Will Fremont's.

"That means you, too, boss," the newcomer said, stepping into the firelight. Will Fremont ignored Buchanan and held his Spencer rifle on Haywood.

The rancher was surprised to see him, though not to have been blindsided by him. The unease of the horses was one of the things the night watch counted on, and they knew Fremont. He made a point of not leveling his gun at the trail boss. The men would have backed Fremont on this. It would have ended the drive here and now. But he also had no intention of accepting this insubordination.

"Lower the rifle, Will," Buchanan said.

"Uh-uh."

"You don't understand—"

"I heard enough of what was said to know all I need to know. This valley is good for the ears. We *all* heard. I woke everyone in case I needed 'em."

Buchanan turned toward the others, who were clustering like moths around a campfire. "Okay, you heard!" he said, loud enough for his voice to carry across the camp. "What do you intend to do?"

"Boss, I know this man's done some good turns, but

they don't make up for the bad. Even though I didn't like it, I was content to let him be. But not to let him leave."

"He can do more for us with the Double-D men than here," Buchanan said. "He could have slunk away. He didn't have to tell me he was thinking of going."

"He shouldn't be thinking at all, except what a bunch of snake bellies he works for. I don't care what he says about reforming. He gives them one more gun and he knows how we work and where we're goin'. How do you know that wasn't what he was sent for in the first place?"

"It wasn't. I believe that."

"Dammit, boss, he had his guns! Reb checked the chuck box just now, found 'em in his bedroll. I wondered why he didn't use it since he's been here. He's been plannin' his leave-takin' from the moment you took him."

"I knew about the guns," Buchanan said.

The trail boss looked as though he had walked into a tree. "You . . . *knew*?"

"Mr. Haywood told me. I didn't like it at first, an armed Dawson man in our camp. But he helped us *after* that. Far as I'm concerned, he's proved his good intentions."

"Then you're the only one. You and Deems. He'd forgive Herod, I think."

"Isn't that what we're taught?" Haywood asked.

"You don't get to speak, mister, unless it's to tell me your epitaph. You bloody snake, makin' ready to shoot us, then findin' a way to become friends with the boss so you can mosey away. I took a vote among the men and you ain't one of them."

"A vote on what?" Buchanan asked. "All they agreed on was to let him stay."

"Stay, yes. Go, no. Go with his guns, a double no."

"What do you propose?" Buchanan asked. It was the only play his whipped mind could think of.

"We tie him to his horse and take him with us. If we need a hostage, we got one."

"Having me as a prisoner won't change St. Jacques's plan one bit," Haywood said.

"For the love of God, don't *make* me shut you up," Fremont threatened, holding the rifle tighter.

"Dammit, Will, he's right," Buchanan said.

Lit by the fire, Fremont's expression was wounded, like he'd been shot. "Boss, don't you take his side over ours. Not after all these years."

"That isn't what I'm doing, Fremont—*all of you*!" he shouted, looking past the trail boss. "This fuse got lit almost a year ago when we tangled with Dawson's boys. You named me the men involved and I reported that to their boss. George Haywood was not one of them. He's had his guns since yesterday, could've left anytime. Could've shot men, horses, anytime. I tell you, if you do this now, we will all be wounded by it, every one of us!"

"He came to try and talk you outa the herd, no different than in the flatlands," Fremont said. "Failing that, he and his boss will do what they did then: take 'em at gunpoint."

"We will not let that happen!" Buchanan assured them. He turned to Haywood. "I do not believe that this man will either."

"Not if his hands are bound behind his back," Fremont said.

Haywood fixed his gaze on him. "That will not happen to me again. You will have to shoot me first."

"I can oblige you," Fremont said.

For the second time in too short a period, Buchanan's tired brain and his proud heart were in conflict. He knew he should not hammer a wedge between himself and his men. He also knew there was a matter of frontier justice before him. Once again he went with his heart.

Setting his rifle against the rock, Buchanan put himself between his trail boss and George Haywood. He faced Fremont, both faces leaping in the light. The ruddy animation was an illusion; both men could not be more set or somber.

"I will not allow this man, who is unarmed, to be shot."

"Then arm him or tie him up," Fremont said. "There ain't no third choice."

"Do what he says, Mr. Buchanan," Haywood said.

"I am running this drive, not you and not Fremont. Will? You gonna go through me to take him?"

Reb Mitchell said from the side, "He won't have to, boss." The man was holding his six-shooter. It was aimed at Haywood's side.

Buchanan remained where he was but turned to face Mitchell. The former Confederate did not lower his gun.

Just then, Buck Griswold strode into the group. "Ya cain't get heatstroke at night, but ya'll clear lost your minds! Fremont, holdin' a gun on the Sachem? Aimin' to shoot a man who helped me get up that first slog, then cut a path for me out of a *mountain*? And not with dynamite but with his own hands! Ain't we better than the Dawson gang, or are we the same kinda creature?"

"You can shoot me for talking but you won't tell me not to," Haywood said—proudly, almost defiantly, Buchanan thought. "St. Jacques will find you whether I help him or not. He is almost certainly riding with more men than before; my guess is up to twenty. That's the number of guns he hires when he needs them. I said many times I don't want bloodshed and I will try to prevent it; I swear to it again before Almighty God—which is a solemn oath, since, if your finger moves, I will meet Him. You can tie me up and waste a man watching me; that's up to you. Up to me? I'll give you this much to keep Mr. Buchanan from having to shoot his own man. I will ride out the way I rode in, without my guns. You can shoot me in the back if you want, Mr. Fremont." His eyes drifted to Mitchell. "Or you can plug me in the side that'll be facing you. But I *am* leaving."

Fremont and Mitchell stayed as they were. So did Buchanan. In the background, beyond the fire, no one moved until Griswold did.

"I'm tired," the cookie said, turning and throwing his arms up in disgust. "Don't wake me up with any shootin'."

As he walked away, López and then Prescott followed. Deems remained, regarding the others with a look of horror that had settled on his face when he arrived and had not changed.

He wanted to say, "This is against God's law!" but thought better of speaking. A shroud of reconsideration seemed to have settled on the proceedings, and he did not want to disturb it.

Buchanan had no such reservations. "I think we all need to sleep this off—you included, Mr. Haywood, if you're willing. I'd prefer you not ride out of here with the hate I see in your eyes."

"Well, I can make no guarantee it will be gone with the sun."

"I'll take that chance," Buchanan said. He regarded his men. "But I give you my word you will be unmolested, now or then."

The standoff continued a few heartbeats more, after which Fremont and then Mitchell lowered their weapons. Without a word, they turned toward where the other men were folding themselves back into their bedrolls. Deems departed as well, leaving Buchanan and Haywood alone.

"I promised my wife I would turn back if there was trouble," the rancher said. "I don't think I knew how much I did *not* mean that until now. Mr. Haywood, if St. Jacques were to ride out with twenty times twenty, I would not sell him my cattle. I may die trying, but I am taking them to Mexico."

"I did not expect to hear anything different." He turned to where his saddled horse was tied to a tree. "I will see you in the morning, Mr. Buchanan."

With a sigh—deeper, longer, less refreshing than usual—Buchanan returned to his rock, put his rifle across his knee, and looked out at a valley that was peaceful once more.

CHAPTER SIXTEEN

GRISWOLD TOOK THE opportunity to bathe in the river just after sunup. Breakfast would wait: He would be making griddle cakes and he liked for the pan to heat and the batter to harden a little before he poured it. The men were going to roll them up anyway and more than likely dunk them in their coffee.

"Eat, drink, and slobber—all at the same time" was how he described flapjack mornings.

Haywood was just finishing up at the river when Griswold arrived.

"Mornin'," the cookie said.

"Good morning."

"How'd ya sleep?"

"Quite well. Haven't had a warden in quite some time."

"Eh? Oh, y'mean the Sachem? Yeah, his wishes is pretty much law among the rest of us." Griswold pulled off his white cotton shirt and knelt by the river. He splashed his chest and arms and rubbed them down, shivering from the mountain-chilled water. "Everything that's happened so far—and just a few days out! I wouldn't've tried to get my wagon across that ledge for nobody else. Nobody."

Haywood thought of the men coming after them. They were hard workers, too—for pay. He was not sure which earned greater loyalty.

No one spoke to Haywood that morning, nor did he attempt to engage any of the hands. When the herd was ready to move south, Haywood rode up to Buchanan.

"Be seeing you sometime, I suspect," Haywood said.

"Where are you headed?"

"I'm going to have a ride north toward the forest," the tracker said. "I don't expect those fallen trees south of the Mohave stopped St. Jacques the way it did the drive, so I'll likely meet them there."

"I see."

Buchanan appreciated the information. Offered in answer to a question, it did not quite have the taint of treason.

Haywood threw off a loose salute—a show of respect for the men who were watching—before riding off. Buchanan did not expect camaraderie to return to the camp at once, although he hoped no permanent damage had been done.

The day passed without incident, and night found them in a spot almost identical to the one they had left. That evening, shortly before sundown, Buchanan had a conversation with Griswold about a plant growing by the water, after which Fremont and the rancher sat on a large, flat rock and reviewed his map. Both men tried hard to be as they were before the previous night's standoff.

"We made good miles today," Buchanan said, noting the distance on the map and transferring the information to his journal. He pointed with his pencil. "Tomorrow should bring us to the start of the desert. At least, we'll start into the north end that has heat and less grass. The next day we hit the main expanse and go from water to water."

Fremont looked at the three red X marks on the area marked "Desert."

"What do we do if there's no water where it's supposed to be?" He put a stubby index finger on the first X. "We can still turn back here. After that, next one's about twenty miles. If it's dry, we start losin' cows."

"I expect that'll happen whether we water 'em or not. López says it's baking heat out there. And we'll have to watch out for rattlers."

"They get up to six feet long," Fremont said.

"You learn that from Miss Sally?" Buchanan said. There was lingering tension between the men. He hoped that mentioning her would break it.

"Nah. That trinket-peddlin' Luiseño mission Indian in San Bernardino. You know the one, sells beads, feathers, skins, and the like."

Buchanan nodded.

"Mebbe I shoulda consulted Medicine Man Grant, that half-breed at the tavern who sees visions when you buy him whiskey. Coulda showed him the map, made sure it was right."

"Y'mean the one who used to be Medicine Man Jefferson till the Union won the war?"

"That's him. Yup."

The conversation suddenly ran out of leg.

"Then there's the other thing," Fremont said, starting it up again, his tone was cautious.

Buchanan continued to stare at the map. "What's on your mind, Fremont?"

"The Dawson men. We suspected they would be coming. Now we know it."

"You got any suggestions?"

"Seems to me that a valley where we have food and water, for the cattle and us, is as good a place as any to make a stand. We put men along the valley walls, our best shots—"

"They won't just ride in. They'll go up those same walls and signal the others."

"I figgered. Those are the ones we pick off."

"So we start the fight? I've been figuring, too, Fremont. They know how many hands we have. St. Jacques is a veteran of many a drive. He sees that we're down two, three men on the valley floor, he'll know where we had to position them to contain the herd. He's gonna set, what, three or four men after each? And what if the Dawson gang starts shooting steers instead? Twenty or so men, wouldn't take long for them to cut down the entire herd."

Fremont was silent as he considered the options. "You can't hope to outrace them to Hidalgo."

"No, and I could be wrong, but I also don't believe they will do anything until we cross the border."

"Track us, wait till the desert takes some of the fight from us?"

Buchanan nodded.

"You think Haywood went back to him?"

"I do. He doesn't really have a choice."

"You think they'll trust him?"

"I don't think they woulda trusted him in the first place if they hadn't had to. Man doesn't seem to make friends real easy. As long as he tells them the truth, they'll trust him again."

"He'll tell them where we are?"

"I expect so, but any cowboy worth his saddle could see where we went. I also expect them to try and head us off instead of following us up that muddy slope. Maps'll show it all leads to the Valley of the Ancient Lake."

There was another silence, and Buchanan suspected what was coming next. Fremont was not one to let troubles sit.

"I'm sorry that last night happened," he said.

"Most of us are, I suspect."

"Yeah, but I led the charge."

"Well, best to forget it."

"I can't. I'm sorry, but I'm also sore."

Buchanan knew that tone of voice. "What'd I do?"

"You didn't confide in me what you knew about the guns."

"I didn't want you or anyone else in an uproar over it. I kept watch on him. And he left without them, didn't he?"

"He did, but only because—"

"You called him on it. I know. I still don't think he would've turned them on us, do you?"

Fremont shook his head.

"I'll tell you this, though, Will. One thing about your position last night made me think hard about my own."

"What's that?"

"Your reasons for mistrusting the man were because of his affiliation, not his skin color. You were an abolitionist. You were concerned about a man as a man. That's why I couldn't just kick your concerns to the ground."

"I appreciate you telling me that." He gave a small, hollow laugh. "Funny thing. I took to Haywood easier than I first did to Reb. Gettin' over his loyalty to the Confederacy—that took a bellyful of forgivin'."

Buchanan clapped the man on the shoulder and rose.

"I can't ignore this either. I did not take you into my confidence. I'll talk to you first before something like that can happen again. Now, how about we get some sleep?"

Fremont nodded and, lighting his stub of a cigar, rose and went off to join the others. Buchanan sat on the rock and considered something else he had not thought about before leaving. On a drive you know, you also learn to expect your own reactions to things. Here, the challenges and his moods were different. That was something he would have to watch going forward.

Once again the drive had an easy passage, covering some eighteen miles of valley until they reached the first scrubby sands of the hot flatlands. It was not quite desert yet. But outside the verdant floor and walls of the valley, the sun would rise early and its heat would increase swiftly. The night they arrived, the air was already different. Although they remained nestled in the low walls of the valley, the dry, dusty air from the south mingled with the cool dampness of the hills. It changed from spot to spot, even within the camp. The change in the heat was noticeable even before the sun rose, which was when the men made their preparations for departure. The drive would go from sunup to sundown without stopping. They had left the river behind on the previous afternoon and had lingered long enough for the cattle to drink their fill. They were going to have to travel the entire day without reaching any of the mapped streams or small lakes. Beyond that, the Big Salt Creek itself would be of no help because it was not fresh water. It was his plan to go along the western side where there were foothills of a small range; on the east was a continuation of the long, wide desert they would already have spent days crossing.

There was a restless mood among the men as they set out, a sense that the day would be hard and the terrain unforgiving. They had washed their clothes of dust in the river in expectation of the sand and sweat that would take its place. These men had never driven across desert, and López was the only one who had spent any time here. He took point with Fremont. As much as Buchanan wanted to see what was ahead, he felt that his place was on tail, watching for any sight, sound, or smell of the Dawson men.

Griswold was uncommonly quiet as the drive was renewed, the sun low to their left, throwing long shadows beside them. The cookie was tired; he had filled every pot, jug, and barrel with water, working well after dark. The washing-water barrel was for the horses if they started to foam. The drive could afford to lose steer but not their mounts. But the cookie was also wary of what was ahead and what was behind.

"If there's banditos ahead, mebbe we can sic 'em on the Dawsons," he said as Buchanan rode past.

"Don't think too much," the rancher warned as he rode past on his way to the rear. "We'll handle things as they come."

"Dam breaks, locusts swarm, Apaches raid—always smart to have a plan, even if it's just runnin' in the opposite direction. 'Cept in this case we got no opposite direction from trouble."

There was no reasoning with Griswold when he was in this state. A time and place for talk was something Buchanan had learned, and not just about one man.

Managing men is something I couldn't have thought of back when I was fourteen, he thought. He vaguely recalled the skills he thought he would need or acquire as he made his way west. Learning that someone like Fremont could be talked to and that someone like Buck Griswold had to be listened to was a talent you grew into; you did not learn it like branding a steer or roping a horse.

The herd was kicking up clouds, which, along with heat rippling upward, limited visibility. Buchanan pulled his kerchief up nearly to his eyes, raised his collar to protect his neck, and drew his hat low to protect himself from the sand. The horses in back of the chuck wagon were somewhat protected, but the horses in front had their heads low and were taking their guidance from Griswold.

The sun was unforgiving as well. There were no peaks or clouds to shield them and the heat rising from the ground made him forget how chilly everyone was just two nights earlier. It would be worse, of course, when there was no brush on the ground—just sand that, as López had explained it, made you pray for the relief of a breeze, then curse it for stirring the heat. The only good thing about the rising heat was that it was something new to Buchanan's mustang. It boiled the fight right out of him.

The sun was on its way to noon when Fremont came cantering back.

"There's somethin' funny going on with the black

cattle," he yelled through his kerchief. "They're slowin' down more than the rest, an' wheezin'."

"Must be their dark coats reacting to heat," Buchanan shouted back. "We got, what, forty or so afflicted head?"

"About that."

"Cut 'em out so they don't hold the others back."

"That's my thinkin'. I'll put Prescott and Mitchell on that bunch. Looks like we'll have a rearward guard at that."

"Good point. I'll stay with them instead of the main herd. You hear shooting, you let the herd run. Don't try to stop 'em."

"They'll kick up too much of a storm to get near!" Fremont pointed out.

The trail boss turned back and Buchanan rode up to inform Griswold.

"We're carving out a small group of slower cattle so you just keep your eyes on the main herd and follow that. We'll be grouping the other behind you."

"Sachem, I'll foller whatever grandfather clock tail is tick-tockin' in front of me, an' I'll be lucky to see that, never mind which herd it's in."

"Griz, you're gonna have to mind me on this," Buchanan said sternly. "The steer'll be scattered left and right for a bit. Do not follow a tail that's black. Could take you hours longer."

"To do what? Get deeper into sand?"

The man had a point, and Buchanan let him be. Handling Griswold was a unique skill that the rancher believed he would never master.

The sounds of cattle complaining loudly began to roll toward Buchanan as Prescott and Mitchell moved the individual steers to the east and to the west. Falling back, Buchanan rode from one side to the other, herding the cattle together behind the chuck wagon. The mustang was also expressing displeasure now, with justification. It was nearly impossible for him to see or breathe through the mix of stirred sand and swirling dead grass, and several times Buchanan had to yank the horse one way or the other to avoid colliding with a steer. As soon as the secondary herd was organized, Buchanan instructed Prescott to ride tail on the main herd while Mitchell rode lead on the darker herd.

"We'll let 'em take their own pace for now," Buchanan said. "Keep in contact with Prescott. If he starts to gets too far ahead, we'll move ours along."

"What about behind us?" Mitchell asked.

"My ears are on the back door," Buchanan assured him.

"Listen, about that fracas over the tracker . . ."

"Like I told Fremont, we were all spent. Forget it. I have."

The former Confederate soldier accepted it, even if he did not believe it. Tipping his hat, he rode ahead. The gesture had a touch of melancholy. Unlike St. Jacques, Mitchell was not highborn, but he affected the same manners. With all that was wrong with the Confederate way of life, politeness was not one of them. Buchanan hoped that, at least, lived on.

The danger of the front herd pulling too far ahead vanished by late afternoon. The edge of the main desert was still a mile or two distant—invisible to the eye but marked on Buchanan's map—when a dust storm blew over them, stirred by the westerly winds.

Buchanan left the tail position and rode to López, who was leading the forward herd. Just that short ride was a challenge. The gale was hot and pushed stove-like temperatures before it. Grit clung to the sweat wrung from the exposed parts of his body from scalp to neck. In just moments, windblown sand had created uneven footing for the mustang while continuing to prickle its hide. The rancher did not make it easier on the horse, having to turn slightly into the wind in order to move forward. He could only hold the reins with his right hand, as he had to keep his hat on with the left.

"How long?" Buchanan shouted when he rode up.

López pulled down his kerchief as he looked away from the winds. "I don't know! I was here during summer when no one wanted to chase us in a desert. I never see wind like this!"

"Stop the herd! I won't have them tumble blind into rocks or gullies!"

"¡Sí!"

"I'll let the men know!"

López acknowledged and passed the word to Fremont, who was just a few yards away and had not been able to hear the exchange. Up front, the winds were shrieking louder as they tore through untrampled grass.

Buchanan rode along the line, first up one side and then down the other, telling the men to stop. He looked up from time to time, hoping to see sky, some sign that the tempest was winding down. There was nothing but sand above, from near his face to as far up as he could see when eddies of wind churned the particles some other way.

The rancher finally reached the second herd, knowing the chuck wagon by its sound, since he could barely see it. He heard the canvas flapping hard and was not sure it would hold. At sea, canvas tore free and became ghostly shapes in winds less than this.

"We're holding up!" he told Griswold. Buchanan had to lean into the front of the wagon to let him know, the man having retreated to inside.

"*Whoa!*" he shouted, pulling the reins.

The man had nothing else to add. That was how the rancher knew this was too much for men and beasts. Buchanan continued to his spot in back, letting Mitchell know and then dismounting. The rancher stood beside his horse, positioning himself beside the animal's head with his own back to the wind. Despite being shielded, the mustang was agitated by the force of the storm and the howling it made as it tore over land and cattle. The rider calmed his animal as best he could.

Buchanan could not be angry with López: the man had said he had come through once, in the summer. He knew that, from one season to the next, this part of the country experienced different kinds of weather off the Pacific Ocean or from over the mountains.

Mitchell had dismounted and walked his horse over to help shield the boss and his mustang.

"Way it just came up on us, like hell opened up to say 'Howdy!'" he said.

Mitchell's horse bucked then and he had to pull the bridle to steady it. "I think it's the beeves spookin' him. They sound like the spirits of the dead my grandmother used to tell about!"

The Southerner was referring to the cattle, which complained even louder after they were bunched together. The sand bit the backs of the steers in the middle. For the ones on the outside and for the horses there was nowhere to hide from wind that prickled their flesh like thousands of stinging ants.

"Boss, this is gonna give St. Jacques time to get closer. You want me to go back and look?"

Buchanan shook his head. "All hands'll be needed to start the herd up. Let him do the chasing!"

Mitchell nodded then stood still, like Buchanan, like the others, like everything in the sandy plain. The men were indistinguishable from cactus or rock, even to their boots being planted the same way with mounting sands. The rancher had the feeling of suddenly being timeless and ancient, as if he had been set in this spot for an eternity.

And then, barely perceptibly, the wind stopped pushing quite so hard. That was the first sign of the storm dying; it fell off quickly after that moment, by halves, and died in less than a minute. Dust and grass fell back to earth like a million shooting stars, first in an arc and then straight down like Rocky Mountain snows. All that remained was the roar in the ears of the men, echoing inside their heads; then that, too, fell away to nothing. It left every sound around them heightened, including birds that had been unable to find shelter and had been blown to ground; they dotted the sandy landscape like rot on fallen logs, many mute and struggling with broken wings, others chirping for lost kin.

The birds were not the only things that captured the attention of the riders.

"Sweet Jesus," Mitchell said when the air had cleared.

CHAPTER SEVENTEEN

WITH THE WINDS and the animals both still now, and the sun higher in the sky, what had hitherto been a tan-powdered haze was now daylight crisp. Ahead lay an expanse that would have given a man pause even if he had not just pushed through a mountainous sandstorm.

"The plagues of Egypt," Deems muttered, his voice carrying in the new silence.

There were just two colors before them: blue sky and golden sand. They met at a nearly straight line on the horizon. The distance was difficult to gauge; the only vegetation was cacti, and they could be stunted or faraway—no one was sure.

Buchanan rode to the point of the first herd. None of the men he passed spoke, and the cattle were now strangely silent. If they had the ability to wonder, Buchanan suspected they would consider what a strange thing it was to be stopped not on a grassy plain near a river or lake but on hot, barren sand.

This time Buchanan went to his trail boss and not to López. Fremont had drawn his kerchief down. The top half of his face was a powdery off-white; the bottom half was soaked with perspiration. His lips were slightly bloated and dry. His eyes were glazed and staring ahead.

"You all right, Will?" Buchanan asked.

"Yeah." The answer was flat as beaten copper. "Sittin' here thinkin' whether we go ahead or turn back to the river."

"Some cattle won't make it either way," Buchanan said. "We'll have trouble just turning them round in these conditions. And we could walk into trouble."

"Right. I'll start 'em out."

Fremont mustered his energy to get the horse to do the same. The animal protested as the trail boss faced the lead steer, which seemed equally disinclined to move.

"Let's go!" Fremont shouted at him.

The animal mooed back and settled into its previous state. Reluctantly, Fremont roped the steer's horns and backed his horse into the desert, drawing the reluctant beef with it.

Slowly, like a logjam clearing on a river, the cattle moved out one at a time. The only thing the elements of the drive had in common was that they were trudging ahead.

Sand dripped like water from the hooves of the cattle and horses. Light winds blew the covering of sand to the east as the drive moved south. Patches of scrub returned, but it became sparser as the cattle were pushed to the desert.

The steers in back were keeping up with the herd, but Buchanan knew that they could not maintain that pace. Spittle fell from open mouths and sometimes the animals would just stop and cry out before being coaxed to continue. There was no sign of water ahead; even with a cautious reading of his map, Buchanan felt they should soon encounter what was drawn as a pond or small lake. He only hoped it was accurately marked within a mile or so.

As morning became afternoon and more and more of the steers in the rear struggled to move, Buchanan told Mitchell he wanted to stop the back herd. The men got in front of the cattle and held them back by blocking the path forward. As the first steers stopped, so did those behind them. That done, Buchanan rode up to the chuck wagon.

"Stop here," he said.

Like a machine, Griswold braked and just stared ahead as Buchanan instructed Prescott, on the tail of the front herd, to keep going.

"We'll catch up when we can," the rancher added. "You don't see us, keep moving."

"Yes, sir," Prescott said, with more of a rasp than before.

"And water yourself up, even if it's just a spill. You'll be alone back here. You gotta be alert."

"You gonna drink, too?"

Buchanan took the canteen from his pommel and swallowed a mouthful.

"Thank you," Prescott said, before taking a drink from his own canteen.

The gratitude was in earnest; the man clearly needed water. But Buchanan's men prided themselves on being tough, and believed that adversity made them stronger and competition made them stronger still. This was not the time to prove that.

Buchanan returned to the chuck wagon, went around back, and waved Mitchell over. Then he summoned Griswold to the fold-down serving area under the chuck box. The cookie bent to look out.

"We're going to have to water the cattle," Buchanan said. "We'll use the pots and pans and walk the cattle by. There may be enough water to save many of them."

Griswold reacted with surprise. "They ain't hounds."

"They won't last to the next water. We have to try."

"We use up a barrel and don't find water, *we* don't last."

"Should we turn back, Griz? Would that be your plan?"

"I ain't sayin' that."

"Good. Then let's get this rolling."

With a lazy shrug, the tired cookie began collecting every receptacle he owned. Meanwhile, Buchanan moved the two extra horses around to the side and climbed in. He unlatched the top of one of the two water barrels and got the ladle that was hanging above. Griswold stacked the iron pots and pans on the floor.

"We're gonna put two pans side by side on the serving board," Buchanan told the men. He gave Griswold the ladle. "Griz, you set up and fill 'em. Mitchell, you bring one steer over and I'll get another."

Griswold arranged two pans and filled them while the other two men stepped into the broiling afternoon sun.

It was a sluggish and tiring task, as the cattle were not inclined to move until they saw the water. Finishing the contents, they were unwilling to move away. But the men created a rough pattern that got each of the forty cattle enough of a drink to keep them going.

Griswold closed up the chuck wagon, which was noticeably lighter as it got underway. He did not complain about it. For all his grievances, he respected Andy Buchanan and trusted his judgment on this.

Mitchell took point and moved the herd past the chuck wagon. After Buchanan had returned the spare mounts to their place, Griswold started his team up and Buchanan once again fell in at the rear. Water was on his mind, but also how many miles they had yet to cover to Hidalgo. Over the years, every drive had been a challenge. But each was met with skills he had learned—partly by making mistakes, partly by watching other herds and talking to veteran cowhands. His herds became increasingly larger, but he always took them along the same route, with few surprises. He made money and came back upright.

Maybe Dad knew something I didn't, he thought. Or else the sun was frying his brain. It was time to stop thinking.

The cattle were largely cooperative and the water seemed to have renewed them to a point. Buchanan did not see any dead cattle from the first herd, which he took to be a good sign.

Either that or we are off our course, he thought.

But walking was harder in the sand, the air was drying to the lungs, and the steers began stopping just as the sun was going down. Some simply refused to walk any farther; others dropped to their forelegs, struggled to get up, and then simply fell over. Buchanan lost four heads before twilight had begun to thicken. Griswold lingered to cut some meat from one of them.

Buchanan rode up to Mitchell and told him they would be pressing on.

"Figured on it," Mitchell replied. "I caught the herd's dust, and there's nothing between us and them.

We go due south, we should connect." He took a brass-encased porcelain-face compass from his pocket. "Should be enough moonlight to read this."

"Good job," Buchanan said as he dropped back to let Griswold know.

Mercifully, the temperatures did not just drop; they fell. Whereas the men had cooked under the sun, they felt a chill in the light breeze. At first, the cooling of Buchanan's hot sweat on every inch of him felt good. Then it raised goose bumps and he actually considered rolling around in the sand to swab it away. But then he'd have grit on every square inch of him. He hunkered into his shoulders and buttoned his jacket and shivered until just that shaking warmed him.

The cold white of the moon and stars seemed to reflect the nighttime chill. Falling stars were plentiful, slashing icicle trails across the heavens. Even when Buchanan looked ahead, he could see them out of the corners of his eyes. He wondered if they were angels, maybe guardian angels, traveling here and there, leaving their mark the way the drive did with their hooves and wheels.

Here, then gone, he thought, looking down and seeing the sands quickly fill in those tracks almost as soon as they had been made.

It was funny how darkness brought on those thoughts. What did they call it—philosophy? That seemed right.

Tracks are here and gone; people are the same. What stays? he wondered.

The ranch may or may not; groves may or may not. It's the children, he answered himself. He felt a sudden, unexpected, and unfamiliar longing to see the girls and to see them wed and having little ones of their own.

He wondered if Mitchell and Griswold were having

similar thoughts. Maybe Griswold about his former wife and Arizona home, Mitchell about the Confederacy and the vanished world he had grown up in.

Or, like sane men, are they half asleep in the saddle?

No. He suspected Mitchell was keeping sharp eyes out for any sign of a campfire. So far, they had seen no trace of one ahead.

Thinking such thoughts could make a man lose sleep, or maybe his ambition. It was an unfamiliar and unlikable path for the rancher. But, like a stubborn steer, it refused to move.

But there were distractions. Little ones. Like the flatlands beyond his spread, like so many plains Buchanan had crossed, the desert came alive at night. Unlike other places, where trees and skies were filled with hoots and howls, the sands themselves seemed to breathe. The ruckus made by the chuck wagon likely kept any larger animals at bay, if there were any. But large flying insects buzzed loudly by—flying beetles, he suspected—and wiry, runty reptiles made their way up the horse and onto the saddle. Buchanan swatted them away, but in the still night, with the cattle too parched and tired to moo, he could hear Mitchell address each and every one with a fatherly voice: "Who are you, sir or madam?" or "Did we wake you, little fellow?"

It was like dreaming while being awake. Even the presence of an animal skull and half-buried bones seemed not quite real. It was not like they had been gnawed clean like on the prairie. It looked like the skin and meat had just vanished like morning dew.

Night bled into morning, with a line of red forming to the left of the small drive. Dawn was heralded by a stronger stirring of the wind. Seeing it through half-closed eyes, Buchanan felt his heart speed up. He silently prayed that the first herd was in view, and close by. If not, then they might have turned in search of water or else his own herd had turned during the night. Either way, not seeing them would likely mean they'd have to use their last barrel of water for the cattle. That would leave only what little was left in the canteens for them.

Buchanan left his tail position to ride up beside Mitchell.

"Morning," the Southerner said.

The rancher inhaled slowly and deeply through his nose.

"I don't smell 'em yet," Mitchell said. "Air's dry and wind's movin' west, so I wasn't expecting it to carry. I don't much smell our own herd."

Mitchell was right.

"Funny how things change," the man went on. "At the ranch, I go out before sunup and there's a whole mess of odors, all of 'em familiar. Same at home, growing up. Flowers, cooking, perfumes. I've never been in a place that *don't* smell."

"Critters except for men are too smart to come out here. And if they do . . . I saw some bones a while back. Horse, looked like."

"I noticed that, too. Had the same thought," Buchanan said.

The sun finally broke the surface and threw yellow light across the desert. It crept ahead, dissolving stars above and exposing sand below. It was the opposite of what Buchanan had seen Old Greyback do at night as its long shadow inched across the flatlands. Riding side by side, both men peered through the clear air.

Blasphemy it might have been, but Buchanan felt what Moses himself must have experienced upon laying his tired eyes on the Promised Land.

Ahead, facing in their direction, sat Prescott on his horse, waving them on.

CHAPTER EIGHTEEN

"One day I want to build a statue to you right here," Mitchell told Prescott. "A beacon to every traveler."

Buchanan and the Confederate veteran had just ridden up, trailing the heat-shimmered vision of thinned cattle and a sand-slowed chuck wagon. The waiting cowboy seemed refreshed and even relaxed. His bearing and expression renewed Buchanan's heart.

"Before you pour the cement, Reb—Lewis, where's the herd?" Buchanan asked.

"Just southwest of here, boss," Prescott replied. "Either the map had it wrong or we was off to the east. Pretty far off, to tell the truth."

"Maps I checked were not so precise on that first water. Future ones will be."

"No matter. We found it. Or, rather, the cattle did. They kept wanting to go southwesterly and Fremont finally let 'em."

"That's why we didn't see a campfire," Mitchell said.

"Anyways, soon as we got to the water, Fremont told me to drink up, then he sent me back to lead you in."

"He's still there?"

"He figured you'd need rest, and on top of that it was stupid to try and travel during the heat of day, so we set up camp."

"Bless y'all," Mitchell said, echoing Buchanan's sentiments.

"Will also instructed me to watch for the Dawson boys. Ain't seen a sign of them anywhere."

"Not surprised," Buchanan said. "They probably figured to rest up and let the heat take some of the fight out of us and, more important, exhaust the cattle."

"Unhappily for us, they got someone in their party who can read those signs," Mitchell said with blossom-petal lightness that could almost have been a whisper.

Buchanan did not know whether the man was being informative or critical. He let it pass.

"Everything they do makes me even more determined to go on," Prescott said. "I had a bellyful of the Dawsons even before this." He eyed the cattle and the wobbling chuck wagon as he waited for the herd and Griswold to reach them. "You lost some head, I see, and Griz is riding light. You watered the herd?"

"Had to."

Prescott smiled and turned the horse. "Well, come on. There's plenty of water at Lake AB—at least, that's what we're calling the watering hole. Deems carved a sign on what was left of a wagon nearby."

"That must be where those horse bones came from," Mitchell said as he fell in behind Prescott. Buchanan returned to his tail position, keeping far enough from the chuck wagon so he did not cover it with sand.

"Was that Lewis who met ya?" Griswold asked.

"It was. Camp's at the water hole."

Griswold smiled crookedly. "I'm proud o' you, Sachem. Ya did it."

"Somehow, yeah." Buchanan looked at the older man's stubbled face with its deep-set eyes. "Let me ask you, Griz: Was I crazy to start this thing?"

"A little late to be inquirin'."

"Tell me anyway."

"Depends what ya do with this 'thing,' as you call it."

"I don't follow."

"What y'asked me the other night, about those mushrooms growin' on the riverbank—"

"That may have been wrong of me."

"No it weren't. You was bein' prepared. You were thinkin' to poison any water we find, to stop the Dawsons if necessary in their iron-shod tracks. An' I gathered 'em like y'asked. But I been thinkin' that if we make it to Hidalgo, it should be 'cause we did it on the square. Otherwise, it's worth dirt."

"I don't disagree, mostly. But if they're intent on stoppin' us—"

"If y'ain't learnt this yet, it's a good time to start. People who start bad things always stop themselves. Lookit the war. Rebs got hotheaded and started fightin' without the supplies or manpower. What about the Alamo? Who lost the war? Not Texas. The Redcoats got tossed off these shores—should never have tried to stomp on us. You worry about gettin' cattle to Mexico. The rest will take care of itself. Besides, we may need that same water on the way back. Pretty funny if y'end up killin' yourself."

Buchanan had never thought of Griswold as a man of peace, but then, the subject had never come up before in all the years they had been together. The rancher did not agree with the man on all the points he raised; he would have to reach the water, see the condition of the main herd, before deciding whether they could hold up against a large, armed force—

Or whether the earth will just swallow 'em up, like in some biblical passage.

The camp was a balm to Buchanan's tired body and conflicted soul. There was camaraderie among the men, if not outright good humor. And although there was still a distance to go in the desert, it would be easier at night, when the sun did not squeeze the water from man and animal.

As soon as Prescott came in, he filled his canteen and went out again to watch for St. Jacques. He would not fire a shot to warn them lest he tell the Dawson men where he was.

"The idea me an' López worked out—both of us havin' fought in wars and all—is simple," Fremont told Buchanan. "Prescott rides in with a warning, we threaten to kill steers and poison the water. The Dawsons won't have enough to get back."

"They'd take yours."

"We'd bury them first. Not enough anyway."

Buchanan chuckled. The men were sitting at the body of water some three horse lengths across and twice as wide. The herd was opposite them, on the southern side. Fremont was puzzled by his boss's reaction.

"What's so amusin'?"

"Griz tried to talk me *out* of a similar notion."

"Griz? Why?"

"Basically called it immoral and uncivilized."

Fremont snorted. He looked over at Griswold.

Deems had helped him unharness the horses and bring them to the pond.

"What d'you think of your sign?" he asked, pointing.

Buchanan looked over at the small board tied to a stake in the ground. "AB" was crudely carved in capital letters.

"It's not just mine. We all did this."

"Yeah. That woulda been too much to fit."

The men made themselves comfortable under tents made from their bedrolls. Buchanan made a few notes in his journal before doing the same. He remembered that he had forgotten to eat—but was asleep before he could do anything about it.

It was dark before Fremont woke him. Buchanan started awake.

"Boss, we're ready to move out."

It could not be very late, since the air was still warm. The rancher rose and brushed away the sand that had blown over him during the night.

"No sign of the Dawsons?" Buchanan asked.

"Nothing. I had the last watch; moon showed nothing but clean desert."

"I guess that's good, 'less they found a way to get ahead of us."

"That'd be a lot of hard riding," Will said.

Buchanan washed himself at the lake, then made his way through the ghostly light of the moon toward the hanging lantern of the chuck wagon for whatever leftovers were there. He was not surprised to find Griswold awake.

"Did you get any sleep, Griz?"

"Enough. Deems refilled the barrel for me and López cut up the beef I took from one o' the dead steers. Here." He handed a plate down from the chuck wagon.

A large, slightly burnt steak sat invitingly on it. "Saved it for ya. The Lord taketh but the Lord giveth."

"Much appreciated." There was no time to sit and cut. Buchanan stabbed the meat with a fork and chewed it.

"Sachem, I had a coupla thoughts about those hombres chasin' us. What if they *ain't* comin'? What if they got waylaid by Injuns?"

"If the Dawsons are riding fifteen, twenty large, as Haywood suspected, it'd have to be a war party that attacks them. We'd've seen signs of one."

"Okay. Then what if they telegraphed ahead and hired *el pistoleros*? Ya considered that?"

"Hired guns work for gold, and you can't telegram that."

"Hmmm. Okay, hadn't considered that."

"Besides, St. Jacques will want the pleasure of doing this himself," Buchanan said between bites. His eyes went to the moonlit horizon. "He'll come. Maybe not soon, but he'll be on us."

"If such is the case, I believe Haywood will try and let us know."

"I hope you're right and not just for that."

"What?"

Buchanan grinned. "It'd be good for me and the men if I was right about him."

"Won't do me any good to be wrong either. Don't forget who else stood up for the man back at that prairie trial couple o' nights back."

"The men need you if they want to eat," Buchanan laughed, handing back his empty plate. "I'm the one who'll be facing desertion and mutiny."

Now it was Griswold who grinned. "Say, there's a tip o' the hand."

"What?"

"Seafarin' terms."

"Doesn't mean anything, Griz, I promise you."

"Don't be so sure," the cookie replied as Buchanan turned to get his horse. "Man reaches a certain age, his thoughts get backward-lookin'. Take it from one who has a squint in his brain from all the mighta-beens."

"I truly don't think so," Buchanan said, walking away but surprised by the older man's remarks. The rancher's unintended sea reference did not suggest Boston but something else: Jacob's notion that he go to sea for Widmark. Being his own boss had always been a certainty in Buchanan's life. After facing down his own men—whose lives he had put at risk not just with Haywood but with the drive itself—he was not so sure.

THE DRIVE WAS soon underway, Fremont conferring with Buchanan about the creek that was marked on the map.

"If the distances are right, we got more'n a day to the next water," the trail boss said.

"The map shows where the creek was situated relative to the San Jacinto that feeds it, though the flow may be seasonal."

"Well, springtime shouldn't be a problem when it comes to that. If we push, we get there faster, we lose head from exhaustion. I say thirsty, complainin' steer are better'n dead ones."

"Agreed, though it means we travel into the afternoon without stopping well."

"We can rest at the water," Fremont said, "make camp till the next morning. Map says our last stretch of desert is just beyond the creek. By afternoon tomorrow we're back on hard plains."

"Yeah. Y'ever think we'd be glad for flat scrubland?"

"Boss, there ain't been one thing about this drive that even Medicine Man Grant could've foretold at his drunkest. Miss Sally warned me that this drive'd be a passel o' learning. She ain't been wrong so far."

Buchanan folded up the map. "You still think she'd be glad you were on this drive, knowin' what we know now?"

"I do. That lady's still got pioneer blood from her girlhood. Can outshoot me, truth be told, six-shooter or rifle. I got her beat at hatchet throwin', though."

"Wish I'd known. We could've used her."

"She would've loved to be on a drive, if women was allowed to and teachin' didn't mean so much." Fremont smiled contentedly. "She's gonna make a great mother."

Thinking about a future that did not involve water or rustlers was a refreshing change, one that Buchanan tried to hold on to as he left Fremont and took tail position behind Griswold.

As much as he tried not to think of it, ignoring the present was not possible, and Buchanan found himself turning regularly to look at the open sands bright with a three-quarter moon. . . .

CHAPTER NINETEEN

THE CREEK WAS where Buchanan had expected it to be.

It was early afternoon when Fremont spotted the overflowing banks and called out; he also saw the first greenery he had seen in days, small clumps of grasses half underwater, gathered where the banks typically lay.

"You're beautiful," he said to the sparkling waters before turning to rope the horns of the tired, lean lead steer and guide it over. The other animals did not need any such urging. Within minutes, pushing and crowding, all of the remaining cattle were spread along the banks. The men rode wide upriver to drink and water the horses.

It had been a challenging night, with some steers slowing because they were tired, others hungry, and one because he had breathed in so much sand that blood was running from his nose. He stopped and did not start up again. The drive lost another four head, but not as many as Buchanan feared he would lose, and Griswold was able to take more meat. It was also a challenge for the men, as the slow pace and sameness of everything around them bade them to drift asleep in the saddle. Some did and woke instantly; López did and stayed asleep, his horse keeping the pace and distance from the cattle; Prescott did and fell from the saddle, scaring some steer as he scrambled to get back up.

As it had a way of doing, the sun made the men forget the trials of the night. Once more the light, along with the water and just being out of the hard saddle, brought renewed life to the cowboys.

If not for the expanse of sands behind them, the terrain on the other side of the creek could be any plain on any drive. The land was familiar and low-lying, with enough grass for the cattle to feed on. Buchanan told Fremont to make camp on the other side and they would stay until dawn.

It would have been a satisfying end to the hard desert crossing if Deems had not noticed a plume of dust headed their way. He thought at first it might be a dust devil, a small tornado of wind picking up sand. The winds were blowing gently south, so its movement was right. But then he saw, emerging from the cloud, the figure of a man on horseback. He was riding hard, which caused the horse to kick up the enveloping cloud.

"Rider!" Deems said, not concerned that the cattle would scatter at the cry. They were much too content to stay where they were.

Buchanan had crossed the creek with Fremont to organize the layout of the camp. Still in the saddle, the rancher sent his mustang splashing back to the opposite bank.

Deems would have announced who it was if he could see; Buchanan knew at once that it was Haywood. A man running from Indians had a frantic manner about him, whipping his horse with his hat, spurring him, shouting. This man sat like a forward-facing ramrod and came in a straight line. He was running *to* something.

Griswold leaned over the left side of the seat to have a look; the rider had to cut wide to keep from knocking the cookie from the wagon. The frothing horse slowed as Buchanan rode out to meet it.

The new arrival was indeed George Haywood. He was wearing fresh guns and the look of a man warning settlers that floodwaters were coming.

Both men dismounted and stood facing each other. The man's canteen hung full from the saddle, so Buchanan did not offer him a drink. It was the horse that did all the work.

"Mr. Haywood?"

"They're twenty-one strong now, which includes me," he said without preamble. "Half of them are cowboys, half are from town, a couple lately in jail for fighting, drunkenness—you know the breed. They camped at the lake last night." He grinned. "At your AB Lake, which they spent an hour arguing about."

"Arguing?"

"They figured you might've poisoned it and did not want to lose any horses. They decided to draw lots and let one of them drink."

"Did they?"

"No. I drank—myself. Filled my canteen right up."

"That was quite a gamble. I appreciate the faith."

"I didn't think you'd do it. I wanted to show them up."

Buchanan was too interested in what else Haywood had to say. Otherwise, he would have considered the irony of the gang losing time debating a thought he himself had rejected.

Fremont had walked up with hardtack, biscuits Griswold kept on hand when there was no time to cook. Haywood shook his head but thanked him. That mutual show of gratitude was a first for both men.

"So you showed them up," Buchanan said. "Then they sent you ahead to scout for us?"

"They didn't send me to scout for *you*. They have maps; they knew where you were headed. It's about water. Took St. Jacques a while to find that lake since their map had it wrong. Even I couldn't find a sign of it, not even a smell, since we had the wind to our back. I told St. Jacques I'd go ahead to look for the next one, make sure it was where it was supposed to be. I wanted to warn you about their nearness and numbers. And also their plan."

"Which is?"

"They mean to secure your cattle or kill every last head. Some of the men they brought are rustlers of Dawson's acquaintance. They've got some story about a grudge against Reb Mitchell. They agreed to shoot the herd, then ride south with two hundred dollars each."

"Jesus. I want to crush him like you did to that orange," Fremont said.

"Were they staying at the lake or setting out?" Buchanan asked.

"They planned to set a spell, shake loose some of the dust, then press on."

"I was thinking they'd wait until we've crossed the border to strike. That ain't so now."

Haywood shook his head. "They want to get to you before you reach the Big Salt Creek."

"Any particular reason?" Fremont asked.

"Our man González is from there. He says there are two rivers forking from the southeastern side."

"They're on the map," Fremont confirmed.

"What's not shown are the villages built up around there," Haywood said. "St. Jacques is concerned there'd be people to hear the killing, find the dead herd, tell the local *policía*. Down there, his lies wouldn't have the protection of him being Dawson's man."

Buchanan considered the explanation. "May I know what you plan to tell St. Jacques about the location of the water?"

The man shrugged. "I've got to tell him exactly where it is and, when we get here, show him signs of where you camped. Otherwise he'll never trust me again."

"There's someone whose trust I can live without," Fremont muttered.

"Then there's information you would also be living without," Haywood said. "I don't know if and when I can come back, but I wanted you to be prepared."

"Once again, I am in your debt," Buchanan said.

There was something in the rancher's voice that sounded reserved, guarded. Or maybe he was just thoughtful. Haywood did not have time to reflect on it. Nodding in farewell, he rode off, trailing dust.

When he was gone, Buchanan gave final consideration to what he was about to say.

"Will, get the drive moving. Pronto."

The trail boss looked over with surprise. "You mean while there's still some daylight or—"

"I mean 'or.' We're going to continue through the night, no stopping. I'll want you on tail. Oh, and send López to me."

"Boss, you gonna try to outrun men who don't have to move cattle?"

"No. But we gotta beat St. Jacques to the sea and keep going. Otherwise we're finished. Go, please. Now."

Fremont was confused, but Buchanan's tone was grave and his instructions clear. The trail boss went off to rouse men and cattle. Buchanan broke out his map. He compared it to the prairie before him. The dimensions of the desert they had just crossed, compared to the ground that lay ahead, suggested they had about twenty miles to cover. That was a day and a half of pushing. The plains would be rougher in some ways than the desert because of gullies, exposed roots, and harder earth on worn hooves. Nonetheless, it had to be crossed.

López came riding up as Buchanan folded away the map.

"You came to California through the Valley of the Ancient Lake," the rancher said. "How well do you know it?"

The Mexican shook his head. "I came to north along the western side of the valley. That's where our hideouts had been, in the foothills of the mountains."

"All right, that's good. We're going back that way, as planned. I want you in front with me."

"What do you intend to do?"

"The Dawson gang is coming after us, Miguel. They're about a day behind and some twenty-two strong."

"Maldita sea todo," the Mexican muttered, rubbing his scruffy chin thoughtfully.

"You fought wars. You know that numbers can make a man overconfident."

"With good reason, Señor Buchanan. That's a lot of guns."

"Hopefully not this time. I plan to stop them. To accomplish that, I'll need you to do something."

"What do you need?"

Buchanan explained what he was thinking. As he did, the former revolutionary perked up like a rose in the morning sun. When the rancher was finished, López voiced his support for the plan, then galloped off to help the other riders rally the herd.

"Don't break your neck in a sand pit!" Buchanan warned.

"I will tell my horse," López said with his typical good humor.

War was god-awful in every way. But Buchanan reflected that it took men who had been in combat to be uncowed by most any other challenge and discomfort that arose. He himself had crossed the American continent, but it was war that had prepared him to lead these men and rush without hesitation into fresh hardships.

That, too, was something he had never been able to explain to Patsy. He thought of her and the girls before he turned to join the men. What he was planning had to work, or all he would have of the ladies was his final, mortal thought. . . .

CHAPTER TWENTY

THE PLAIN AT night left the steers less than a herd of almost three hundred head of cattle with a mind in each head.

Every man knew that it is the tendency of steers to wander or stop altogether when they are not penned by fence or herders. On the prairie, in the dark, every one of the six riders was as busy watching for unseen obstacles as they were tending cattle. López was the only man at the head of the herd. Fremont was in back but in front of the chuck wagon. Buchanan was once again behind. His official task was to listen for the Dawson riders. In fact, he and Fremont spent more time leaving their posts to round up stray beef.

The reason for the strays was that the men were watching the ground more than they were the herd. Even so, there were dangerous stumbles and sudden halts. The near-full moon was low, and although the expanse was illuminated, the light threw long, long shadows that concealed flaws in the surface. Not just cracks and holes but large rocks, clumps of tumbleweed, even hollow anthills. The danger was heightened by the fact that Buchanan had set them the task of moving at a daytime pace to keep some distance between the drive and St. Jacques.

After several hours the moon gave them a respite by passing overhead. By then the herd was a snakelike force weaving generally south; on the sides, Prescott, Mitchell, and Deems had drifted farther apart than they had realized. The men took the opportunity to reassemble the cattle before the light slanted in the opposite direction. It was not long before the herd—tired now as well as unguided—had flattened into a mob.

Fremont rode back to Buchanan.

"I figger we got about two hours till sunrise, when there won't be no light at all," he said.

"That's about right."

"I counted about a half-dozen strays that the boys couldn't grab without losing more. I say we stop, give everyone a rest, while we go back and get them."

"You sure? We stop now, we lose cattle to thirst."

"Maybe. But if we don't, we definitely lose steers."

During a drive, Buchanan relied heavily on the opinion of Will Fremont, and the rancher considered three things that were part of Fremont's request. First, the trail boss was making a strong recommendation. It usually came with equal consideration of cattle, men, and conditions; it was dangerous to ignore that. Second, Fremont was the number two man; it was bad for morale to dismiss him. But, third, St. Jacques would not be stopping.

"What is this, Will?" Buchanan asked.

The trail boss peered into Buchanan's dark face, with specks of moon in the eyes. "I don't follow."

"Is this drive about getting as many cattle as possible to Hidalgo or about beating St. Jacques?"

"Now that you ask, it's both I guess. But we—"

"How many steer do we have to lose before we make less selling them to Mexico than we do to Dawson?"

Fremont's head jerked back like he'd been snapped at by a dog. "You actually considerin' that?"

"I don't know. I truly do not. Things are different than when we set out. Like I said, what are we after *now*?"

"Boss, even assumin' that bastard would buy the herd now—and that's no guarantee—Dawson would own you. That would be the end of your ranch. The AB sign comes down and the Double-D goes over the gate. What do you do then? What do *any* of us do?"

Buchanan did not answer. His expression told Fremont that he had an answer but did not want to say it.

"Oranges?" Fremont read into the silence. "You'll plant groves?"

"And raise horses. You, me, Griz, maybe Prescott."

Fremont exhaled. "I don't say that's the worst idea in the world, given what's set in motion. But to go on bended knee to St. Jacques and Dawson? S'pose he wants your land next . . . and he may. Mitchell says his cows are grazin' more and more on your grass."

"We got enough."

"That ain't the point. Bein' neighborly ain't gonna buy you his gratitude. He will want to own the land, the ranch, and you. You won't have any place to plant Jacob's crops! And, boss, I thought you didn't want to work for Dawson or Widmark or anyone."

"That's true. It's the reason we're having this talk."

"This is a lot for a man to consider in a hurry and

sober," he said. "But speakin' for the hands, and I think I can, we'd rather go back free men than slaves. I fought a war because I believed that in my guts. Miss Sally—she teaches the kids about how folks fought in these parts to overthrow the tyrant Santa Anna." He shook his head. "I will back you whatever you decide for your own brand, but for me? I would rather die than submit."

Buchanan had listened with his heart as well as his ears.

"Before we left, I gave López orders," the rancher said. "At sunup, he's to ride ahead, into the foothills, make his presence known."

"To who and why?"

"He has said that many of his compadres live in the western hills. They did not want to farm or build railroads, so they rob travelers. I had intended to stay east of that region—but we need more guns."

"Bandit guns. How do you know they won't take our cattle?"

"We'll give 'em some. López says they'll cotton to being treated like men, like partners getting paid instead of like pirates."

Fremont seemed to fill with the same enthusiasm López had shown back at the creek.

"We stop now, we round up the strays like you say," Buchanan continued. "But the Dawsons gain on us and López may not reach whatever help is out there in time. We can move faster when the sun's up, but we won't make up time and the steers'll be two hours more worn down. Plus we may lose cattle for lack of water. So what do we do?"

"We go on," Fremont said without hesitation. "I'll fall back and round up those head that I can. I don't know that there's a great plan out there, but this is a good one."

"Glad you brought it up, Fremont. I been chewing cud on this thing, always arriving at the same words you just stated. Oh, one thing you should pass along—any cattle drop, shoot 'em."

"But the sound of the gunshot—"

"St. Jacques finds a live steer, he knows we're just two, maybe three hours ahead. Dead steer—buzzards will come. Picked-at carcass could add a couple of extra hours to St. Jacques's thinking."

"That's true."

"Also, let Miguel decide when to head out himself, though sooner is better than later."

"He already told me. He was thinking first light. That way he doesn't fall in a gopher hole, he said."

Buchanan managed to find a smile. "That's fine."

The trail boss rode on to rope the strays he could. Buchanan was not only grateful for the talk but for having men who, unlike himself, had an almost eager willingness to listen.

He was thinking now that he could learn from the men.

Fremont was able to save three head of cattle, although he almost lost his horse in an old Indian wolf pit. Migrating tribes would dig pits and cover them with a latticework of branches covered with grass. The goal was to protect children from predators and also to obtain pelts. One of the steers he approached took off and fell into the brittle trap; it broke its neck, hindquarters twitching as they stabbed up above ground level. That is what Fremont's horse would've done had it continued on its course.

The trail boss decided not to go back for the rest,

because he was needed to keep from losing more. He paraded his horse from side to side in the spreading rear of the herd, coaxing stragglers back into the group wherever they happened to be.

Griswold had an easier time negotiating the terrain and moved his wagon along both sides to offer the men coffee he had made before they broke camp. He reheated it with a small iron pot in which he had packed sticks and brush he'd collected at the creek.

"I warmed it best I could without settin' fire to the coach, embers bouncin' and flyin' like they do," he apologized to each man. "It won't heat ya but it'll wake ya."

The night was colder than Griswold's coffee, and the hands were appreciative.

Buchanan fell back farther than before. Like the night before he encountered Haywood, he found himself putting more and more space between himself and the herd. He was almost at the point where his hold on the drive was just listening to the distant banging of Griswold's wagon, which had returned to its position in the rear. Buchanan was angry that he had to deal with St. Jacques on top of what was already proving an expectedly difficult drive. He was distracted trying to puzzle out what Haywood would do, whether they could count on his help or at least his neutrality. Buchanan thought he knew folks' natures well enough, but this one was a puzzlement. At the same time the Dawson distraction was in some ways a welcome one. The rancher was not out doing what he would have been, searching for strays in the dark. In doing so, he might have ended up like Fremont almost had.

The plains gave way to more and more sand, and then the drive was back in desert. The heat was not an issue, even as light began to break, because the country was bordered on both sides by mountains. The peaks provided relief from the direct sun, although they also blocked the easterlies and westerlies that had provided some relief against the daytime heat. From time to time a poor steer stopped and fell to one side. Some would struggle to regain their feet; others just lay there. Buchanan regretted that he had to leave them to the mercies of thirst and desert predators.

It was the first drive on which he had regrets. He thought it strange that that had never occurred to him before. From the time he conceived this undertaking it was always succeed or fail, with nothing in between. He had not, in fact, felt anything like this since leaving his inactive, grieving father in the care of his mother.

She told you that you had your own life to live. What does this *tell you?* he asked himself.

The only thing that occurred to him was to listen more closely to the woman closest to him. It was a strange thought to have while in the middle of doing something that a man was born and raised to do. He liked it better when he was just puzzling over whether he could trust George Haywood.

Griswold poked his head around the side of the wagon and shouted. "Ya smell it?"

Buchanan did not. He had lifted his kerchief to keep out the sands kicked up by the chuck wagon wheels. He moved aside and lowered the cloth.

"Salt air," the rancher said.

"Has to be that big salty creek, yeah? Unless there's a salt desert ya don't know about."

"López would've mentioned such."

"I seen him ride off a while ago," Griswold said. "More'n scoutin', it looked like. Reminded me of one of them

Pony Express boys I saw just after I left Arizona. He was beatin' dust like he was tryin' to outrun a *hvirfilvindr*. That's what my granpap used t'call a whirlwind."

Buchanan pulled his kerchief up and fell back. Griswold never expected an answer to his speeches. He gave them whether anyone was listening or not.

"Hey, boss!" Griswold shouted.

"Yeah?"

"I'm seein' tired horses! They're fightin' the boys a bit!"

"Thank you!"

Buchanan was not surprised by that, or by the fact that Fremont had not come back to tell him. They had the spare animals if needed. It would mean dumping whatever provisions they were carrying or finding a place for them in the wagon—although repacking would slow them down.

The rancher rode a little to the east of the herd so he could look ahead as well as back. In the distance he could see what looked like a necklace of small diamonds like his mother used to wear. They were strung across the horizon: the first hint of Big Salt Creek.

IT WAS EARLY afternoon before the drive came within direct sight of the salt creek. By then the herd was strung out nearly a half mile, a group composed of individual steers moving at their own lazy pace. There were little flashes of color and sound, the arms of the cowboys cracking whips in the air to urge the strays and stragglers forward.

The scent had an uplifting effect on the men and horses, as though some ancient urge, some primitive memory, drew them toward the sea. When Big Salt Creek came more fully into view, Buchanan saw at once that the name did not fit. Either that, or it had grown since it was first called that. What spread before them was more than a lake. It was an inland sea of an inland empire, so vast that it cooled the air of the desert immediately to the west.

"It's like a rabbit pelt on my left cheek," Griswold put it as they stayed on the eastern side of the sands, closer to the lake.

They could not stay there long, however, as access to the foothills required a turn to the southwest. Fremont brought Prescott up to help him turn the steer into the warmer air. The lead animals resisted and had to be roped and tugged. That caused protest from the tired horses; Fremont's horse had to be swapped out for one of the animals tied to the chuck wagon. Mitchell brought it up, Griswold stopping the wagon to take on the necessities that the Confederate had stripped from the horse and left in the sand.

"Least ya coulda done is handed 'em to me!" Griswold complained.

"No time, Griz."

The man rode off to bring Fremont the fresh mount. Buchanan turned and watched along the trail they had traveled. The breeze was covering their tracks somewhat, but Haywood would have no trouble finding indentations from the wagon, patties, even spits of tobacco.

Mitchell returned with Fremont's horse and tied it to the wagon. He mounted to return to the herd. He happened to look back and stopped.

"Hey, boss?"

"Yeah. I see it."

A mound of dust lay on the northern horizon, still in the plain. It was at least four times as wide as it was high.

"Tell Will to get them into the foothills, Reb. Hurry. Griz, leave the rest and get the wagon outa here."

"Ya may need an extra—"

"Jabber all ya want as you join the drive."

Griswold threw a final armful of tools into the cart, leaving sacks of flour and bundles of jerky. He hurried back to the driver's seat, muttering.

"There better be more mountain goats or somethin' to hunt, 'cause I won't have the men yellin' at me for just servin' beans."

Buchanan weighed putting guns in his hands. He decided against giving them a reason to shoot. He also knew this above all: Armed or unarmed, his being here was not going to stop their pursuit.

The last sounds he heard were Griz's indistinct mutterings and the fading clang of the pans.

Then he was alone, not lying in wait for one man like last time but facing twenty-odd charging cowboys.

CHAPTER TWENTY-ONE

BEFORE DISMOUNTING, THE only questions in Buchanan's head were whether St. Jacques had the men riding shoulder to shoulder to create a terrifying dust storm or surround him, folding him in like the wings of a bat, and whether they would gun him down or trample him.

It did not matter. Very little did as Buchanan dismounted. The one thought that counted: You lived and died like a man. He would miss his family and they would miss him, but that came second at this moment.

Maybe that'll come after I'm bleedin' out or my bones get broken. . . .

The unit group of different colored animals and all kinds of riders came nearer, their image rippling a bit from the heat before plowing through. It was a nightmare of faces twisted and possessed with anger, hot skin dusted with sand, and snorting, frothing animals that had been ridden hard. There was so much to fear that Buchanan found himself free of it. He stood as if he were waiting for a coach to pull in.

In the center of the line was St. Jacques. He reminded Buchanan of one the figureheads on his father's ships, stalwart and upright, immune to the spray of the sea or the assault of the wind. Haywood rode on the east side, at the end of the line. He had been far from St. Jacques during that first encounter, too, when they had tried to buy the cattle. The rancher did not know whether Haywood had been put there or had chosen that spot so he would not be seen holding fire, if it came to that. As ever, Buchanan could not read any emotion on the man's stone face.

St. Jacques spurred his horse ahead of the others as they neared. The stallion pushed up dirt about ten feet away when the rider reined him to a sharp halt nearby. Buchanan's own horse started and had to be steadied. The other animal turned one way and then the other as the other riders stopped a horse's length behind. St. Jacques steadied his mount and looked down at Buchanan. The Double-D foreman was wearing a partial smile, more catlike than human. He had come to play.

"Impressive spot," St. Jacques drawled. "Glad I got to see it."

His white wide-brim hat was held to the back of his neck by a leather chin strap. He smoothed the eagle feather in the band, then fixed the hat on his head. He leaned forward casually as though he were courting. "It's quite a thing you've done, getting this far. Haywood told me some of the troubles you faced while you held him in servitude."

Buchanan made a point of not looking over at Haywood. If the man had used those words, it would be to explain his long absence, to protect himself.

"My offer remains if you care to accept it," St. Jacques went on. "And honestly, sir, I suggest you do."

"Or?"

The man straightened and spread his arms to indicate his gang. "Or, sir, like honeybees, we will go around you. Eventually, some member of your party will sign my paper so you get paid. It is fair of Mr. Dawson, I think, being willing to pay for dead cattle."

"You speak wickedness with the voice of a pastor," Buchanan said.

"Do I? Sir, I have seen wickedness painted across a great swath of land and people by men like you. No, not *like* you. You were a part of it."

"So were most of the men you ride with, I reckon."

"There are victors and there are losers, and we make what peace we can. Your own man, Reb, has done that, it seems. He fought for the same cause as I, and I hear from Haywood that the man's belly is no less roiled by what he has been forced to swallow."

"I hired a man, not a flag. Reb would never do the kind of thing you propose."

"And I would never call myself 'Reb.' That's a Northern designation, not mine. It suggests loyalty to one's home, nothing deeper. No, I am an idealist. I repudiate the term 'Reb' and I repudiate the one you just used to describe me—'wickedness.'" St. Jacques's grin had faded. "This is a business transaction, no less than what Chester Jacob proposed to you. You have a choice to accept profit or to accept loss. Now, we are tired from our long ride, hungry, and ready to cook beef. I ask one more time: Do you accept payment for your stock or not?"

Buchanan looked along the line of men as St. Jacques spoke. He did it only so he could pause on Haywood. As expected, the man sat still as a Sequoia, his eyes unreadable. The rancher did not believe he could expect help or a sudden defection.

The rancher knew that he was cornered. What the Double-D deployed had not been an artful entrapment, just manpower, but it was enough. Buchanan felt regret but no shame in his position. It would be like staying angry at the desert or the ocean. The cattleman had exhausted everything he could do short of a last stand that would surely result in his own demise. And if he drew, his men would hear the gunfire that cut him down. Some, maybe all, would fight. Then they, too, would die.

Yet he still was not decided. Like St. Jacques, he would have to live with surrender, haunted every day.

You can be done with this burden with a word, plant oranges, be with your ladies, said a quiet but insistent voice.

As the rancher resisted accepting either outcome, he felt a soft, barely perceptible change in the ground; it was the smallest vibration, like an earthquake still far off. He felt it before he heard it or saw the cause. It was not even enough to shift the sands beside his feet.

"We are waiting, sir," St. Jacques said.

Even as the man spoke, there was a stirring up and down the line. Because he was looking at Buchanan, St. Jacques did not initially see it—the cause of the growing thunder in the ground. When he did, his eyes narrowed and twenty guns were raised.

With relief filling his chest like clean, fresh air, Buchanan turned. Behind him was a cloud every bit as big as the one that had brought the Dawson gang to his drive. The pounding of hooves and wall of sand announced the arrival of López and his fellow Juaristas, fighters of the Restored Republic. As the men neared, Buchanan saw Prescott and—God bless him—Reb Mitchell on either side.

The group stopped at roughly the same distance behind Buchanan as the others. López was in the middle. He smiled at Buchanan, who smiled gratefully back. The rancher choked down a swallow as he turned toward the men of the Double-D.

"I was waiting, too," Buchanan said. "I am not waiting any more. My answer, Mr. St. Jacques, is that I decline your offer."

Now it was the Southerner's turn to consider his position. He certainly knew his men; within moments of the party arriving, and without turning, St. Jacques had thrown out both arms to stop his men from taking any rash, individual action. Like Buchanan, the Double-D foreman was dead center in the line of fire.

When St. Jacques was certain that his men were at least briefly in control of themselves, he lowered his arms. He smiled. "I see a few ribbons and sashes that are known to me. How fitting that you are backed by rebels, albeit those who won."

Buchanan made no response. A few impatient horses snorted. That was answer enough.

"Might I suggest a brief truce?" St. Jacques said. "Perhaps you and I could go off and discuss matters. You still have a long and difficult journey ahead, and the trail is already littered with dead AB cattle."

"I'd shoot them myself before selling them to you."

"Ah, the brash impulse speaks. Very well, we will talk here, openly. I suggest you consider reason. Accept payment and everyone in your outfit goes home early, safe, and with a profit. We will be generous: Your Mexican friends get the cattle, which they will use locally. I am sure Mr. Dawson would not object. I have heard you run a somewhat democratic outfit. Why not talk it over?"

"Tell you what, Mr. St. Jacques. I'll do that." Without turning, Buchanan shouted, "Reb, what's your vote?"

Sitting at the eastern end of the line, Mitchell rode forward. He stopped beside Buchanan and looked at St. Jacques. "Only man who gives orders on this drive is Mr. Buchanan. That's my vote."

St. Jacques was openly disapproving of the man's actions. He nodded slowly, then shifted his eyes to Buchanan. "Your final word, sir?"

"The answer is no sale," Buchanan said.

"Very well. Our dispute is not with your Mexican guests, nor did our instructions anticipate an international incident. But be assured, sir, this matter is not yet ended."

The man pivoted in a single, rearing maneuver. In that display of horsemanship, Buchanan saw the qualities that he had admired in the enemy and got a small show of the world St. Jacques had lost.

The rancher turned to Mitchell. "Thank you, Reb."

"I meant what I said, boss—but I confess it was not easy."

"Because of St. Jacques?"

"Yessir. I didn't know him but I knew those like him. They were my countrymen."

"They still are," Buchanan said.

"Yessir," he said again, both men aware of the chasm between the two ideas.

Mitchell returned to the herd, taking Prescott with

him. Buchanan got back in the saddle and trotted over to López.

"A timely arrival, *sí*?" the former rebel smiled.

"I'll never forget this. I hope you will convey that to your compadres."

"They already know, I think."

"What do they want? What can I give them?"

"To succeed."

"That's all?"

"That's a great amount," López said. "I tell them you are trying to feed the people and they asked for nothing more than that. Some men"—he nodded after the retreating St. Jacques—"they fought for ideas. We fought for people. They live in the California foothills to protect our border from men like Dawson, not men like you."

Buchanan did not know which was the stronger emotion, being surprised or being impressed. In either case, he was overwhelmed by the display of generosity and compassion.

"They would like to ride with us into the lower range, show us water and a path to Mexico that does not include very much sand."

"That will be greatly appreciated," Buchanan said to the group.

He took a moment to look at the faces of the revolutionaries. They were weather-worn and scarred, more so than the Double-D men. Yet there was a humanity in their eyes that St. Jacques and his men had lacked. That quality had saved him from loss and humiliation he would have carried for the rest of his days.

As they turned back to the herd, Buchanan glanced over his shoulder. He was looking to see if and when Haywood might cut out from the group. It was probably too early for that, while they were still in view. But he did not doubt it would happen, or that the Dawson gang would resume their pursuit. The rancher was disappointed by the man, even though he was not sure exactly what he had expected him to do.

All Buchanan knew now were two things regarding Haywood. First, that he did not especially wish to see Haywood again. And second, that his wish would likely be denied.

CHAPTER TWENTY-TWO

WEEKS OF TRANQUILITY helped the men to recover from, if not forget, the ordeals they had faced to that point. There was a lingering sense of pride and good humor—both went hand in hand—due to the repulsing of the Dawson hands. Everyone knew they would have to be dealt with at some point, but it made Deems, if not the others, certain that God was on their side.

The former revolutionaries proved to be excellent and companionable guides for the first three days. To a man they were devout Catholics, and Deems's prayerful grace before supper was a solemn time for them. They thanked God still for their deliverance from oppression and prayed for the lives of their countrymen and their nation.

The leader of the nineteen-man band was a sixty-three-year-old grandfather known only as León. Only after they had been together for several days did Buchanan learn that the name was more than a name; it was his title: Lion. During the wars, he had used his soldiers shooting from cover as a distraction so he could enter an enemy camp and kill the French with knife and machete.

A stout, balding widower whose family lived on a farm in Veracruz, León was especially fond of the writings of José Joaquín Fernández de Lizardi, El pensador mexicano, whose ribald poetry he carried in his saddlebag. He could often be heard laughing for no reason, which he explained as suddenly remembering a favorite passage.

"Was he like this during the wars?" Buchanan asked López .

"Always. He would be reciting poetry while we waited in ambush, then continue when the attack was done."

Buchanan was surprised by this loose confederation. He could not imagine any of his superiors during the war comporting themselves that way.

López translated the stories of their experiences during the war. Unlike the stories of most Civil War veterans, the tales were devoid of the kind of boastfulness the Americans sometimes heard at the taverns and around campfires—usually from people who had to inflate the minor role they played in this skirmish or that reconnaissance. Also, these rebels had won their war. That helped to settle the effects of battle in a way St. Jacques and even Reb Mitchell had not experienced.

The two groups stayed together until the southern end of the Cocopah Mountains, in sight of the towering Black Butte. By heading to that, they would come to the Colorado River. The Mexicans would not accept the gift of several head of cattle. They wanted them all to go to those who needed it.

The drive had been touched with nobility, Buchanan thought. What had started as commerce had developed into something richer. That made him grateful for being able to continue.

When the groups parted, López, Fremont, and Buchanan reviewed the map. The Mexican had made various notes based on what his countrymen had told him.

"We only must avoid the fields of mud volcanoes," López said as the cattle started down a rocky ridge. "The cones are not very big, maybe as high as a man on horseback, but the mud is hot and the ground is very, very soft."

"That wasn't on the damn maps," Fremont remarked as they prepared to descend from the foothills.

The herd had not lost any animals since the desert, and there were 239 head as they reached the plain. Black Butte was slightly behind them to the northeast, a tower as dark and foreboding as Old Greyback was bright and proud. Buchanan was still in the tail position, behind Griswold. He did not think St. Jacques would risk open pursuit now. The Juaristas might be watching for them.

But Haywood—Buchanan *wanted* to see *him*. He wanted to know what the man had actually told St. Jacques.

The day was hot and muggy, and as they proceeded, the men smelled the mud of the volcanoes. The cones themselves appeared after a while, churning out thin plumes of smoke beneath an increasingly cloudy sky. The volcanoes were quite a distance off, over a mile, and the men stayed well clear of them. Even this far away the foul, charred quality of the mud was like an old, open grave, and the ground had a spongy quality.

Although the steers did not get stuck they were unable to wander. The men had the least to do here since the drive began.

That changed at sunset.

The men made camp near a southern bank of the Colorado. It humbled Buchanan to think that this was the same river whose banks he crossed in Arizona during the war. He had seen the Mississippi River on his journey west, but only a part of it—not two distant sections.

The sun had gone down and the campfire was burning some yards off to keep predators at bay.

Fremont said, "This is damn nice country. I wonder why nobody's ranching here?"

López answered, "Someone will, when there is the railroad."

Suddenly the fire began to hiss and sputter. Moments later, even as the men were throwing off the top of their bedrolls, a warm and then cold wind tore into them from the west and raindrops that felt as heavy as grapes began to pummel them—first from above, then slashing sideways.

The cattle did not seem perturbed, though the instantly ferocious winds frightened the horses. What alarmed the hands was not the storm itself but how close they had settled beside the river.

"I was listenin' to the waters!" shouted Prescott, who had been on watch. "Wondered why they sounded louder!"

"Storm's moving west to east, same as the flow!" Buchanan said, his back to the pelting rain. "Will, come with me. Everyone else, stay put till I get some light!"

It was a dark night, and he had to use his toe, carefully set, to feel his way in the dark. Fremont was directly behind him; their destination was the chuck wagon. When they arrived, Griswold was already poking his head from the wagon's door.

"Now, there's a blow!" he said. "Horses out back shook me awake!"

"Light a lantern, hand it down!" Buchanan shouted up.

Griswold disappeared behind the curtain and, like a magician, emerged moments later with the lantern.

"At least the heat is gone!" Griswold cheered as he handed the light down. "I'll light the other in case it goes out!"

"We'll need it anyway!" the rancher told him.

Buchanan and Fremont ran to the riverbank, where the herd sat. The animals were lowing now but not because of the slashing rain. The men hurried around them. They felt the fresh softness in the grassy bank before the wildly swinging circle of light showed them the height of the fast-flowing Colorado.

"Jee-sus wept!" Fremont said as they looked out at the surging black water.

"Move 'em away," Buchanan said gravely.

Fremont was already in motion when Buchanan spoke. He was charging back along his own steps toward the camp.

"Get 'em back!" he shouted. "Griz, get the other lantern!"

"I'm comin'," the cookie shouted not far behind him, the yellow light moving to and fro. He stopped as his cart shook noisily behind him. He hung the lantern from the nearest tree branch. "Sachem, I gotta handle the horses!"

Deems was nearest and Buchanan gave him his lantern before slogging off to get the other. It was knocking against the tree, rain dripping from its sides, and he shielded it as best he could with his arm.

Buchanan went to join the others. He digested the scene fast and whole as he trudged toward his men. The world around him was eerily like a storm at sea, even down to the faint smell of the Pacific blowing in. He refused to believe he had come all this way to meet the same fate as his brother.

The horses were rearing wildly, and riding them was not an option. It would have taken energy that needed to be applied to the steers. The men moved them first, fearful that they would run off and be lost in the lush pastures. They tied the animals to a tree behind the chuck wagon, moving Griswold's animals there as well. They were bucking so much on both sides, the cookie was afraid of the wagon falling over or snapping its brake.

Buchanan had experienced severe gully washers before, but never beside a river. He also felt a smaller crosscurrent coming from the north, possibly off the Big Salt Creek.

"Boss, I say we leave 'em go," Fremont said. "They run, they probably won't go far! The cattle need us!" The trail boss and Buchanan were the only ones trying to calm them now.

"You go! I'm worried about them hurting themselves!"

Fremont signaled okay and, putting his head and shoulders down, made his way to the nearest lantern. They had been tied to trees near the herd, giving light where it was immediately needed: the cattle that were slowly being shoved, kicked, and whipped away from the river. The men had started by trying to push the cows nearest the water outward, but they bumped against cattle that were disinclined to move. Three men went around the other side to rope individual animals and try to drag them into motion. Prescott had the most success, actually encircling steers around the head with his arms as he had done in the rodeo.

The storm showed no sign of relenting as the cattle were maneuvered from the riverbank. Fremont was still on that side of the herd as the rising water reached his boots. He turned to the other man farther down that side.

"Miguel, go around and help move 'em out! These steer get too wet, they'll stampede into the others!"

The Mexican sloshed ahead on the muddy earth. Fremont had never felt anything like the seething mass of beef in front of him as he stopped pushing and let the water do that job for him. All he wanted to do was make sure that they did not turn into the river in a panic. Steers' sense of direction was poor under normal conditions; in this situation it could be fatal.

To the west, Buchanan saw it first: a surge of water that was at least waist-high and twofold more than the banks could contain.

"Fremont, get out!" he cried.

The trail boss could not hear him—ironically, because the wave was so loud. Where Fremont was standing, about three hundred yards away, it would still sound like rain.

Buchanan grabbed a rope, left the horses, and ran forward, half slipping as he raced the floodwaters to reach his old friend.

"Fremont! *Fremont, get back!*"

Whether the trail boss heard the water or Buchanan

or both, Fremont turned as the water came rolling at him, catching him before he could take a step. The man had his legs swept out from under him. He landed facedown, his legs in the water and his body pinwheeling as he was pulled downriver. He dug his gloved hands into the sod, cutting long ruts as he was dragged.

"Miguel! Lewis—anyone!" Buchanan yelled. But the gale was too loud and the men too far away to hear him.

With the wind at his back, Buchanan took a chance by throwing his lasso from ten feet away. The rope landed on Fremont's shoulders and he raised one arm from the watery mud to put it through. Just then the current spun his head toward the river while simultaneously dragging him downstream. Once again he dug into the bank with both hands, although they did little to slow his progress. The rope slipped away and Buchanan yanked it back. Still running forward, he scooped the loop up and heaved a second time, trying to get the rope in the water as far below the man's left hand as possible. He succeeded in dropping it near Fremont's elbow so that he drifted toward the loop. While Buchanan watched anxiously, the trail boss raised his arm from the water and slapped around until he had it in his fingers. Buchanan dug his boot heels in and tightened the line as Fremont got his arm through and grabbed the taut rope.

"Both hands!" Buchanan yelled.

Fremont released his grip on the bank and put his left arm through the loop. He also grabbed the rope with his right hand.

The torrent wanted the man but not as much as Buchanan wanted him back. He leaned back. Even as the waters rose and lapped over the rancher's boots, he pushed against the earth with his heels, trying to walk backward, arms straining to pull Fremont in.

Suddenly, an extra pair of hands grabbed the rope. Buchanan did not see who they belonged to until the man bent low enough into the glow of the lantern.

It was George Haywood.

The tracker was grimacing as he pulled with strong arms, leaning back so far, he appeared to be seated. He started working the rope hand over hand. Pulling together, the men drew Fremont from the raging water onto muddy ground and then several feet beyond. The trail boss lay still.

Buchanan dropped the lariat and ran over. As rain continued to pour down, he flopped Fremont onto his back. The man was unconscious.

"You are *not* going to die!" Buchanan screamed.

He straddled the man's waist, pushed Fremont's face to one side, and put both hands flat on his rib cage. He pressed upward slowly, repeatedly, leaning into each push the way he had learned at the seaport in Boston. The man's cheek had felt cold, very cold.

"Come *on*, Will!"

By this time López and Mitchell had seen what was going on. They ran over, Mitchell skidding to Fremont's side on his knees. He pulled off his glove with his teeth and stuck two fingers in Fremont's mouth as deeply as he could. The trail boss lay still for several moments longer; then, abruptly, he coughed hard and a stream of warm water spewed from his mouth. He retched, turned onto his side, and spit more.

"Let's get him up!" Buchanan said.

The rancher took him under one arm, Mitchell under the other, and they got him to his feet.

They walked him toward the chuck wagon and leaned him against the side, away from the river and sheltered from the slanting rain. While they held him there, letting him cough out what water remained, Buchanan looked around. He saw Haywood standing shin-high in the river, pushing the cattle toward solid land. Some went; those that did not ended up in the torrent and then moving downriver against their will. Their struggles sent up high splashes but did not get them any nearer to the bank. They cried skyward but the sounds were soon lost in the storm, the steers vanishing into the night.

Fremont finally raised his arms and then his head.

"You look bad, friend." Buchanan smiled.

"Feel worse," Fremont said. "Felt like I swallowed half the river."

"Not quite, but enough to nearly drown ya."

Fremont looked at Buchanan in the dark. "You pulled me out?"

"I tried, but it took me and Haywood to get you to ground."

"He—he's back?" Fremont coughed again.

"Yes, and timely enough."

Mitchell released Fremont. "I'm goin' back to help the roundup."

"Thank you," Buchanan said.

"Yeah, from me, too," Fremont said weakly. He shook his head, which was more like letting it just flop from side to side. "I thought I was done."

"Wasn't gonna let that happen," Buchanan said.

"Haywood," the trail boss muttered. "Jeez. I'll thank him, too, when I can move."

Buchanan looked out at the faint light. Although

the river continued to leap and pour from its bed, the storm was weakening and the men seemed to be getting a handle on the herd. There would be time enough for Haywood. For now, cold and shivering, Buchanan was just grateful to be standing there with his friend instead of mourning his loss.

CHAPTER TWENTY-THREE

THE STORM HAD passed before the steers had been settled. The oppressively hot day gave way to a cool night. Griswold made a fire using dry wood he kept in the chuck wagon for just this purpose. While the men pulled off their soaked clothes, the cookie hung the lanterns on trees so he could see as he fashioned a drying rack between two upright branches that had come down in the storm. He lay sticks he had kept to make torches across the top. When he was finished, he carried it over to the campfire and jammed the ends in the sodden earth.

"Cookin', doctorin', laundry," he muttered. "I oughta get the pay o' three men. Four, if ya consider pullin' teeth, which can still happen."

"I'm grateful to be alive," Fremont said. "That's pay enough for me."

The trail boss was seated beside the fire, covered with a blanket from the chuck wagon. His knees were pulled to his chin as he contemplated the brash actions that had nearly cost him his life and the heroism of the ones who had saved him.

"And bartender!" Griswold exclaimed suddenly, a cloudburst of complaint. "Don't forget who it was ran barefoot through the mud to get the whiskey that brought back yer warmth and color!"

"I will never forget that."

"Dribbled half of his down yer chin, so don't blame me if we run out."

"We'll get tequila over the border," López said. "You will like it more."

"I believe, Griz, that every man here will give up his personal claim to the four head we lost tonight," Mitchell said.

"What do you need money for, anyway?" Prescott asked. "The ladies at the Horn and Hide stopped takin' yer money two, three seasons ago."

Griswold began draping shirts over the center of the bar, chaps—which did not need as much drying, being leather—toward the end. "Mebbe I'll strike, see how you all like it. That's what I'll do."

"Then you won't get nothin'," López laughed.

The Mexican's laughter, like the conversation itself, was born of relief. Talk drifted and shrank as the men lay back around the fire, their flannel undershirts and cotton drawers drying on them as they tried to rest if not sleep.

Buchanan took the watch, since the men needed sleep. Besides, his muscles were still charged, his arms looking for something to do. He even considered chopping wood and cutting away the bark for more firewood, but he had something else more pressing. After checking to see that the horses were secure, he tucked his rifle under his arm and walked to the chuck wagon.

Haywood was drinking coffee that he had made himself with Griswold's blessing.

The men had learned the drill already: George Haywood showed up and the others paid him no attention. They were not being rude but watchful. This man who had helped get them off the ledge and had now helped save their trail boss was still the man who had stolen back his guns and then tried to steal their cattle not once but twice.

The backboard was open and Buchanan put his foot on it. It was dark back here, the sloshing of the river full and ominous but all else was silent, even the owls and coyotes.

"Brew smells good," Buchanan said.

"I make it strong," Haywood said. "Every man's got a particular smell, lest he smells like coffee. Have some."

"Not just now," Buchanan said. "Seems I have to thank you again, Mr. Haywood. Were you out here scouting?"

"That's what St. Jacques called it when he sent me. But I don't believe St. Jacques trusts me anymore."

"Why? 'Cause you lied to him about what happened in our camp."

"No, Mr. Buchanan. He believed what I told him."

Buchanan looked at the man with open disapproval. "That you were our prisoner."

"That's right. There was nothing else *to* say."

"Then what makes you think he doesn't trust you?"

Haywood drained the cup, poured another from the pot. His movements were certain, trained for activity in the dark. "He did not tell me what his own plans were. For all I know, he turned round after I left and went hunting for Juaristas in the foothills. In case you didn't catch it, St. Jacques has had a bear's bellyful of losing battles."

The rancher considered this. It made no sense, but he respected Haywood for being honest about lying.

"What's your guess about his plans?"

Haywood hesitated—too long, Buchanan thought. "I truly do not know."

"Would you tell me if you did know?"

"I was just contemplating that," Haywood said. "I'm not sure. See, I can still go back if I want to. I throw in with you, I'm a hunted man. St. Jacques, given what he is, and me, given who I am—he would never give up trying to hang me."

"Can a man live like that?"

"Like what? I saw you back there at the foothills, Mr. Buchanan. For all your high ideals, you were considering St. Jacques's offer."

Haywood was not wrong. Now that he was safe, and with hindsight, the rancher felt ashamed.

"You're not wrong," Buchanan said as he took coffee for himself. "That wasn't a matter of lying. I was faced with a tactical decision."

"You and me, we grew up with different ways of surviving," Haywood said. "You make decisions because you have choices. I learnt how to yield on the outside while staying strong on the inside."

"I understand," Buchanan said. "Would you have joined them, firing on my cattle?"

"I most likely would. Cattle are not people; they're food. And you would have been paid."

"I don't like what you say, but your honesty is appreciated."

"You probably won't like this either," Haywood said. "I can't swear to it, but I don't think St. Jacques gives a spit about the border anymore. Crossing it won't make you safe." He pointed with his tin cup. "You're one Yankee he does not intend to let win."

"People make mistakes when they're mad," Buchanan said.

"*Or* they whip you near to death. I've seen him break horses, permanent. And there's something else you should know. I don't like the man, but he's no fool. Commanded cavalry during the war and knows all the tricks and tactics. I heard the stories, like circling horses in the woods to make it seem like he's got more than he does, leaving uniforms stuffed with hay on the ground to make Union boys walk into ambushes. With nothing to do but ride and think since those Juaristas surprised him, he will find some way to surprise you."

"And you?"

"And me. I don't think like a reptile."

Buchanan wasn't sure what he meant by that. "You mean a real one?"

"I do. He's watched them chase locusts. How they wait, dash, keep their distance, then strike with their tongues, sometimes working in pairs. Said he heard during the war that Chinese learned to fight that way, so he did the same. Didn't much care for foreigners, but he was smart enough to learn from them."

"That's a little too philosophical for me," Buchanan said. "And I'm not a locust."

Haywood said nothing.

"That still leaves us with the question of what you're going to do," Buchanan went on. "Where are you supposed to meet him?"

"North, same way I came. I just can't be sure he'll be there. Could be using me to make you think he's coming up behind you."

"But you don't know."

"I do not," Haywood said. "St. Jacques—he doesn't like confiding in former slaves."

"Yet you stay."

"Yeah. They mostly leave me alone. Man like me, that's a welcome thing."

Buchanan had met a number of former slaves and each had his own measure of what freedom meant. To some it was leaving their old existence behind. To others it was exacting revenge against those who had abused them. He tried to respect them all, although Haywood presented a challenge: his employer was out to get them.

"You mind if I stay the rest of the night?" Haywood asked. "It was a long ride getting here and I'd like some sleep before thinking any more."

"Of course."

"I'll bunk by the horses, like before," he said.

"You can stay by the fire."

"Actually, it looks drier over on the rocks."

Buchanan shrugged and left it at that. He went toward the river that had so lately threatened his foreman and the drive, the waters turbid and still flowing hard, though not as turbulent as earlier.

St. Jacques was not giving up. That left the Dawson man just two options, as far as he could figure: chasing him west of the Big Salt Creek or making a rush along the eastern bank, hoping to cut him off.

If I was him, I'd send Haywood west and go east, he thought. *Make a dash toward Hidalgo.*

Unfortunately, there was no other location that Buchanan knew where he could sell his cattle. The confrontation with the Juaristas had humiliated the proud Southerner in front of his men. He wondered if the Dawson foreman would bother to give him the same offer a second time, or whether he would just shoot the cattle—and possibly the men—on sight.

And I'm still outgunned, he thought. *I can't risk that possibility.*

Another standoff was not likely to work, even if more soldiers could be found on this side of the border. Buchanan needed a better solution, and there was not much time to find one.

Frustrated, he decided to clear his head. He went to his horse to get his journal and record the events of the evening. While he felt for a pencil, his fingers touched several folded sheets of paper. He moved them aside, then stopped. With a sudden rush of excitement and hope, he fished them out with two fingers. He also grabbed the map. It was too dark to read here, so he went over to the campfire. Griswold was still tending to the clothes.

"Ya want to watch these, Sachem? Make sure they don't catch fire? I'd like to go back to sleep."

"Hang on awhile longer," Buchanan said. He stood under one of the lanterns and opened the papers.

"Patsy slip ya a secret note? 'Don't open till yer up to yer chin in river water'?"

"Hush," Buchanan said as he scanned the notes he had made in San Bernardino. He looked them over and fastened his eyes on one of the entries. His pockets all being wet, he slipped the papers between his lips. Buchanan unfolded the map and angled it under the lantern. After studying it for several moments, he muttered, "I'll be damned."

"What's wrong? We goin' the wrong way?" Griswold asked.

"*Quiet,*" Buchanan said again as he looked at one of the markings he had made. Without looking up, he asked, "Miguel, you awake?"

The Mexican groaned, raised himself on an elbow. "I have been up ever since you got here and Griz had someone to hear his fresh *mierda*."

Griswold huffed. "I don't know what that means but I don't like the tone."

Buchanan ignored the cookie. He stepped closer to López and spoke softly; he did not want Haywood to hear.

"Miguel, Santa Rosalía de Camargo," he said. "*Traqueros* travel between there and Chihuahua with railroad supplies. From Chihuahua they are building north to Texas."

"Señor Buchanan, forgive me, that is all new. I have not seen any of it."

"That's not what I'm asking. Chihuahua is what I'm interested in. Looks to me like it's half the distance from here to Hidalgo."

"It's closer, about as far as we have traveled so far. I fought there once. Maybe someone still knows me."

Buchanan felt his spirits rise. "The terrain?"

"Plains and hills," he replied. "A number of villages, farms."

"Thanks. Sorry to have woke you."

"De nada," López replied, even as he was falling back to sleep.

"Is that where we're going?" Griswold asked. "Gotta know account o' water, rations."

"You know what? Go to sleep," Buchanan said, and walked over to the cookie. "Say nothing of this."

"Okay, okay. I know how to keep my mouth shut."

Griswold continued to mumble about his silence as he checked the drying clothes. Buchanan returned to his horse to consider the plan that was forming in his mind . . . and what it would take to carry it out.

CHAPTER TWENTY-FOUR

THERE WERE NO birds to rouse the men before sunup. Any that lived there had gone to their nests during the rain and stayed there. Whatever four-footed plains dwellers lived there found puddles of water nearer to their abodes. Pooled rain was everywhere.

Some men woke with the sun, others with the sudden change brought by the returning warmth after the storm-chilled night. Except for the four dead steers lying this way and that along the sloppy banks of the receding river, there was a freshness to the surroundings that felt like a fresh start. The cleanliness faded quickly as buzzards began to descend on the carcasses, followed by shrikes. Soon the four carcasses were covered with feathers, the rank smell and sounds of birds rising above the rush of the river.

The men looked away as they dressed with clothes that were stiff but dry. Griswold had left the garments on the long stick; there had been no need to watch them, as the fire had subsided. The cookie had been up before any of them and to every man the smell of his butchered beef frying was a powerful reason to greet the day.

Fremont was wobbly at first but got his footing quickly. Buchanan had napped a little; mostly, though, he was up considering the route forward. He still had his map, his notes, and his journal. He wished he had asked to take the map book Miss Sally had shown him. He had not noted places he had not expected to be going. There was a dot for Chihuahua because it was a large town and gave him a sense of scale, but he had noted nothing else between it and Hidalgo.

"You all right?" Buchanan asked his trail boss when they met at the chuck wagon. The men were silent, still recovering from their shared ordeal.

"I will be in the saddle and the horse does the walkin'," he said. "Fightin' water ain't something my muscles was used to."

"Come with me," Buchanan said, looking around. "Miguel?"

The Mexican already had his biscuit with a thin slice of meat tucked between the halves. He walked over. The three men were clustered far from Haywood, who had made his own small camp with his clothes drying. He was washing a ways downriver.

"Fremont, I don't know if Haywood is staying—I expect not—but you tell this to the men one at a time."

The trail boss nodded as Buchanan shifted the papers so the open map was on top.

"We are going to Chihuahua instead of Hidalgo," he said, pointing to his pencil dots. "I believe that Mr. Haywood was sent to make us think St. Jacques is in pursuit." Buchanan used his finger to trace a line slightly north—the direction the Dawson gang was last seen going—then turned abruptly south along the western side of Big Salt Creek. "He can travel faster'n us, catch up by tomorrow. I reckon the storm woulda slowed them some, but I suspect he kept going north, around the top of the Salt Creek, then down the eastern side."

"Why would he do that?" Fremont asked.

"Simplest reason of all: We won't be expecting it. St. Jacques covers ground, takes up positions, picks off the cattle as we come through."

"Boss, do they even know where we're headed?" Fremont asked.

"I mentioned it to Chester Jacob; maybe he let it fall. I have to assume they know. In fact, I hope they do."

"Why?"

"Because we're not going there. We're gonna sell as much beef as we can directly to the rail bosses in Chihuahua. That was where Hidalgo intended to move most of it."

While he spoke, Buchanan traced out the new course on his map, drawing features from memory.

"Way I see it, St. Jacques is gonna cross the Gila River south of the Salt Creek and stay east of the Sierra Madre mountains, thinking to hop from water to water—Lakes Guzmán, Santa María, Los Patos, as I recollect. That'll let him keep the horses fresh. Then either he goes south along the Rio Grande and follows the Gulf of Mexico coastline or else waits for us to come along."

"Señor, that is a lot of territory."

"And he's got a lot of men, more than he needs. He may fan 'em out to the west, watching for us. Only we won't be passing anywhere near because we'll have cut off sooner than he was expecting."

"Let me have this, please," López said, reaching for the pencil. He made a small circle. "Somewhere here is the town of Arizpe. I fought there once. To the east"—he drew a line—"is a cut through the Sierra Madre mountains. It is not easy terrain I believe, but I think we can cross it."

"Cross mountains?" Fremont said.

"No—there are a number of valleys. I have not been there, but they were on our own maps during the revolution."

Buchanan was trying to compute the distance. "That'd be about seventy, eighty miles?"

"*Sí*, about that."

"Very good. Fremont, that's where we're going."

The three men looked at the crude map before Buchanan folded it away.

"What if St. Jacques *doesn't* know we were intendin' to go to Hidalgo?" Fremont asked. "Jacob might not've said. The Dawsons could just as easily figger wrong that we'd head to the Gulf o' California, sell some cattle, and mebbe ship what's left south."

"My father was a fisherman in Guaymas," López said. "A drive might make that its destination."

"I talked by telegraphy to someone about going there. They can't take more than a dozen or so head. Dawson surely knows that."

"If that's the situation," Fremont said, "then he has to be behind us. He'll catch us for sure. Thing he won't know is how far the Juaristas did or didn't come with us."

"Unless Haywood tells him," López said.

"Yeah," Fremont said. "Dammit, that could happen."

"That's right," Buchanan said. "Haywood could do that. Haywood *should* do that. He works for the man. But I don't think he will."

Fremont was thoughtful. He looked over to where Haywood was just finishing up by the river. "Man saved my life. I owe him. But, boss, we got a job. We got *our* men to look after. The tracker can hurt us."

López said, "I say we keep him with us. At least we don't kill him."

"We're not gonna do anything," Buchanan said.

Fremont's expression went from uncertain to certain. "We can't just let him ride out."

"That's exactly what we're gonna do. Long as he doesn't know our plan, he can't harm us."

López shrugged, nodded, and walked away. Fremont just shook his head.

"I'm not gonna stand here and tell you you're wrong," Buchanan told him. "But I thought about it during the night and there's nothing else I can do."

"Night isn't the best time for thinkin'," Fremont said. "I tried it. Yer worn-out and the world looks strange."

"That may be," Buchanan agreed with a smile. On their wedding night, Patsy told her husband that it had to be nighttime when the snake tricked Eve to taste the apple and Eve convinced Adam. "My mind is like a longcase clock winding down," she had said.

"You stopped him back at the Mohave," Fremont pressed.

"That was different. I trust him, even when I don't."

"I'm not sure I follow that, boss—"

"Not sure I do either," Buchanan laughed.

"—but you know I'm with ya."

"I know, and I value it.

The men regarded each other a moment before Fremont walked off. What the rancher had meant was about more than just Haywood. Going to Hidalgo was impossible, but there was no guarantee that the railroad office in Chihuahua would accept his herd or have the money to pay for it.

I'll risk that but won't take Dawson's money, he thought as he put his papers away. *What was it Jacob had said about me not that long ago? That I was a stubborn man without a head for business. . . .*

The shipping agent was possibly right about that much, at least.

Buchanan helped Griswold fix the four horses to the chuck wagon.

"Sachem, you know what I ate this mornin'?"

"From the smell, I'd say one of Jacob's oranges."

"That's right. Strings caught in my teeth, the ones that's left, but it wasn't bad. I'm thinkin' maybe I'd like to set aside some land when we get back, grow some of 'em."

"I think that's a good idea," Buchanan said.

Griswold seemed pleased and he climbed into the seat with a bounce in his boots. That was not something he heard often.

The rancher rode out with him to help with the final preparations to resume the drive. He believed that the country ahead was like the country behind, flat and dusty prairie. He knew there was water throughout the region. It was not that he remembered that specifically, but if it had been otherwise, he would have noted it on his map.

As the drive set out in its stages, with the lead steer moving and the others following in fits, Buchanan walked toward his horse. The rancher was not surprised to see the animal alone at the tree, Haywood having mounted up and ridden off. With the ground still damp, there were only a few hoofprints to mark his departure north. The hills concealed man and horse and there was no cloud of dust to indicate whether he had gone straight or headed northeast.

"Did you go to where you left St. Jacques or to where you suspect he might've gone?" Buchanan wondered aloud.

He did not want to believe that Haywood had lied, that he knew for certain St. Jacques intended to cut southeast and was riding to let him know the position of the drive.

The morning was a slog through the damp earth, but the trail became more welcoming as the sun rose. The grasses were plentiful and the men had to urge the cattle along to keep them from feeding. Like the cowhands, they had expended a lot of energy the previous night.

The weather was warm and then hot, just like the day before. Buchanan watched the skies, relieved that they were cloudless. After what had been squeezed from them the night before, he was not surprised.

The drive left the Colorado behind after noon, where the river turned eastward. The cattle grazed and watered there for less than an hour and then were moved on, due south to where López said Arizpe should lay. During the sojourn Buchanan had doubled back to scan the northern horizon with his spyglass. He was searching for any sign of St. Jacques and his men but saw nothing.

There are too many ifs and maybes, Buchanan thought.

If the gang was coming this way, and if Haywood had told them there were no longer any rebels with the drive, then they could charge ahead and be on the AB men as early as the next morning. That assumed Haywood had ridden hard to the north, the gang did the same to the south, and they had already met.

If. Maybe.

That was why considering things at night was better. A woman's heart and a man's gut spoke clear then, pushing aside their fuzzy brains.

IT WAS A little over three days before the town of Arizpe appeared on the southern horizon. At some point, without a mark or village to announce it, the drive had crossed into Mexico. A passage that should have made Buchanan feel safe had just the opposite effect. He had never been in another country. and the United States he loved and had served suddenly seemed not just far away but unreachable.

Arizpe was situated below the mountains, near enough for sheep to graze in the foothills. The pass was barely visible due to the angle of the afternoon sun and would be too dark to enter well before nightfall. Buchanan rode from the tail to the head of the herd to tell Fremont that it would be best to wait until morning before attempting to enter.

As they approached, the first structure to become clear to them was the rust-colored tower of the Nuestra Señora de la Asunción de Arizpe. Like many churches throughout the American Southwest and Mexico, the mission was over a century old and the town had grown both around it and because of it. Buchanan felt some peace when he saw it; although the colors were different than the ivory bell tower and stark walls of the Mission San Luis Rey, Nuestra Señora de la Asunción reminded him of the first time he set eyes on his future wife.

The town turned out to see the unexpected sight. The women stood in a row waving colorful blankets. The men were behind them, some armed with old rifles that, Buchanan suspected, had not been used for years and quite possibly would not fire at all.

To the west, excited children had to be held back by the older men—in some instances forcibly—from running to the herd. They contented themselves with cheering and waving sticks. The children were only accustomed, if at all, to having in their midst a few milk cows and a bull and maybe some calves. They had never seen anything like a herd of longhorns growing in size and sound as it emerged from the plain. Nor would they have any idea what it meant, other than spectacle—like an army moving through or horses being rounded up.

An elder rode out on a burro as the drive came nearer. Watching him were eight men, all in old, worn uniforms, each with a rifle. Fremont had the animals stop while López rode out to greet the man. The cowboy threw away the cigarette he had been smoking; during the revolution it had become a sign of casual disrespect to ladies, suggesting a ruffian and not a caballero.

The man was dressed in white cotton trousers with a red serape and black and gold sombrero. His hair and beard were gray and long. Both men showed one other *cortesía* as they approached. López dismounted and bowed as he led his horse over. The older man inclined his head as a show of courtesy.

"We are sorry to disturb your tranquil morning, but the cattle—they have their own time for things," López said with a smile.

"You are welcome anytime, along with your cattle,"

the man replied. "I am Alcalde Nicolás Barragán—a term larger than this man and his duties, I admit."

"Don Barragán de Arizpe, I thank you for your greeting." He looked beyond him at the ragtag band behind him. "And may I assure you, the *guadias* are not needed.

"They like to do this," the alcalde said with a wink.

That was likely true, López thought. It was also true that every stranger who came to any town was not trusted—until he was.

The village leader eyed him carefully. "You were a part of the *revolución.* I see this fire still in your eyes."

"*Sí,*" López answered. This was always a moment of truth during the revolution, when a man like the alcalde would welcome them back in the dark or drive them away with a warning never to return. It was an unexpectedly emotional moment for López, whose survival had, for years, depended in large part on the fearless generosity of patriots like this man.

"We can offer you water and a bit of food, but not more, I am afraid," the older man said. "Bring the cattle to the eastern side of the village, where you may also make camp. There is feed at our corral. You may leave your horses there."

López replied with relief and emotion, "We want nothing except to cause as little disruption as possible."

"It is too late for that," the alcalde chuckled, pointing a thumb at the forty or so children. They were a roiling mass well behind him.

López informed Buchanan of the invitation, which he gratefully accepted. The herd was relocated, the children following at a distance. When the herd was settled, López invited the children to come closer provided they stay behind the cowhands. Many of the youthful crowd were as excited to see American cowboys, the boys imitating how they stood, walked, and threw a rope to keep the steer from wandering.

After discussing it with the men, Buchanan ordered one of the leaner head butchered and a meal prepared for the village. There was a large and celebratory dinner, richer to the villagers for being unexpected. Even Griswold was relaxed. The extra work was a bother, and he said so many times. But the widowed señora who ran the kitchen at the local *taberna* was very much to his liking. He was delighted, after the grand supper, when she asked to see his chuck wagon.

After the meal, while the men listened to one of the local young men play guitar and danced with a few of the ladies, Buchanan spent time listening to their host talk about the valley and the range in which it sat. The alcalde sat with him and with López, who translated. The rancher was particularly concerned about bandits.

"He says they only come where and when there are crops to steal," López said. "The villages in the north are small and far apart, so it is not worth their effort, and Arizpe trades with travelers for much of what they eat."

"The blankets we saw," Buchanan realized.

"It is also months early for banditos, who will be in the south, where the growing season is earlier."

The night wound down quickly with everyone well-fed. Most of the village turned out to see them off the following morning . . . including a set of eyes that had not been present at the previous night's festivities.

CHAPTER TWENTY-FIVE

EXCEPT FOR HAVING to return an adventurous boy who had hidden in the chuck wagon, the entry into the valley was accomplished quickly and without incident. Lewis Prescott, the former rodeo rider, took the stowaway home using backward-riding tricks that convinced the frightened boy never again to leave his village without permission.

The passage through the Sierra Madres was not what Buchanan had been expecting. It was narrow and zigzagging, with steep walls and slanting piles of rock and dirt on either side. Here and there were edges that seemed to have been left when the surrounding wall cracked from seeping water and fell away or were knocked down and shattered by rock sliding from above.

"We gonna have to fix some maps when we get back," Fremont noted as they rode in. "Ain't more'n a gorge."

Deems, riding nearby him, added, "It's like the Lord

extended His hands and pulled the mountain apart just enough."

Mitchell snorted. "He didn't finish this place any better'n He finished men."

There was an unearthly echo of hooves and animal sounds, and movement slowed where the morning sun did not yet reach. The herd would frequently stop where large, craggy boulders, sheared from the cliff above, blocked their way. Coaxing the steers around them required stopping the lead animals and those behind them lest they be crushed against the obstacle. The chuck wagon fell behind, having to make right-angle turns to get through blocked, narrow passes.

"Wasn't built to go sideways," Griswold complained. He had to get out to lessen the weight and walk the team through.

Buchanan, riding beside him on the seat, had untied the spare horses and trailed them so that the wagon could slide sideways a few feet where it had to.

"Some country, Mexico, where I never want to come again," Griswold said. "Refugee behind my flour, wagon movin' sidewards, givin' away our beef! It ain't *natural* here."

"You seemed to enjoy the señora."

"Well, man does not live by bakin' bread alone."

"Also, I seem to recall you felt the same when we first met the Grand Canyon," Buchanan said.

"We didn't try to go *in* it," Griswold said. "This Mexico place—the whole thing is upside-down, even the lingo."

Buchanan knew he had played out the rope of reason and let the conversation go back to being one-sided.

Progress through the valley was unexpectedly slow,

and a day that had begun well quickly turned caustic to Buchanan's spirit. The narrowness of the pass was one problem: there was also the length. For a rider, neither would have been an issue. But the way the herd was moving, they might not reach the other end by nightfall. That would make them easy, trapped targets for anyone approaching from the opposite side. If not bandits, then possibly—if not imminently—St. Jacques. The rancher knew it was unlikely, and he continually referred to his papers to try and remember what he had seen on the more detailed printed maps. If the Dawsons took an inland route, it would not put them close to the current route, but it would put them closer. If they fanned out, a rider might see or hear them. Within these walls, they were creating quite a ruckus.

"He thinks like a reptile," Buchanan said suddenly. "Has nothing but time *to* think."

"What's that, Sachem?"

"I'm considering our situation aloud," the rancher answered.

"Which situation? This crack in the mountains that ain't suitable for a drive?"

"No, I'm talking about St. Jacques," Buchanan replied. "If we were all troops during the war, I'm wondering how would he find us and attack."

"One way he ain't is from the high ground—unless he plans to throw rocks." Griswold chuckled. "That'd chafe Deems!"

"What would?"

"To be stoned, like some sinful whatnot in the Bible."

"St. Jacques won't do that. Going into the mountains would slow him. What he has now is more men and greater speed. How does he use that?"

"I don't know. I woulda gone home by now. I can't think moon-looney like that."

But St. Jacques could and did, and as Buchanan rode alongside, he weighed the naked facts of the situation. The Dawson gang had information available to them that he had unavoidably left behind in deeds and tracks, along with the testimony of Haywood should he choose to give it. St. Jacques also had speed and numbers on his side, and a devious mind to deploy them.

A plan was beginning to form itself, one that concerned him more than anything they had faced till now.

Tying the extra horses to the seat rail of the chuck wagon, Buchanan rode to Mitchell at the back of the herd.

"I'm gonna tell Fremont to keep the herd moving hard till we're out of here," the rancher said. "Keep up, and if you can't, forget any strays."

"Something happen?" the ex-Confederate asked.

"No, and I want to make sure it doesn't," Buchanan said as he rode ahead. There was room for him to maneuver around his riders and the herd, but not a lot, and there were jagged rocks to his left side.

Fremont was in the lead with López riding slightly ahead to watch for holes and narrow passages.

"Miguel! Over here," Buchanan said as he rode up.

The Mexican cantered over. The men continued riding, Buchanan in the center.

"Will, I want you to push the herd. I want to be out of this gorge before dark, if that's possible. Miguel, you ride ahead. Let me know if you can see the end."

"*Bueno,*" López said, and rode off. He stayed to the northern side to avoid the deep shadows on the southern half.

"You think the Dawsons got the draw on us?" Fremont asked.

"I truly do not know. But I'm thinking if I was him, with more'n twice the men, I'd've split 'em up, sent one west and one east. A party moving south along the western side of the Sierras will learn from our tracks, maybe from Haywood, maybe from the alcalde, that the Juaristas did not stay with us and we're headed to this clog of a valley."

"Which means they could be close."

"It does," Buchanan said, "and it's my fault. We probably should've pushed on last night, but—"

"That's bosh, boss. The men needed that fiesta. So did that town. So did you."

"Well, we got it. They still don't know where we're going, which is why, if we can get out of this, we can still beat a west- or east-moving band to Chihuahua."

It was late afternoon before López returned. The shadows had shifted but there was still enough light to show his face when he reported to Buchanan, who was back beside the chuck wagon. The Mexican's expression was grim.

"If we do not stop, we still do not arrive until it is dark," López said. "Very dark."

"How is the passage?"

"The same as we have seen. And very soon the shadows will be everywhere. We will have to go slower."

Overhearing, Griswold said, "An' this time we ain't got torches. Used my last sticks to dry clothes."

"You have instructions for point?" López asked.

"Give me a moment."

Buchanan took out his map and studied it as the mustang loped along. He used his index finger to approximate distances down the eastern side. He looked up, around, and back. Then he regarded López.

"Tell Will to slow 'er down, Miguel. We're not going to try and finish the passage today. I'll come up a bit and explain. Also, send Prescott and Deems here."

"You will set up—how do you say it?—guards for the rear?"

"That's close enough," Buchanan said.

López threw off a small salute before leaving.

"What're ya gonna do, leave 'em behind to hold off any Dawsons that come through?" Griswold asked.

"That's the idea."

"Okay. Once we get out, an' assuming they survive, we need 'em on the herd. What, then?"

"I'm working it out," Buchanan replied. His strict tone told Griswold to stop talking.

The two men arrived as the herd slowed. Without the swing riders in place, the center of the drive bulged toward the sides as the cattle gave themselves room.

Buchanan stopped and faced them. He had the extra horses, both of which had bundles of tools on their backs.

"I don't know for sure, but we may have Dawsons coming up behind us. We gotta prepare as if we do, anyway."

"Pharaoh's chariots," Deems muttered. "We need the Lord of Hosts to do battle alongside us."

"I welcome any assistance with wide-open arms, Joe, especially His. But, barring that, we need defenses. The valley floor will be in shadow soon. I want ya to take a shovel and pick and get to work digging as many holes as ya can. Not a trench they can walk over. Keep digging into darkness: I want enough holes to trip up a horse, make them lose one or two or three so they have to stop till they can see again. I don't like it, but if they're coming, we gotta make 'em stop for the night."

"I'm gonna enjoy this, boss," Prescott said. He had already guided his horse to one of the extra animals. He dismounted and untied the bundle on its back. He handed Deems a shovel and kept a pick. The two men headed west, Deems assuring Buchanan they would be two Horsemen of the Apocalypse, resolute and bringing their own brand of wrath down on the Dawsons.

"He's crazy," Griswold said after they had departed.

"We're probably gonna need more of that quality before this is finished," Buchanan said with solemnity.

The drive continued until late in the afternoon, when the shadows were too wide and deep for the men to see. There was no wood for a campfire, nor would they have made one. In addition to the light giving away their location, Buchanan was concerned that the crackling would prevent them from hearing anyone who might approach from either side. He also asked the men not to talk for the same reason.

Several of the hands had bedded down by the time Prescott and Deems returned.

"We made it like a mess o' cannonballs went off out there," Prescott said. "No one's getting' through from that direction."

Buchanan told them to go to the chuck wagon for beans; supper was cold but abundant. The rancher went over to Fremont, who was still awake. He was sitting on a rock that had fallen at some point in the past and buried itself deep in the dirt. He was chewing a cigar too stubby to be lit. Its only use was to keep the man's mouth busy.

"I hate waiting," Fremont said as Buchanan leaned

against the cliff beside him. "Used to feel the same way the night before a battle. At least in the war you knew what you was waiting *for*."

"Think about moving the herd out in the morning," Buchanan said. "That's the only job we got any control over."

"I know. Got Mitchell out front, but I don't think I'll be sleeping much. It's this place. Every movement I hear, I think, 'Is that us or them?'"

"I'll listen for both of us. You lie down."

"Sure, sure," Fremont said. He took the cigar from his mouth and tossed it. "Ain't nothin' left o' this anyway."

The camp fell almost entirely asleep. Without a campfire, even the herd seemed to settle into quiet repose. Before too long, Buchanan saw what Fremont had meant. The rancher felt the heaviness, the closeness, of the cliffs closing in. He was used to open spaces, not this. Even after the flooding of the Colorado, there had been a freshness to the abused camp and exhausted men. This place and the imminence of danger preyed on him.

Maybe Will was not wrong, he reflected.

Waiting, too, was the enemy.

Buchanan sat where he had been standing. From time to time he slept, only to be wakened by sounds from the west—distant noises that were heightened by the stone walls and silence of the camp. They could be animal growls and trees creaking back toward Arizpe.

Or they could be horses and riders falling.

If so, the traps have worked, he thought. After weeks of accepting whatever fate and men had hoisted upon them, that was a tonic to his soul.

CHAPTER TWENTY-SIX

THE MORNING BROUGHT a wash of cooler air from the east. It was a welcome relief from the humidity that had collected in the gorge. It was also a beacon bidding the drive to come forward.

Neither that nor the hint of deep blue in the sky were what had wakened Buchanan. What roused him was the sound of hoofbeats in the distance—to the west.

"Will," he whispered to his sleeping trail boss.

The man flustered to wake. "Yeah?"

"Wake the others. We may need guns. Keep 'em on foot."

Fremont crawled from his bag and, still on his knees, went from man to man. waking them and giving the order. Buchanan rose, his rifle in both hands, across his chest the way he had carried it in war. He listened carefully; after a minute, he was certain.

Men were coming from the west. Buchanan heard horses, some with an uneven gait.

"They fell into the holes," Fremont said, walking over with his Springfield.

"Sounds like it."

The men of the AB were silent as they watched the twisted angle of the gorge to their west. They stood shoulder to shoulder; tucked behind them was the cookie peering from the back of his wagon, his own six-shooter in hand.

There was a sharp turn some two hundred feet distant; as they looked on, three men on foot and then seven on horseback came into view. The mounted men all had rifles under their arms. The men who were walking led lame horses behind them. The animals were still carrying their bedrolls and supplies. One of the men on foot was St. Jacques.

The Dawson trail boss raised a hand to his men when he saw the row of five men ahead. The newcomers stopped.

"That was a clever thing you did," St. Jacques shouted. "We need three horses."

Griswold muttered, "You're gonna need a whole lot *more* horses if you make another move."

"Quiet," Buchanan said.

St. Jacques left his horse and started forward. "There are more men coming up behind you. I suggest you set aside your arms. They will shoot your beeves and those nearest you will, I fear, trample you down."

"Mister, I've had a bellyful of you," Buchanan said. "You want to shoot, shoot. We will all get bloodied."

"I have no intention of shooting. There's no need. You're the one who is trapped."

"Well," Fremont whispered to Buchanan, "you was right about them splittin' up."

St. Jacques continued to walk forward. Buchanan could not fault him for guts if nothing else.

"I say again, Mr. Buchanan: Give me three horses to replace the ones you lamed. We can shoot these and then wait for our companions like civilized people. And before you ask, the drive ends here. There will be no further offers to purchase your beef. That time is passed. It's to be a feast for buzzards and wolves now."

"The question is: What will they be feasting on?"

The voice came from behind the Dawson men. Even before he saw him, Buchanan knew the man who had spoken: It was Haywood. The tracker was perched on a small ledge, his rifle aimed at St. Jacques.

"Haywood," the Southerner said as he turned. "I wondered where you had gone."

The other Dawson hands turned to various degrees, raising their weapons.

"Lower the guns or you'll have a lot fewer horses," Haywood warned.

"Do as he says," St. Jacques ordered.

The Dawson trail boss walked slowly toward his own injured mount. His rifle scabbard was on the right side. That was the side he was headed.

A shot cracked; the animal flopped over, blood jetting from its head. Buchanan took a few steps forward. His rifle was smoking and his eye was dead-set behind it. To the west, the Dawson horses jerked here and there from the shot and had to be steadied. Behind Buchanan, the herd stirred and mooed unpleasantly.

"Will, take the men and steady the cattle," the rancher said.

"Lead 'em out?"

"Not yet. The cliffs will help contain them. There may be more shots."

"Yes, sir," Fremont said with fresh enthusiasm as he motioned the others to mount up and follow him.

St. Jacques watched the proceedings with a look that had gone from rage at the loss of his stallion to a haughty contempt—like a low Yankee had no right to shoot a fine horse. Maybe, to him, this was now a duel between gentlemen, with only one of them fitting that description. Buchanan suspected the man's glare was a challenge like the slap of a glove. The question he asked seemed like a formality, since the conclusion was obvious.

The AB men must surrender or die.

"What do you propose to do now, Mr. Buchanan? If I give the word, you and Haywood die."

"And you. And a bunch of your hands."

"Such is war."

"You're the one who made it such."

St. Jacques snickered. "You talk like a boy of ten, pointing a finger. The West is changing. The railroads are here, the telegraph connects towns and cities, settlers are coming. This is about a new order of things, and Mr. Dawson intends to have a strong voice in how it grows."

"And who's included or pushed aside," Buchanan said. "Well, we ain't gonna settle that here. All I want is to get my cattle to market."

There were shouts from the east: Buchanan's men followed by gunshots and the mooing of the cows in the front.

St. Jacques smiled. "That, Mr. Buchanan, is not going to happen."

There was a commotion behind the rancher as cattle backed into the valley, pushed by those in front of the herd. Griswold shouted as steer caused the horses to rear. He tried to simultaneously steady them and turn, both of which were impossible.

"Now, sir," St. Jacques went on, "lay down your arms, leave me with two—no, three—horses, and you may leave."

"I make you the same offer!" Haywood shouted.

"Kill that bastard," St. Jacques said through his teeth, without turning.

St. Jacques was presenting Haywood his back, daring him to shoot. He was glaring now at Buchanan, challenging him to do the same. He heard nothing except shuffling on the dirt. His eyes on the rancher, he saw the man grin behind his gun.

The Southerner looked back. Entering the valley and taking up positions behind boulders were seven Mexican men in ragged uniforms. They were on horseback, rifles at the ready. One of them was leading Haywood's horse.

"You made a foolish mistake, St. Jacques," Haywood said. "Mr. Buchanan here rode into Arizpe with beef. You rode into the village with threats. I managed to explain to the alcalde what you proposed to do. He sent these men to help persuade you otherwise. We saw you all start to stumble and curse, so we waited just outa sight."

St. Jacques did not repeat his order. His men waited.

The uproar of beef and chuck wagon had abated slightly since the last gunshot. The steers had nowhere to go on three sides, and the din of the chuck wagon had prevented them from pushing forward.

"Y'ain't like stampeding buffalo, ya dumb 'horns!" Griswold shouted at them. He had gotten the chuck wagon far enough away so that it was silent, a sea of calmed cattle behind him. "Hey, St. Jacques? If ya got men out there, they ain't gettin' through! Not with this wall o' rawhide!"

Haywood's sharp voice broke the silence that had settled on the gorge. "I'm waiting for your answer, mister. Hell, I got no education like you, but I can count. This 'bastard,' as you called him, may die but so will you and all of your men."

Buchanan was still not convinced, as Deems was, as Patsy was, that there was a God who had nothing better to do than to look after him and the small efforts of the AB. Nonetheless, three times now St. Jacques had been in a position to bully and then had to retreat.

The Southerner turned back to Buchanan, his look ferocious. "I surrendered once before. I would rather die than do it again!"

He stalked forward, his rifle snug in his tight fist. As he approached, he raised his gun toward Buchanan. After initial reluctance, the rancher was forced to do so as well. St. Jacques shouldered his stock and aimed. Buchanan did not. As his rifle came up, he dropped to his belly. St. Jacques's Enfield cracked but the shot went high. Buchanan's reply did not. The Dawson foreman stopped as the bullet struck and shattered his breastbone and continued into his chest. His head had snapped back slightly at the impact, causing his hat to fly off and fall to the ground, the feather fluttering as it did. Bullet and bone fragments perforated his lungs and heart and he stood still for a long moment, his face registering shock from the impact. His mouth fell open as he tried and failed to draw breath, as the skin of his face paled, as his knees wobbled. His men saw a great red spider form and grow on his back, seemingly alive as it finally sought the ground, pulling him with it.

No one else fired. After the echo of the gunshots

faded, and the anxious cattle were once again steadied, the standoff ended with Dawson's men lowering their guns.

Behind the tableau of dead horses and a fallen man of the South, Griswold sat staring from the seat of his chuck wagon.

"First time I ever seen a showdown with rifles," he murmured as he looked out at the split chest of the late Yancy St. Jacques. "God help me, I pray it's the last."

CHAPTER TWENTY-SEVEN

ST. JACQUES WAS wrapped in his bedroll and buried under a pile of rocks. His death was Mexico's problem, if the local *alguacil*, the county sheriff, chose to pursue it. If he talked to the people of Arizpe, that was not likely.

For his part, Buchanan was sad and then angry that it had come to that. But he was grateful not to have been the one who perished.

With the defeated men of the Dawson gang leading the way through the relentless sun, the herd moved toward the eastern mouth of the gorge. The men were on horseback, including the two extras the drive had brought along. Two of the Dawson men rode double. All had been disarmed, their weapons in the chuck wagon.

With the prisoners in front of the herd and three AB guns behind them, Buchanan did not think they would have trouble when they ran into the rest of the Dawson crew. His thoughts, as he followed the chuck wagon, were with the man at his side.

George Haywood explained that he had not left that morning back at the Colorado River. He had tracked the AB drive from a distance, waiting to see if St. Jacques or any portion of his team showed up. He did not follow the herd into the gorge but watched as St. Jacques rode in and threatened the alcalde. After the Dawson gang rode out, it was an easy matter to secure the cooperation of the Arizpe militia.

"Which brings us to what you're going to do now," Buchanan said.

Haywood offered a rare smile. "Makes a man damned unhappy when there are a couple of 'right' things in conflict under the shadow of a great wrong. You having a right to the drive, me owing allegiance to Dawson, but St. Jacques being a wicked son of a bitch. I'm glad that weight's off me. I tell myself, 'You're alive and you're free.' For now, I will go north, because I discovered I do not know *near* enough Spanish to survive here."

"I don't think Dawson or his men are going to give you any trouble," Buchanan said. "St. Jacques was the troublemaker. And the rest of 'em have reason to stay clear of the law. Paying for cattle at gunpoint is still rustling, and they won't want to face that."

"I know those men, and the stink of St. Jacques corrupted some of them. I like to think they'll come back to their senses."

"Either way, would you consider staying with the AB?"

"I heard a rumor that you're considering some other trade."

Buchanan chuckled. "Considering it."

"Oranges?"

"Considering it."

Haywood's smile settled a little as he grew introspective. "I don't know. Tracking and cattle have been my life for six years. I like the work and I don't think I want to give it up."

"What's your immediate plan, then?"

"Soon's we're in the open, I'll ride with the Dawson men, see what is on their minds and in their hearts."

"Makes sense."

"But I thank you for your consideration, Mr. Buchanan."

"It's a small thing compared to what you did for us. I'd be the one in that stone grave if not for you, an' St. Jacques would've gotten away with it."

Haywood rose a little in the saddle and saw daylight ahead as well as above.

"I think I'm gonna ride out, see how many of those boys are in a forgiving mood."

"I hope to see you at the ranch sometime."

"I'll be there. *With* your horses."

He extended his hand and Buchanan shook it warmly. "What is it they say down here? *Vaya con dios*?"

"'Go with God,'" Buchanan said.

The tracker smiled, blew a gloved kiss to the sky, and rode ahead, waving at Griswold as he guided his horse around the herd.

Buchanan remained where he was, on tail, well behind the chuck wagon and Griswold's chatter, contentedly alone. There was nothing—not one thing—that had gone the way he had planned since they left the ranch. For that matter, his life had been like that since Boston. Maybe it *was* time for that to change.

The herd emerged into the sharp light of the afternoon. The foothills were long and sloping but not very high, with a bright prairie beyond. The Dawson group was still at the opening, having been pushed backward by the cattle. There was no challenge from them. The reasons for the small-scale war still existed, but without St. Jacques, the longing for a fight was gone. Half the Dawson men had no guns and half, having ridden hard for nearly two days, had no belly for a showdown. They headed north in the company of Haywood, who seemed to Buchanan to be both safe and content.

"If that wasn't the most unexpected day I ever lived . . ." Griswold said as the cattle began to move.

"Don't say that," Buchanan told him, falling in beside the seat.

"Why not, Sachem?"

"Because there's still a few hours of daylight left, Griz."

The cookie frowned at that, but Buchanan intended to enjoy his first afternoon in quite some time.

The journey to Chihuahua took just over a week. They arrived very late in the afternoon and once again their first sight of the town was a house of worship. In this case it was the cathedral at the Plaza de Armas. Buchanan, Fremont, and López were at the head of the herd as they approached.

"Four years ago we fought the French imperialists here. They had taken up positions in the church, barricaded doors with pews, bales, everything they had except the horses. We could not enter, so we attacked with a cannon. We said many prayers for the violence we did." He pointed. "You can still see the damage to the bell tower and the poor bell."

It happened that López was remembered in the

town, by the padre whom he and his revolutionaries had liberated from the French. Father Angel Sáenz was shopping for a straw hat in the plaza marketplace when shoppers began to gather and point to the north. He walked out, both puzzled and interested by the unexpected arrival of cattle.

"Padre Sáenz!" a voice called from the front of the drive.

The portly clergyman shielded his eyes—the unfulfilled purpose of the hat—and walked toward López. The padre's brown frock appeared nearly golden in the western sun. His face glowed even brighter when he recognized the man at the head of the drive.

"Miguel López!" he shouted. "The man who broke my bell!"

"Do you forgive me?" López cried back.

"Every day that I do not see Frenchmen in my village! More importantly, my son, I am sure God forgives you as well!"

From Father Sáenz, through López, Buchanan learned that the railroad office was on the other side of Chihuahua, something he had suspected when he heard the sounds of banging and yelling the nearer they had come.

Buchanan and López dismounted and walked their horses while Fremont settled the drive.

"It is a constant discomfort to the ears," the padre said as he walked between them, "except on the Sabbath, blessed as the Lord's day *and* a day of peace! But—*but*—our town has never known such prosperity! Look how many tables are in our marketplace. You remember, Miguel, when we only had what the French left us?"

"I recall," López answered. "Including the diseases."

"Yes, there was misery. The Good Lord tested us, we proved worthy, and so we accept this bounty . . . along with the noise."

The three men walked through the dusty town, the padre greeted with much the same respect as the alcalde in Arizpe. Faith and the wisdom of age were the cornerstones of these villages, perhaps of the new Mexican nation. It did not seem a bad way to conduct the business of a country.

The man in charge of the railroad was not Mexican.

"His name is Horace Caine, a surveyor who lost part of an arm and all of his patience in Gettysburg," the padre explained. "He is from a railroad family that wishes to build what they call the Corpus Christi, San Diego and Rio Grande Gauge Railroad from here to your southwest."

That'll make Dick Dawson happy, Buchanan thought.

"It may be that is the true reason Dawson did not want us to make friends here," López suggested.

"That may very well be."

"But first," Father Sáenz said, "Señor Caine must demonstrate that he can turn farmers into railroad workers. So far . . ." The padre waved his hand the way Buchanan had seen rowboats roll on choppy waters.

The three made their way among stacks of wooden ties and steel rails, then maneuvered between men working machinery that created a level track bed. Horace Caine stood in front of a single ramshackle engine that was being used to test laid track. A ribbon of wood and steel stretched out behind the train, running south.

Barking three separate instructions at once to a supernaturally calm translator, Caine initially greeted the two Americans as bothers. Then he learned why they were here. His big, open face turned from devil-red to angelic before he could snap out another command.

"Food, hell," Caine said with a mildly apologetic look at the priest. "I've been asking Hidalgo for more men. We'll eat half—the cows, I mean—and use the others to haul steel. What do you want for them?"

Buchanan named a price, the same he had quoted to Hidalgo. And just like that, the entire herd was sold. Buchanan and Caine retired to the small hotel on the south side of the plaza overlooking the construction site. He had his own safe in an office so small, the hotelier had to leave so the other two men could fit. Caine paid Buchanan with a sack of gold coins.

"Not sure this new 'gold standard' will take, but if it doesn't, you can melt these down and you've still got gold."

"That is entirely satisfactory," Buchanan assured him.

"Get your herd bedded down," Caine said. "If you stay till I can get a capable team over . . ."

"It'll be done," the rancher replied.

"Good man. I'll have some of our grub sent over."

The rancher left the office with his chest tight and tears behind his eyes. If he had been undecided before about planting oranges, he was decided now. Upon hearing about the plans for the railroad, he knew he would have the same problem here that he had in the States: Men like Dawson would crowd him out with cows. But that was not the main reason for making the change; he and his men did not shy from a scrap.

What tilted the scales toward planting was the fact that he suspected he would never again have a day like this.

Buchanan met López in the plaza and walked toward the men. Like the rancher, the Mexican seemed choked up when he saw what Buchanan was carrying. The rancher sought out Fremont first, then gathered the others for a celebration that had not only been earned but was much-needed.

Only the man who found his stores of spirits seized and then depleted before sundown had cross words for the celebration.

"Don't complain t'me when yer whiskey beans ain't got no liquor taste in 'em."

Buchanan said they would buy more before they left Chihuahua and that he did not think anyone would be complaining about anything during the journey home.

The trip to the north began three days after the men had arrived. The cowboys had celebrated, slept off the celebration, then finished transferring the cattle to the camp and resupplying. As in Arizpe there was a celebratory atmosphere in the town. Buchanan realized that it had as much to do with being a free people as it did with the spectacle of beef on the hoof.

It was ironic, he thought, that the Civil War had not produced a similar feeling among his countrymen.

Buchanan did not retrace the route they took, which had proven to be less favorable than he had expected; the thought of crossing the ledge that Haywood had helped them hew from the mountainside was reason enough to follow a different trail. They set out to the northwest, around the Rio Conchos and for four days made their way past the three lakes to El Paso. There, after the men spent a little of the gold they had earned—and Buchanan purchased church gloves for his three girls—the cowboys picked up the old Gila Trail. It was not as direct as some of the other wagon ways, but it followed the San Pedro, Gila, and other rivers, and the men wanted a rise that was easy, not necessarily fast.

Riding beside the wagon—now out of habit, not necessity—Buchanan was relaxed . . . and thoughtful.

"What're we runnin' back to, anyway, Sachem?" Griswold asked a day out of El Paso. "I like the oranges we took, for once in a while, but that smell all the time?"

"We can still raise some cattle for our own use . . . horses. You don't have to live near the groves."

"'The groves,'" Griswold said. "Sounds like you already got 'em laid out in your head. You're decided."

"I believe so," Buchanan said. "I don't much like drives that end with killing a rival, even if it was him or me."

"I don't imagine Jacob would be drawin' on ya," the cookie agreed.

Saying out loud what he was thinking made the notion even more real to Buchanan. It *was* decided. He would hereafter be an orange grower, not a rancher. The name did not sit well.

But Buchanan had over a week to get accustomed to it as they made their way along the trail. They passed a sign that announced a new town, Shakespeare, where silver miners were already staking their claims. Mitchell and Prescott came forward there, asked Buchanan about his intentions.

He confirmed the rumors.

"Would you mind, boss, if we took our share and stayed here a spell?" Prescott asked.

"We gambled goin' over and through the mountains," Mitchell said. "We figure to continue tempting fate."

He said it with a wink; it was clear both men preferred this risk to the certainty of oranges. They departed with good wishes from the others and rode off to a future as risky as every future those two had known in war and peace.

The remaining four men cut north toward San Bernardino.

It was on a warm day, early in the afternoon, that they passed the cabin where Mitchell had lived to tend to the grazing cattle.

"It's gonna be tough, boss, givin' all that up," Fremont said.

"You think of starting your own spread? You'll have good money to buy starting stock."

"I ain't sayin' no, but on the other hand this was a couple weeks that I didn't think we'd see the end of. I ain't felt so mortal since the war. Not sure I want to feel that again."

"I don't think Dawson'll own up to what St. Jacques did, but I can't see him giving you a sampler for the ranch house, either."

"I believe that's true and—well, who knows? I'll try growin' fruit or vegetables or whatever they are, an' if it ain't to my likin', maybe I'll take up Jacob's offer to go to sea."

"You can grow whiskers," Buchanan said. "Keeps you warm in a squall."

It was another day before they reached the main house, riding in under the noon sun. Pete Sloane had heard the horses approaching from a distance and informed Patsy Buchanan. It was a home day for the girls, and, following their mother, all three ladies walked quickly and then ran toward the four arrivals. Sloane stayed back, giving them their time. Buchanan broke from the others and galloped forward, waving the sack of gold coins in his hand. It was his way of letting them know that all was well. He stopped well short of the three so he would not cover them with dirt and flung himself from the saddle.

Just then, King bolted past them all at a run. He leapt all over his master, licking whatever section of cheek he could reach and kicking loose the dust of the trail.

"Did you keep good watch, boy?" Buchanan asked.

As unselfish as he was faithful, the shepherd backed off, now barking with joy as his mistress arrived.

"You did it!" Patsy cried, hugging her husband.

"We did something," her husband said. "It wasn't what we planned . . . we didn't make it to Hidalgo . . . but—"

"God had His own plan," she said, stepping back, smiling and crying at the same time. "He always does."

"Funny. That's just what the padre said in Chihuahua where we sold the herd."

Just then, the girls arrived and slammed into their father, hugging him. Patsy stepped back and waved at the other men, who were taking their time coming in.

"It's so good to see my two doves," he said, crushing them both to him. "I got gifts for everybody, which I'll bestow, but only after I wash, take off my boots, and hug you all some more."

"Where are Reb and Lewis?" Patsy asked.

"They decided to try their hands at mining," he said. "Seems they have no appetite for groves." His eyes found Sloane standing in the shadow of the smoke pots set for the hornets. Buchanan nodded toward him and the cowboy nodded back.

Patsy's eyes snapped back and she looked at him for a long, soulful moment.

"Like you said, God has His plans," Buchanan told her.

Patsy made room for herself between the girls and threw her arms around her husband's chest even tighter. She wept with joy into her husband's dusty garments as the four Buchanans held tightly to one another and to the challenge they would share together.